PENGUIN BOOKS
LIVING HELL

Vivaan Shah is a theatre and film actor. He made his Bollywood debut with *Saat Khoon Maaf*, which was based on a short story by Ruskin Bond.

He has been doing plays since childhood, movies since he was twenty years old and writing since early adolescence. An amateur film historian, he has also directed a play, *A Comedy of Horrors*, featuring the works of Edgar Allan Poe.

VIVAAN SHAH

LIVING HELL

PENGUIN BOOKS

An imprint of Penguin Random House

PENGUIN BOOKS

USA | Canada | UK | Ireland | Australia
New Zealand | India | South Africa | China | Singapore

Penguin Books is part of the Penguin Random House group of companies
whose addresses can be found at global.penguinrandomhouse.com

Published by Penguin Random House India Pvt. Ltd
4th Floor, Capital Tower 1, MG Road,
Gurugram 122 002, Haryana, India

First published in Penguin Books by Penguin Random House India 2019

ISBN 9780143445760

Typeset in Aldine401 BT by Manipal Digital Systems, Manipal

Printed at Repro India Limited

www.penguin.co.in

This is a legitimate digitally printed version of the book and therefore might not
have certain extra finishing on the cover.

Prologue

Flat No. 502

The exact time on the wall clock hanging over the kitchen mantelpiece in flat no. 502 was 2.31 p.m. Each and every switch in the house had been left on, even the ones next to empty plug points, and the ones Scotch-taped with markings saying 'Do Not Touch', even the lone double switch that lay dangling in a corner from a disconnected table lamp. Thankfully, the gas had not been turned on, as there was no one to attend to or enjoy the facilities and amenities of this abode. The empty glass plate in the microwave kept rotating without any apparent purpose—the timer had been set to half an hour and fifteen seconds and as the twentieth minute approached, the mechanism itself seemed baffled at what it was supposed to have been doing.

The knob of the fan regulator had been left at '2', a speed that made more noise than doing any good. The television kept trying to peddle a variety of wares to an audience of inanimate objects that seemed least interested in what it had to offer. One advertisement was followed by the next in descending order of utility. An ad that promised to cure blisters on the soles of calloused feet with the able assistance of a crack cream was televised with as much zest and vigour as an Indian armed forces commercial enticing potential prospects to get recruited in the navy.

Over all the more menial sounds insidiously inhabiting the kitchen and living room, there chirped a silent dripping from the toilet, as if in background to the restless recital of the household. It came like the whisper of a wind chime, discreet yet glaringly apparent, and impossible to not take notice of. Even though there wasn't anyone to take note of anything, each drop that fell into the bucket landed quick, with one clean swoop, echoing all about the four corners that surrounded it, its friendly reverberations hinting at a latent malice . . . a malice that lay distilled in the objects of everyday life, which one normally accustoms oneself to if one intends to enjoy the comforts and splendour of easy living. Every article in the flat, every furnishing, every gadget, every piece of technology, every object, every function, every service, every purpose in the house was devoted solely to the welfare of its inhabitant who lay in the lowest place of all, bereft of all support, helpless and dispensable. Locked in the bathroom, still as a stopcock, his legs spread out wide on the damp floor, his arms hanging from the shoulders, his neck tilting backwards and his eyes widening in anticipation of rigor mortis. Death itself seemed disappointed at how unceremoniously its latest seat had been usurped. As if to die all alone was the greatest sin. And to go on living by oneself the only answer.

Flat No. 303

He sat slouched in front of the television with one arm resting on the cushion and the other hand wrapped firmly around the remote control. He was ready to use it at a moment's notice—the second his attention would begin to waver. His eyelids were threatening to close shut any minute and his feet began to slowly drift apart as the ceiling fan above him rotated like a windmill, contributing to the stagnant ventilation that made his forehead involuntarily wrinkle in irritation. He was gradually dozing off and there wasn't a thing in the world he could do about it. He lay suspended in mid-air, swaying left and right . . . Nadeem Chipkali, the lizard . . . hovering halfway between consciousness and slumber, not quite sure himself whether he was awake or asleep.

His flatmate lay passed out on the couch beside him, the palm of his right hand vacant yet pointing in the direction of the television, as if it were still clutching the remote. The remote control had been an object of much contention between the two, and he who enjoyed possession over it certainly had the upper hand in the household, at least as far as recreational activities were concerned. After all, there wasn't much else to do. The music system wasn't working, the computer had conked out, and the newspapers and magazines that lay scattered on the floor were of more use for mopping up spilt water than actually for reading. His mobile phone, too, lay incapacitated in a corner of the room, like another disenfranchised member of the household whose silence spoke more than the commotion creeping in through the open windows, reminding him time and time again that there was nothing much to look forward to, and certainly nothing to wake up for. He would spend hours by its side like a devoted friend and confidant, waiting for it to ring, for a message even from Vodafone to appear, for any signal from the outside world to rescue him from the sloth he had slowly sunk into.

'If you receive calls from any of these numbers,' declared a sombre voice on the television amidst an array of phone numbers on display, 'asking for credit card details, bank account number, CVV code, PAN card number, GST number, Aadhaar card number, please refrain from doing so and report immediately to 0884532160, or simply dial 0125, that's 0125, for QUANTRA Tele-Com & Cyber Security Notification Centre.'

The intercom attached to the kitchen wall began to ring in its high-pitched burglar alarm blare, tearing through the stillness with a stirring sense of purpose, suggesting that it was a matter that demanded urgent attention. Nadeem had one eye half open as it pierced through the living room. He knew it was the landlord and was not in the mood to address the situation he was presently incapable of finding a solution to. He knew the landlord would give up after three or four tries unless he took the effort to land up at their doorstep—a predicament he was hoping to avoid. But it persisted longer than he would have liked, with each interval in between the rings bearing the promise of silence, but each successive outcry growing shriller and more obtrusive. With it came the beeping of his alarm clock, which was set to go off at 2.45 p.m. for no particular reason other than to drag him to his feet and think about how to spend the day.

'Any offers proposing schemes for real estate, investment, insurance and currency exchange are fraud,' the telecaster carried on in so insistent a tone that it seemed there was something fraudulent about what he was saying. 'Please beware and report at once to 0884532160, or simply dial 0125, that's 0125, for QUANTRA Tele-Com and Cyber Security Notification Centre. 24x7 service. Two outlets in Cyber Hub, one in the MTNL building, Reclamation, two in the India Bulls Building, Lower Parel, one in Jogeshwari (East), three in BKC and another in Navi Mumbai.'

The faint sound of a burglar alarm from a distant vehicle could be heard blaring away.

'Also, any offers on automobiles, discounts, servicing, repair work, purchase and sale, please notify at once to 0228428735 Auto Cell Unit IV.'

None of these warnings managed to arouse his alarm in the slightest. The doorbell rang. He didn't even consider lifting a finger to open it. The only thing that *did* manage to get him to budge was the sound of the caller tune that went off abruptly, breaking the dull monotony of the various household noises as if an eagerly anticipated visitor had arrived at their humble abode. He scrambled to his feet to check his phone, only to wipe his eyes at the dismal realization that the call was not for him. He checked his flatmate's phone, which lay on a small wooden side table at the other end of the couch with a lamp and pocketknife to give it company. The call may have arrived on his flatmate's phone, but it certainly was for him. The letters on the touchscreen spoke loud and clear. It was The Pipsqueak—the little guy, someone he had been avoiding for a while now. He knew the day of reckoning was at hand and wondered how much longer he would manage to ignore him before having to confront the matter. Procrastination was his motto: Do later what one can do now.

'Please call 0125 . . .'

The glistening image before him on the television, reminding him of the harmonious world outside, suddenly burst into static. The cable had evidently gone and the scrambled fuzzy sound emanating from the television grew louder and more disconcerting as he stared blankly into it. The intercom was still ringing away, harmonizing uneasily with the beeping of the alarm clock. The bell rang rhythmically at equal intervals, the sound of the burglar alarm was consistently growing louder and the caller tune from his flatmate's mobile phone still insisted that it be answered.

He arose from the couch sullenly and sauntered over to the washbasin, splashing his face with water until he felt that he was equipped with the alertness required of him. What would it be first?

None of the options seemed even halfway agreeable in the vagary of the passing moment. Answering the door was without doubt the most immediate concern, but what if it meant having to deal with the electricity bill, or the gas bill, or worse still, the pending monthly bill from the neighbourhood department store? He opened his wallet to see how much he had on him and glanced through his driver's licence and various other forms of identification, hoping to be revived with the cheerful prospect of seeing his face all those years ago when the passport-sized photograph had been taken. He didn't look any happier, perhaps a little younger, but certainly about as glum and purposeless as he always did.

'Nadeem Sayed Khatib,' it read. The smile he had tried on for size, at the insistence of the photographer, while posing for the photograph, now appeared unmistakably phoney in the glare of the afternoon sun. He didn't like how he looked, his hairstyle, or how he had held his face together like a stuffed fish for the amusement of all those assembled at the photo studio. He didn't even like his name. The passport-sized photo was an embarrassment. He didn't want anyone seeing him in that state. It was taken during the year of the recession and his hair never quite grew back just as thick. He was of average height, thin, in his mid-twenties, had a frame that could slither through any doorway with the ease of an alley cat, and a face with neither a birthmark nor a beauty spot to distinguish him from all the millions of mugshots of lowlifes and losers with a police record.

He tossed the wallet aside and breezily unlatched the door, yanking it open, fully confident that he could deal with whatever inconvenience came his way. It was the kid from the fourth floor, 403 to be exact, the flat right above 303 and identical in layout. He claimed that some of his laundry had fallen into their balcony. Nadeem gallantly guided him over to the balcony, past the clatter of the plates, spoons and forks lying on the floor. The kid nearly tripped over the beanbag, admiring the contents of the dishevelled living room, his mouth curling up into an 'Ugh!'

The intercom was still ringing, the alarm clock had snoozed and wailed every five minutes, the burglar alarm had grown somewhat softer in anticipation of its owner and the mobile phone on the side table still refused to shut up. Nadeem had learnt to ignore such minor disturbances.

Outside in the balcony, water was dripping all over the clip strings that ran alongside the railings. As fate would have it, all their laundry had been soiled with the refuse from the drainpipe above. Nadeem looked at the kid morosely, letting out an empty exhalation.

'How many times have I told you all about shutting that pipe!' he said. '*It's right above my balcony*. Water falls every day on the clothes. What's the point of drying the clothes out here if you can't keep them from getting wet?'

'That isn't from ours,' the kid said.

'Whaddya mean?'

'We haven't had water in days.' He was right. There had indeed been a water shortage a couple of days earlier which was still continuing in those flats that were known to be more liberal in their usage.

Nadeem's head craned up in an instant. He ran the palm of his hand gently along the railings, looking up, squinting through the sunlight overhead and trying to trace the trajectory of the fall. The water was coming from the drainpipe protruding out from the parapet of the fifth floor, the one right above 403, flat no. 502.

'That's that Makhija,' Nadeem grumbled, tilting his head all the way back to get a better look.

'I know,' the kid smiled. 'I took water from his tank once.'

'Now you listen . . .' Nadeem began. 'If you ever steal water from my tank, you've had it.'

The kid picked up his fluorescent yellow Nike nylon shorts from the floor and sprinted back into the flat. Luckily, the drain water had spared it. It was completely dry. Nadeem ran after him, tumbling over the leg rest between the couch and the television, falling face first into the shoe rack. The kid got away, slamming the front door shut right on Nadeem's face as he tried to crawl towards it. He kicked the ground in irritation, nearly chipping a tile, and hauled himself up, throwing his slippers aside. One of them nearly hit his flatmate who had failed to be stirred by all the commotion. Nadeem smacked the alarm clock, sending it somersaulting into the wall. It tumbled open—the glass detaching itself from the circular frame and the seconds hand spinning about indiscriminately as a small circuit board slipped out from beneath the battery case. It kept beeping even though it had been practically dismembered. He kicked the side table on which the mobile phone had been resting, turning it over and injuring one of its legs severely. The phone hit the tiles, bounced off a corner, did a cartwheel and landed on the rug unscathed, thanks to its protective case. Punching the wall with the side of his fist, he charged towards the intercom and pulled the receiver out from the holder with such force that it nearly dismantled the entire contraption. By now, it had stopped and the person who had for so long been trying to get in touch with him would do better to stay away. He punched down on the three digits—502. First, the engaged tone, then a ring. It rang three times before he started to get fidgety. He waited for someone to pick up, but after the fifth ring, it became painfully evident that the supposed vacancy of the household was just as likely a possibility as an outright ignorance to his plight. It was afternoon, perhaps the occupant was in the midst of a nap. Was it an urgent enough matter to address in person even if it meant risking all civility and neighbourly goodwill? Perhaps it was a matter for the society of the building and ought to be put in writing as a formal complaint to the secretary, Mrs Juliet Miranda, a doddering old woman who occupied the first floor and made quite a big deal about it, sitting on watch all day at her window like a pirate trying to sight land from a telescope.

He rang her up and made a big fuss about it, practically waking up everyone in the entire building from their afternoon naps, hollering about how he was going to make sure that the occupant of 502, Mr Makhija, personally washed his clothes for him.

'SHUT UP!' she barked, sealing Nadeem's trap quicker than a blow to the head. 'Now, you listen to me . . . I don't care if the drainpipe from 502 is pissing all over your clothes. It's not my problem. I'm the secretary, not the plumber.'

'But . . .'

'If I ever hear a peep out of your big mouth, I'm going to see to it that you are never allowed in this building again. Am I clear?'

'Uhh . . . huhh . . .' Nadeem mumbled, cut off midstride.

'I don't hear you.'

'Uhh . . . huh . . . ya.'

'First, pay your rent to your poor old landlord . . .'

'Poor old . . . ya, right!'

'You listen to me here now!' she spoke with more severity than before, 'First, you pay your rent, then you talk!'

She also informed him that if he ever spoke to her in such a tone again, she would personally kick him out on his ass and make sure that he spent the night kissing the pavement. She always knew that having a Muslim tenant in the building meant trouble, but she knew how to handle his type.

Nadeem cut the call, shocked at his inadequacy at being assertive, and that too with an ignorant old lady like

Mrs Miranda. Circumstances had slowly reduced him to the rank of a pushover. Whatever little spine was left had been bent out of shape sitting in front of the television all day long. Compared to the kind of people he had dealt with, she was a cakewalk, but the notion of being homeless was not an enticing prospect, so he put it to rest. He could dry his clothes elsewhere. The four walls that surrounded him and the roof over his head were the only sanctuary he enjoyed from the uncertainty of the outside world. He had mortgaged his car and somehow managed to scrape together enough money for an advance and security deposit on a one-BHK with a living room, a kitchen and a balcony, which was the highlight. He had managed to procure it thanks to one of his flatmate's cousins, Howard, who lived in the area and owned a flat in the building, which he had given out on rent. Nadeem had got the kitchen done up, changed the furniture, made it look more like a home and less like a bargain basement deal, which is what it was for twelve-three-seventy-five a month, including a deposit till their lease got over.

The building was called Little Heights, and although it wasn't the kind of place their friends would refer to as fashionable, he felt reasonably secure there. The law had given him a second chance after teaching him what the cool icy breeze of a lock-up felt like. He wished to never experience it again and tried to start afresh from scratch, knowing fully well that his name would be forever engraved in stone in the registers and files stacked away in some sessions court. Nadeem Khatib, aged twenty-seven, no insurance, no former employment, no marital status in hand or in the pipeline. Just him and his balcony, looking far and wide into the Goregaon skyline hovering imposingly over the Western Express Highway, into the hordes of disenchanted flyovers and up the bylines of the BMT subways.

Nadeem Chipkali

Nadeem Khatib, alias Nadeem Sayed Khatib alias Nadeem Sayed alias Nadeem Khabri alias Nadeem Chipkali, was a tipper by trade, a debt collector by profession, a broker by disposition, but a student by practice. He was always eager to learn a thing or two about another person, provided it paid off in the long run. He knew how to size up a stranger before he learnt how to shake hands.

Information was his racket: information of all sorts and in all shapes and sizes, anything that mattered to a party enough for them to purchase it. Although it was his obligation to lend his services in favour of law enforcement, his adeptness at procuring hard facts had brought him to the attention of every thug and lowlife in town. Even the stray dogs that slept in the sewers practically knew him by his first name.

He had been on the payroll of Inspector V.M. Gaekwad of the Byculla police station, ever since he got busted at a *nakabandhi* off the J.J. flyover with Rs 12 lakh cash in hand. He was nabbed by a constable who shone a torch into his red Honda City and asked him to open the briefcase that lay on the passenger seat. An imported semi-automatic Double Eagle was also found in the glove compartment. He was first taken to Byculla police station and then transferred by the authorities concerned to the Crime Branch where he was attended to by DCP Sumant Rao Kaambli, an officer who was known and famous (or perhaps infamous) all over town for his methods of persuasion.

The money belonged to Nadeem's former employer, Taufiq Ahmed Sheikh, alias Taufiq Maharaj. Nadeem had been appointed with the painful task of having to collect it for him from a builder in town by the name of Sampath Bhaveri. Nadeem even half considered that the builder might have tipped them off at the police checkpoint, knowing fully well that there was just one route for him to take back from Pydhonie towards the suburbs, which runs over the J.J. flyover, where a nakabandhi is usually set up at night. He did, at first, think it irregular for the cop to shine a torch through his window and demand to have the briefcase opened. 'Suppose it contained something personal,' he thought. But he kept his mouth shut and didn't make a fuss about it. He didn't want to say anything more than what he had to.

After spilling the beans on Taufiq Ahmed Sheikh, he didn't have anywhere else to go except inside. So, he served his time, spent two months in Arthur Road Jail until he was fortunate enough to have his flatmate, Warren, pay his bail. They let him off with a warning, which was certainly

more agreeable than the five-year stretch for money
laundering they were initially threatening him with, prior
to his decision to cooperate. The briefcase containing the
money was seized and was currently in the custody of the
Customs, locked away in some cupboard, probably long
forgotten about.

Nadeem had told them the addresses of three of
Taufiq Sheikh's major sites. He had given names too:
Irshaad Ahmed Sheikh alias Irshaad 'Batla', Naved
Sheikh alias Naved 'Pathla', Adnan Sheikh alias 'Lamba'
Adnan, Siraaj Mukadam alias Siraaj 'Kaalia', Ehteshaam
Siddique alias Ehteshaam 'Ghapchi', Ehsaan Khurshid
alias Ehsaan 'Khujli' and Sufiyan Nathani alias Sufiyan
'Khapthi'.

Taufiq Ahmed Sheikh—who had been extradited
from the country as an undesirable alien—was currently
in Abu Dhabi and had made the necessary arrangements
to live there for the rest of his days. He was not the object
of Nadeem's apprehensions, at least not in person. The
more palpable threat lay amongst the many members
of his vast and sprawling family who were situated at
different corners of the coastline. One in New Bombay,
Vashi; one in Mandwa, Alibaug; one in Rey Road, at
the dockyards; two in Sewri, two in Nagpada, three in
Antop Hill, Wadala; one in Malwani number three and
one in Dongar. They ran dens, matka parlours, small-
time book keeping outfits and loan-sharking operations.
They bribed the cops, collected *hafta* from every shop,
peddler and hawker in their areas, and were generally
considered public enemies by most respectable citizens

in the neighbourhood. Scrap metal had been their trade (what was less euphemistically referred to as *bhangaar*), but they had infiltrated other areas of enterprise as their accumulations swelled. The bhangaar was used as a front for stuffing transport vehicles and sailing vessels, so that other illicit goods concealed within could go undetected. They started small, smuggling everything from electronics to *chaandi* (silver), then moved up the ladder gradually as they made inroads into the warehousing trade, providing godowns and storage facilities for industrial hardware and equipment, import–export cargo for local merchants, sometimes even contraband such as arms, ammunition, drugs, and uncut gold, which proved to be the most profitable. They knew where Nadeem lived, that he had rented a one-BHK in Malad (West), just off Fire Brigade Road in Jankalyan Nagar 2, where he put up with his friend Warren, a Catholic from St Paul's Road.

It wasn't long before their landlord, Feroz Machhiwaala, took note of the disreputable activities his tenants engaged in. Nadeem would return to the flat at odd hours, was never present for society meetings and his association with the aforementioned parties had threatened to tarnish every equation he had attempted to cultivate, even the one that was in danger of crumbling as soon as the front door was opened.

Feroz Machhiwaala kept pressing his finger against the doorbell repeatedly. He had been trying to reach Nadeem since the morning but Nadeem couldn't be bothered. The thought of having to see his face again was a most bothersome prospect. Many a tranquil afternoon had been disrupted by the intrusive inquisitiveness of the landlord, and Nadeem was only returning the favour to the secretary of the building with the call he had placed earlier.

The peep-peep-tring-tring of the ambushing bells blasted through Nadeem's skull. After having hung up the intercom, he slapped on a moist, urine-soaked white T-shirt and stumbled out the door, closing it shut behind him. Feroz Machhiwaala stood stubbornly outside his door, breathing in some of the mechanical noises that escaped the flat. His demeanour was rigid yet tolerant even to the most atrocious displays of indiscipline. But he still couldn't figure out how two able-bodied young men could spend the entire day cooped up inside the house, vegetating. As Nadeem had anticipated, he had been summoned by his landlord to answer a few questions pertaining to his current source of employment.

'I'm currently working as a real estate broker, Mr Machhiwaala.'

'Really? Then maybe you could be of service to me by finding a tenant for 201.'

'I don't think I can do that, Mr Machhiwaala! My work pertains mainly to acquiring building sites for construction, not for habitation.'

Feroz Machhiwaala glared at him in reproof, gradually turning towards the closed door of his flat. They didn't want to let him in as yet. It was too early in the day for them to even consider tidying up. The exact time according to the broken-down alarm clock was 3.15 p.m., but in actuality it was half past three. Nadeem had set his clock fifteen minutes early so that he could be two jumps ahead of everyone.

'What the hell were you doing in there?' Mr Machhiwaala inquired. 'I've been trying to call you since morning.'

'I'm sorry, I was sleeping.'

He looked Nadeem over from head to toe in disgust, laughing silently to himself before proceeding with a remark, which he put forth with a backhanded matter-of-factness.

'I heard that you used to be a debt collector for Taufiq Ahmed Sheikh!'

'I used to be a lot of things,' Nadeem laughed, evading the intent of the question by trivializing the whole matter with a smiling shake of the head.

'Not exactly the kind of tenant the rest of the society would approve of,' said Mr Machhiwaala, raising his eyebrow even higher than was customary.

'What made you approve of this tenant then?'

'Well, beggars can't be choosers. I needed a tenant for 303. It was lying empty for as long as I can remember, ever since Mr Saluja abruptly vacated without any notice.'

'Yes, I've had the pleasure of having his leftover MTR packets, plastic wrappers and toiletries for company.'

'He always was a particularly messy sort of fellow.'

'Not an ideal tenant?'

'Questionable activities, not that it's any of my business, mind you! But a landlord does have certain responsibilities. Take the esteemed Mr Makhija, for instance. He doesn't have much time left on his lease, and it would be only appropriate if we started looking for a replacement once those dreadful formalities are taken care of.'

Mr Makhija, the tenant of 502 on the topmost floor, was single. He lived all alone and had the good fortune of occupying a *barsati*, a terrace flat, which he liked to refer to as a penthouse. It was about as agreeable an accommodation one could possibly come by in a building such as this, and he had acquired it at quite a modest rate, much to the chagrin of Mr Machhiwaala. He, however, was two months overdue on his rent, despite the monthly amount being much to his approval.

According to Mr Machhiwaala, he was a stingy man and scarcely settled his bills at the bania at the end of every month. He had been living with them for nearly a year now, and the other members of the society had wearied of his reclusive nature and tiresome ordeals. He never paid his society dues, had to be reminded five times before he showed up with the rent and was not the kind of person they wanted to have around. He was generally considered undesirable by each member of the society.

'When do you want to kick him out?' asked Nadeem.

'Once his lease expires, which would be by the end of the month. His notice period starts now.'

Nadeem thought about it for a moment, considering the proposition. If he was clearing the flat by the end of the month, that left him with another fifteen days in which to show the flat to potential clients and put the word out in the market that there was a lucrative deal on a barsati in Little Heights, provided they settled on a reasonable commission or brokerage for him.

'What about Howard's flat?' he asked, 'How much is he making off it?'

'Those are some merchant navy clients,' said Mr Machhiwaala disdainfully, 'Money is not an issue for them. They're paying twice as much as what you're paying me!'

'Well, they're a family and a two-BHK!'

'Which reminds me . . . uhh . . .' Mr Machhiwaala coughed.

'Yes, our rent! I know.'

'When can I expect it?'

'As soon as possible, I'm on it!' With that, Nadeem did a swift about-turn and began prancing off towards his door.

'By the way, two guys came by the other day,' Mr Machhiwaala mentioned, 'They told Kishorie Lal they were going to 303. They even signed their names in the register.'

'What'd they look like?' Nadeem turned around, suddenly interested.

'According to Kishorie Lal, one was tall and thin, in his mid-forties, the other was short fat, stocky, hair slightly balding, with a handlebar moustache. They were both wearing sunglasses and were dressed in formal office attire. Checked rayon full-sleeved shirts and black synthetic trousers.'

'Great! Did he say what kind of shoes they wore?'

'Gucci. Fake.'

'Old Kishorie Lal has quite an eye for detail!'

'He doesn't miss a thing on you either! I get a complete rundown at the end of the month.'

'How reassuring!'

Mr Machhiwaala winked at Nadeem sympathetically, with the intention of winning him over to his side.

'Why don't you go and pay Mr Makhija a visit?'

'Who? Me?'

'Yeah. Tell him it has been two months and he still hasn't paid, and that his lease is closing in. He doesn't have much time left.'

'Not like he doesn't know it.'

'Yeah, but you could go as a reminder.'

'Something you can't do yourself?'

'I've already been five times last week.'

'What makes you think my telling him will make him budge a square inch?'

'Maybe you could help him pack his bags.'

'I'd rather help him do his laundry first.'

'Oh, come on, Nadeem! You know how to do this kind of thing. You're a professional. Or at least you used to be.'

Nadeem looked at him for a second longer than he usually liked to. The corner of his left eye twitched in retaliation. It was quite apparent from the momentary hesitation in his squint that he had taken it personally. He resented the inference. He was too young to be called a wash-up. He liked to think that he was still as bright and fast as he was, maybe the brief stint in the cooler had slowed him down a little, but he hadn't lost any of his bearings. He knew in which direction the wind blew and he had his finger on the barometer ever since he got his head bashed in by a *paandu* (cop) at the Byculla lock-up. He carried the scar like a medal.

'Why would I wanna do anything for you, Mr Machhiwaala?'

'Perhaps it has something to do with the elapsed time period for the payment of your rent.'

'You mean you could extend it a little if I went and strong-armed Makhija into moving out?'

'I could consider it.'

Nadeem patted his landlord on the shoulder confidently and thumped his own chest, assuring him that he was the man for the job.

'What do you want first? The payment or his rear end in the lobby?'

'For now, just last month's rent will do. I have a couple of debts of my own to settle. Just go and have a word with him, talk to him a little, see if he listens to reason. If not, then be firm and take necessary measures.'

'I'm sorry!' Nadeem laughed. 'I left my hockey stick in the last flat I vacated.'

Makhija

Nadeem turned upon his heel to return to his flat with a newly acquired sense of purpose. This time, he didn't care to knock or ring the doorbell as he was certain that his flatmate hadn't bothered to lock the door from the inside when he had left. As soon as the door creaked open wide enough for him to enter, Warren jumped out of the couch as if he had been hit by a bolt of lightning.

'Sorry!' said Nadeem. 'Didn't mean to disturb your afternoon nap.'

'Ah! It's okay,' Warren yawned. 'You got any Fevikwik? The toilet seat's busted.'

'No doing of mine.'

Nadeem walked over to the fridge, which was usually an object of desolation. It never contained anything of any specific household value. No eggs, bread, milk, fruits or even curd, just ice cream and Thums Up. They even had a box of Taj Mahal tea, which was probably as old as the Taj Mahal itself, stashed away in the cabinet over the kitchen platform with a packet of milk powder.

The house was in a shambles. Not the kind of environment a person in Nadeem's line of work would want to conduct his business proceedings in. If only his clients could see the kind of tinhorn accommodation he shacked up in, they'd probably get a better idea of what kind of person their broker was.

The ringing of the intercom had finally ceased, the cable had come back on, the battery of the alarm clock had probably died, Warren's mobile phone, which lay on the floor, had been put on silent mode, and for a brief flicker of a moment, there was absolute silence in the living room.

And then the bell rang. Warren didn't budge from his position in front of the television. He was too engrossed in WrestleMania III to even consider lifting a finger. Nadeem got up to open the door, taking a swig out of a bottle of three-days-old, flat Thums Up. It was the courier guy with Warren's Vodafone bill. Nadeem signed for it and slammed the door shut.

'What's the point of having a cell phone if you're not going to use it!' Nadeem hollered at Warren. 'You don't even pick up the goddamn phone, man! Every time I try to call you, the only answer I get is from the lady who says, "The number you are trying to call is not responding." If you were to count the number of missed calls that you've accumulated, you could build a house with them.'

'Look, man, stop nagging. You're not my mom.'

'Sometimes, I wish I was.'

Nadeem sat down on the beanbag next to the couch in front of the television. He flipped the channels past the NBA game on ESPN, went through several spiritual leaders on DD Astha and Mahua, a rerun of an old Centurions episode on Cartoon Network (which was to be followed by Swat Cats at 3.30 p.m.) and *Power Rangers* on HBO (which he had seen thrice), before settling on a car racing programme which seemed mildly interesting.

'Warren!' he called out to Warren who had practically dosed off.

'Warren!' he yelled louder.

'What?' Warren awoke with a scowl.

'Did two guys come by the other day?'

'What two guys?'

'One short and fat, the other tall and thin!'

'Laurel and Hardy, sure. They come by every Wednesday at 8 p.m.,' said Warren, pointing to the tube.

'Apparently, they signed their names in the register.'

'If they came looking for you, they probably signed fake names.'

Warren had a point.

'Were you around when they came by?'

'Look, man, I can't keep track of every douche bag that rings the doorbell.'

'Did the bell ring more than once?'

'I don't remember, man.'

Warren tried shutting his eyes in order to ignore Nadeem's questions, but they opened involuntarily, as if by habit. Only the whites of his eyes were visible.

His appearance was not by any means likely to inspire any hospitality if their landlord were to catch a glimpse of him in that state. He had been sitting in front of the television in his vest and shorts for two days straight. His long black hair, which was once parted sideways into an earnest picture of acceptability, hung aimlessly over his forehead, partially obscuring his face. His once clean-shaven jaw had been conquered by an attempt to grow a beard like the one he had seen on the lead singer of Metallica. He had failed miserably at doing so and hence wore it inconsolably along with his thick-framed spectacles.

He didn't manage to do much to contribute to the household. He had spent his better years working at his father's garage in Chimbai, and so had neglected developing any other skill that would deem him employable. He was a slacker, liked to hang around, sleep all night on the couch, watch television and eat chips. Temperamentally, Nadeem didn't exactly associate with him but perhaps that's what made their bond so strong. The two of them seldom felt the need to say anything to one another, especially when immersed in the tube. It hypnotized them into a submissive stupor from which no force seemed to be strong enough to extract them.

The sound of the NASCAR tyres screeching on the asphalt managed to awaken Warren. Often, his curiosity did not comply with his pathological tendencies, and even though he wasn't as much of a car freak as his compatriot, he suffered through the programme as a show of companionship.

'Oh, by the way,' Warren broke the morose silence, bringing up one of the few concerns that had occupied his mind over the past few days. 'Uhh . . . did you . . . uh . . . have a word with . . . uh . . . what's his name . . . Feroz?'

'Yup, I was just with him.'

'What'd he say?' asked Warren from the corner of his mouth.

'He said he'd give us an extension if I went upstairs to collect rent from Makhija and notified him of his dwindling time.'

'That weirdo! I wouldn't go anywhere near his flat. I'd probably get rabies.'

'You hate everyone, don't you, Warren,' said Nadeem drearily, as he lifted his rear end out of the beanbag.

'There are some exceptions.'

'Like myself.'

'Don't give yourself so much importance. You don't choose your friends, you're subjected to them.'

Nadeem let out an accidental laugh that was somewhere between a grunt and a cough. He couldn't help but snigger as he ran his fingers through his hair in front of the mirror. He buttoned on a shirt, put on his slippers and headed out the door, forgetting to close it shut.

'Shut the door, you idiot!' Warren wailed.

Nadeem got into the elevator which crankily insisted in its mechanized female voice: 'Please close the door.'

Staying with Warren for so long, Nadeem had always been susceptible to being infected by some of his contagious laziness. He usually preferred to take the stairs, but his newly acquired habits prevented him from doing so, and so he pressed the button for the fifth floor after adjusting the lift door. It always refused to shut properly and would make an awful racket, giving all the building residents another worthy cause for irritation. Careless visitors would often leave it that way, forget to close it, unaware of its obtrusive noise, as a result of which the voice would keep playing until somebody took the trouble to shut it.

The fifth floor had only two flats on either side, unlike the rest of the floors which had three. Little Heights was one of the few buildings in the area which was not blessed with an A-wing and a B-wing. Nadeem had specifically chosen a building of this sort, after having suffered considerable embarrassment knocking on the doors of strangers, only to be told that he was in the wrong wing.

He knocked on the door of flat no. 502. There was no response. He tried ringing the doorbell a couple of times, but again in vain. He got back into the elevator and headed down towards the lobby where the watchman, Kishorie Lal, was snoring into the breeze of a table fan with his legs resting on a desk. Nadeem checked the register for the last two days and found a column where two visitors had signed in for his flat, 303. The time of their visit was 5.45 p.m. and the time of their exit was 6.30 p.m. The names they had given were Ganpat Shukla and Jasmeet Zhaveri. Rather clumsily chosen, thought Nadeem. They were the most obvious ones that could have possibly occurred to the two visitors, and Nadeem half considered that they might have selected the names from the flat nameplates that adorned the ground floor walls. Ganpat was a name native to Maharashtra or Gujarat and Shukla was most certainly an Uttar Pradesh surname. The two didn't go together. Similarly, Jasmeet was most likely to be Punjabi and Zhaveri was a Gujarati surname.

Nadeem tapped Kishorie Lal's legs till he woke up.

'Where's Makhija?' he inquired. 'He stepped out?'

'No,' replied Kishorie Lal, grumpily. 'He's upstairs. He hasn't stepped out in weeks.'

Nadeem got back into the elevator and went back up. He knocked again, louder this time. There was still no response. He put his ear to the door to grasp any sound that would indicate Makhija's presence or absence. All he could hear was the sound of the television. A teleshopping infomercial could be faintly heard, something to do with the Ab-King Pro. Nadeem hesitantly turned the doorknob and, to his astonishment, it opened. The door had not been locked from the inside and there was no one in the living room in front of the television. All the lights were on, the microwave was beeping furiously, the fans were rotating at the slowest speed possible, the living room windows were open, but the grills were securely fastened. The house looked like it had not been attended to for quite some time.

Nadeem called for Mr Makhija but got no response. He walked over to the terrace balcony. The sliding doors were jammed when he tried to open them and the mosaic flooring had withered with the departing monsoons. As he turned to catch a sight of the bedroom, he could hear the sound of water trickling. He called out once again but heard nothing in reply except the incessant flowing of a tap. It was coming from the direction of the bathroom that was in the farthest right corner of the passage. Nadeem walked slowly towards it, looking left and right, overcautious from being fully aware that he was intruding on someone else's private property. The tubelights in the passage flickered. The sound of the water flowing from the tap was becoming louder and more distinct as he approached the bathroom. He first put his ear to the bathroom door as he could see it was occupied. He could tell that the water was flowing into a bucket, but there was something about the sound that suggested the bucket was full and that the water was spilling over the edges and flooding the bathing area. He considered the possibility, wondering whether or not the toilet was empty. He first knocked on the door but got no response. As he glanced down at the latch, which looked locked from the outside, he noticed water flowing out from under the door. He lifted the latch and creaked the door open slowly, keeping an eye out for whatever it revealed. As it opened completely, Nadeem's eyes widened at the sight before him.

Mr Makhija sat on the commode, his mouth firmly agape, his eyes looking on into the distance and his neck greatly swollen and disfigured. An irregular bulge was detectable along the indentation that arched from the collarbone up towards the Adam's apple, which may have been the result of strenuous exertion or force exerted. It was turning violet, abandoning maroon, and spreading clear across the throat, giving his wide-eyed, open-mouthed expression the gawking idiocy of an idiot child staring into the sky. Although the absence of the usual marble-like stiffness suggested a recent demise, the dryness of the saliva that had trickled down the side of his mouth betrayed the evidence on his face, hinting at a longer time period than might be expected by the apparent lack of decay. Around him lay scattered a profusion of toiletries, all possible remnants of some vigorous struggle that might have occurred within the confines of the toilet.

The sight of this gruesome mess made Nadeem sick, but he had a stronger stomach than he thought. God knows how many days he must have stayed in that condition. The water flowing from the tap ceased just as soon as Nadeem mustered up the courage to enter the bathroom. It was apparent that the entire tank had drained but it still gurgled out a few drops. Nadeem contemplated whether or not to turn the tap off. He hated to see water go waste, but given the circumstances leaving his fingerprints at the crime scene was not a good idea, even if it was in service of environmental preservation.

Forensic Lab Inspection

Inspector Praveen Nagpal of Malwani police chowki, surrounded by two of his deputies, bent down to get a good, thorough look at the corpse, after which they covered it and instructed the constables to seal the flat for a forensic inspection.

The house was out of bounds for all residents of the buildings, save for Nadeem and Mr Machhiwaala, who stood solemnly trying to be of some help. The elderly and bespectacled Mrs Miranda, followed by Mr Paritosh Sahoo of the second floor and old Mr and Mrs Sawant from the first floor had congregated outside the fifth floor lift, whispering to each other inquisitively, gesturing towards the door of 502, expressing abject disapproval in their frowns. Finally, a *hawaldar* was sent to shoo them away.

By the time the coroner and the forensics arrived on the scene, it was evening. No one had touched anything in the house, save the fingerprints expert who was collecting samples from glasses and windowpanes, and Inspector Nagpal who was looking around the house, going through the cabinets and drawers. The rest of the hawaldars stood dutifully in a corner, maintaining a mournful silence. They gathered around the body as Inspector Nagpal uncovered the sheet for Dr Laabru of the Crime Lab.

'So?' asked Dr Laabru. 'What have we got here? What does it look like?'

'Possible strangulation,' Inspector Nagpal remarked. 'Lacerations around the neck. His face took some time to acquire the pallor and texture characteristic of such cases.'

Dr Laabru bent down to open the mouth of the victim and gaze inside. The windpipe had definitely been throttled. There were pockmarks and cuts all around the throat, an acute inflammation of the epiglottis, the tonsils and uvula were severely scalded, and the cartilage ascending from the collarbone up to the jawline protruded alarmingly.

'Did he spill any blood?' asked Dr Laabru, looking up at Inspector Nagpal.

'Not enough to suit me. If he did, we couldn't find it. All we got are the mucus and bile lying in the basin.'

Dr Laabru turned back to the victim, confounded, his lower lip rolling upwards and his eyes squinting at the attempt to go over every inch of the upper torso with microscopic precision. He tilted his head, running his fingers all along the Adam's apple up to the chin.

'Did he have goitre or something?' he asked.

Inspector Nagpal took out a piece of paper from his pocket. 'We found a medical prescription slip or definitely a prescription slip, whether medical or not, I don't know. It was found in the pocket of his pants. It's from a doctor by the name of G.D. Vengsarkar.'

Nagpal read from the prescription slip before handing to it over to Dr Laabru.

'The drugs prescribed,' Inspector Nagpal read, 'were Synohydraloxide and Bentamine 350 with a 2 mg measurement of Nimulid.'

'What the hell was he suffering from? Midlife crisis?' remarked Dr Laabru, as he snatched the paper from Inspector Nagpal's hands to get a look at it. He wanted to study the prescription slip, but he could hardly read it. The handwriting was vividly illegible, as if written in some hieroglyphic code or deliberately written not to be deciphered.

'Have you found any of the medication?' he asked Inspector Nagpal.

'No. None of the specified medication.'

He took Dr Laabru towards the medicine cabinet next to the key hanger. The first-aid kit burst open with an assortment of pills pouring out. It contained a wide range of allopathic, antibiotic and prescription drugs, along with ear drops, eye drops, nose drops, aspirin, antacids, insulin shots for diabetes, vitamin B-52 tablets, painkillers, paracetamols, the works. A bottle of Phensedyl cough syrup lay by the windowsill next to the phenyl and mosquito repellent, but they scarcely noticed it.

'Check with this Dr G.D. Vengsarkar, who was his general practitioner, what condition he was suffering from and if he was visiting a specialist,' Dr Laabru instructed

Inspector Nagpal. 'Also check all the pharmacies in the area, show them this prescription slip. To purchase these kinds of prescription drugs, they have to make a note in the files and their system. It can't be sold without registering the patient's and doctor's name.'

Nagpal turned to his deputy, Srikant, and handed him the prescription slip.

'Go first to Apollo Healthcare,' he told Srikant, 'then Noble Chemist, then 24x7 and Asian Chemist. Check if they've registered this prescription slip. If they have not heard of it, check at every hospital pharmacy in the area.'

Inspector Nagpal signalled the rest of the constables to wrap things up so they could load Makhija on to the stretcher.

'How long did you say he hadn't paid his rent for?' he asked Mr Machhiwaala.

'For the last two months!' Mr Machhiwaala replied promptly.

'When did you last speak to him?'

'Just last week.'

'And no one has had any contact with him since?'

'Even the watchman hasn't seen him step out.'

Nagpal told his second deputy, Dilip, to have a word with Kishorie Lal and to go through the register to note down the names and numbers of everyone who had visited the building in the last week.

'You will be required at the police station for a statement,' Inspector Nagpal told Nadeem. As they exited the flat, he stopped to look at Makhija's mailbox, which hung next to his door. He opened it to find three envelopes, one of which was his Vodafone bill, another a circular from Little Heights society and the third was a notice from ICICI prudential funds. Makhija's mobile phone was already in the possession of the fingerprints expert in a ziplock plastic bag and Nagpal summoned him to ask for it. He handed the phone to Inspector Nagpal, who took it out of the packet and got into the lift browsing through his recent messages, contacts and missed calls. Nadeem and Mr Machhiwaala took the stairs.

Downstairs, people from the neighbouring buildings had gathered and assembled around the front gate to look at what was going on. They were peering into the compound confoundedly as they tried to make sense of the reason behind the police presence.

Inspector Nagpal stormed right out of the elevator, past the front lobby and called for his jeep with a dexterous swishing of the fingers. That hand signal seemed to communicate more to his deputies than any number of words. As the jeep pulled over with a screech, he got into the front seat telling Nadeem to get into the back.

'Does he have a car?' Inspector Nagpal asked Mr Machhiwaala, who stood near the lobby with his hands behind his back.

'I do,' said Nadeem. 'But it's not in my possession at the moment.'

'Not you!' Nagpal frowned. 'Did Makhija own a car?'

'Oh!' replied Mr Machhiwaala. 'Yes, it's parked behind. It's a white Indica, 2008 model. He had recently bought it. The watchman has the keys.'

'Dilip!' Inspector Nagpal barked. 'Have the men check his papers, registration, licence and call a mechanic to figure out when the engine must have run last.'

'My . . . uhh . . . flatmate used to be a mechanic,' Nadeem informed Inspector Nagpal.

'Very well, then,' he said. 'Have his flatmate brought down for an inspection of the engine. Whatever you do, don't turn on the ignition.'

Nadeem got into the back seat of the police jeep as Inspector Nagpal slammed the door shut, flicking his fingers to the driver signalling him to carry on. The jeep stuttered out of the main gate past hordes of onlookers and unwarranted curiosity.

Malad (West) Police Chowki

At the Malad (West) police station, a long line of people had assembled at the registrar's desk. When Nadeem got out of the jeep, following Inspector Nagpal, he remembered the days when he was one of those men waiting in line. He remembered the long hours of procedure and the sordid, morose faces that haunted the police station, all rabid with a look of anticipation in their eyes, waiting for any sign of movement in the ever-stagnating queue.

A hobo was creating quite a stir in the waiting room and it was quite apparent from his demeanour that he was wasted. Inspector Nagpal darted into his cabin, ignoring the commotion around him. Nadeem tried to keep up with him as he gazed at the derelicts that crowded the registrar's desk. Tejaswini, the lady clerk in the administrative branch, was getting some papers signed by the assistant sub-inspector. The chaiwaala was doing the rounds, watering the plants, laughing and chatting with the friendlier hawaldars.

As Nadeem walked into Inspector Nagpal's cabin, the duty officer followed, slamming the door shut. He sat down next to Nadeem and opened a rather large and intimidating register where he was to note down Nadeem's statement. Inspector Nagpal seated himself in the chair behind his desk, breathing heavily and staring at Nadeem, trying to size him up. The door flung open as Tejaswini popped her head in to ask the inspector a question.

'What do you want to do about Vicky Sahib's son?'

'Get me the commissioner's report on that,' Inspector Nagpal said. 'Until then, I'm not authorized to do anything. I'm not going to go out of my way to help some big businessman's spoilt son. Let him go through routine procedure, nice and slow, take your time on the paperwork, make him wait. These rich bastards think they can get away with anything. So what if he's Vicky Solanki's son? We've had four fights in the same area, two accidents, three totalled cars and nine busts in town, plus eight instances of exceeding the permissible decibel limit! We've shut down all private parties. The youth is going to the dogs!'

'The educated youth,' Tejaswini correctively added.

'Yup. The educated youth! At least the illiterate are well-behaved. But these bastards with cars and contacts! Send him in later. I want to have a word with the son of a bitch. What's his name?'

'Nicky,' she replied.

'Vicky named his son Nicky! How innovative!'

Tejaswini exited the cabin, delicately closing the door shut, fully aware of the sensitive nature of the conversation that was about to take place. Inspector Nagpal turned his attention back towards Nadeem, as he reclined in his swivel chair and made himself at home.

'State your name and age.'

'Nadeem Khatib. Twenty-seven years.'

The duty officer wrote all this down. Just then, Inspector Nagpal's subordinate, Dilip, flung the door open and entered with an urgency that seemed almost routine yet vaguely ominous.

'We found out about that car, sir. There's no insurance, no registration. It's a Maharasthra number plate. We'll have to file a separate case, unregistered vehicle.'

'Tell them to get the car here,' Inspector Nagpal coughed. 'I want to see it first.'

He turned back to Nadeem with a piercing stare. There was something about him that Inspector Nagpal didn't like, but he couldn't put his finger on it. Maybe it was the way his face was put together, his hairstyle or just the colour of his shirt. Nadeem often had that effect on people.

'What's your line of work?' he asked Nadeem.

'Property dealer, real estate consultant.'

'I've known your kind, Khatib. You change colours and occupations at the drop of a hat. What were you doing in Makhija's house?'

'Well, sir, as Mr Feroz Machhiwaala pointed out, he had sent me to collect Mr Makhija's rent.'

'Forget about that Machhiwaala. For all I know, he could have sent you there to collect fish. What were *you* doing there?'

'As I said . . .'

'Listen, Khatib, we know why you were sent there. What we want to know is what you were doing there?'

'Nothing, just looking for him.'

'And you found him in the toilet.'

'Quite right.'

'You have any witnesses?'

'Mr Machhiwaala . . .'

'Forget about that fishmonger. I'm talking cold hard facts, eye balls, evidence. Did anyone see you enter and exit Makhija's flat?'

'No. As I said, it's on the top floor. No one else lives there except Mr Makhija.'

'Save that Mr Makhija nonsense for the judge. You can call him Makhija in my presence. By the way, what was his first name?'

'Chintan, I think.'

'Chintan Makhija. Sounds like an upstanding citizen. I bet he's got his name plastered on every Lions and Rotary club west of the Goregaon post office. Did he have any friends?'

'None that I know of, sir. He lived alone and there's no one else on the fifth floor except for him.'

'What about the other flat? Is it empty?'

'It belongs to one Naresh Raheja.'

'Break the next door flat open and check the place,' Inspector Nagpal ordered his subordinate. 'I don't care which Raheja owns it.'

Nadeem thought that if this was the way they handled homicide cases, then the living had it worse than the dead.

Inspector Praveen Nagpal seemed sharp and capable though, with a patience that seemed only to be a pretext for what was to follow. Nadeem, however, seemed curious about who his superior was, when he would land up and how he would behave in front of him whether he'd still have his feet up on the table in his presence, or up his ass with a feather duster.

'Also,' the inspector barked. 'Show the house key to every locksmith in the area and check if anyone had asked for a spare to be made.'

He turned back to Nadeem.

'You said the door was unlocked when you reached there?'

'Yes, the main door as well as the bathroom door, and the tap was still on.'

'Sir,' Dilip interrupted. 'We just found out that he was last seen at the neighbourhood hardware store, Shelu . . .'

'Shaalu,' Nadeem corrected.

'Shaalu. We have the receipt,' Dilip continued, handing the bill to the inspector. 'We spoke to the owner of the store. He said Makhija had last visited them the week before last, had purchased a 4x4 sheet of sandpaper, a roll of masking tape and aluminium foil, a box of rubber bands, a plyer, a screwdriver, a pair of tongs, a grinder and a four-foot-long strip of jute rope.'

'What the hell was he trying to do,' asked Inspector Nagpal. 'Tie himself up?'

'I know that Shaalu,' said Nadeem. 'He must have tried to peddle everything under the sun to him.'

Dilip opened the watchman's register and read from it.

'Apparently,' he stated, 'two men came by the day before yesterday to pay you a visit. You forgot to mention that.'

'I didn't think it had anything to do with this case. That's my business. It's private.'

'Nothing's private here,' Inspector Nagpal reminded him. 'What's your business is our business. Who were these two men?'

Nadeem didn't answer. He had the right to remain silent. He couldn't dream of an advocate and he hoped he wouldn't need one.

'According to the watchman,' said Dilip. 'They looked like goons.'

'And according to the building secretary,' added Inspector Nagpal, 'you seem to have had quite a bee in your bonnet regarding this Makhija character. She said you called her up two hours before the body was discovered to lodge a complaint.'

'That has nothing to do with any of this,' Nadeem protested. 'That was before I found him.'

'And next thing you know, the guy winds up dead,' Dilip smirked.

'One hell of a coincidence,' Inspector Nagpal said.

The door burst open again and, this time, Nagpal's deputy Srikant charged into the room with far greater an urgency than Dilip had displayed. He looked wound up, his whole face was flushed with an approaching anxiety. He leapt across the room to Inspector Nagpal's desk and leaned over to whisper into his ear. Inspector Nagpal immediately shot up and told Nadeem to step outside the office. Srikant informed Nadeem that Warren was outside in the waiting room. Nadeem wondered why they had brought him along, as the duty officer escorted him out of the office towards the waiting room. He hoped Warren wasn't in any trouble and looked back towards the inspector's cabin where his two deputies were huddled around his desk. The three men were looking evidently secretive, as if something had hit the fan. The duty officer pulled Nadeem away from there and, yanking his arm tighter than he would have liked, dragged him all the way to the waiting room where he left him with Warren.

'What's the big idea?' Warren gasped. 'Sending up a bunch of paandus to summon me to check Makhija's car. I had to open up the entire bonnet and inspect the axle. I usually don't like to get my hands dirty unless I get paid for it.'

'They were only doing their duty,' murmured Nadeem.

'And what makes you think I wanted to be a part of it?'

'You ought to do your bit for society every once in a while.'

'I pay my dues and keep my nose clean. I wasn't sent to planet Earth to make the police force's job easier for them.'

'Sometimes, I'm not sure what planet you were sent to. A couple more hours in front of that television screen and they'll be hauling your carcass down the stairs.'

Warren looked around trying to make sense of the ongoing activity.

'What are you doing down here?' Nadeem asked, nudging him. 'Why did they bring you?'

Warren hunched down low and whispered. 'Kishorie Lal told them that some guys had come to the flat while you were away and that I was upstairs in the building when they had come. Although I have absolutely no recollection whatsoever of this, they still had to call me down for questioning about this. Apparently, they are the only unidentified visitors in the register for the last two or three days.'

'Tell them you were sleeping when they came and that you didn't answer the door.'

'What happened to Makhija?' asked Warren, visibly agitated.

'That's what they're trying to figure out,' said Nadeem, looking down at the floor.

'You don't think those two guys who came to pay us a visit the other day could have had anything to do with it?' Warren asked, breaking into a sweat.

'I doubt it, considering they had more pressing matters on their mind. If they wanted to make an example, they could have picked our neighbours and they wouldn't have had to go all the way to the fifth floor. But . . . on the other hand, supposing they picked the easiest option. Taking care of a single middle-aged man wouldn't make too much of a noise and it would make their point considerably clear.'

'Well, I guess you'd have to call Taufiq Maharaj to figure that one out, but I still have my doubts. Even bhaigiri has it scruples. They don't randomly harass strangers who mind their own business.'

Nadeem leaned back and looked out the window.

'By the way,' said Warren, summoning his attention. 'He wasn't single. He may have lived alone, but he was a married man.'

Nadeem turned towards Warren and sat upright.

'How do you know?'

'While I was downstairs checking the radiator,' mumbled Warren, 'a lady showed up.'

'What lady?'

'Name of Rohini Makhija. Considerably younger than he was, all dolled up like she was out shopping, and not in the least bit perturbed about her husband's death.'

'When did she turn up?'

'Half an hour after you guys left the building compound. She wasn't dressed appropriately for mourning, I can assure you. Not that I'm a great judge of character, but her blank face hinted that she didn't give a damn, one way or another.'

'Were they divorced? Separated?'

'How should I know? All I know is that no one's ever seen her visit this building, Machhiwaala included. In fact, he said that Makhija had lied to him about his marital status.'

'Are the cops bringing her here?'

'I'm pretty certain they are. They kept bowing and scraping in front of her as if she were the crown jewels. They didn't question her, just showed her around the flat, and she felt free to pick up anything that caught her fancy, claiming it belonged to her.'

'Did Machhiwaala question her?'

'On the contrary, she questioned him. She wanted to know all the sordid details. He kept offering his condolences and saying he was sorry, but she didn't look sorry. She just looked bored.'

Nadeem got up and went to one of the hawaldars standing in a corner next to the head constable's desk. He first requested the hawaldar to tell him what was going on, but the hawaldar just ignored him. He barely looked at him and didn't even acknowledge his presence. Nadeem then politely asked if he could be permitted to leave, but he was simply told to sit down and wait for Sub-Inspector Dilip, who would be with them shortly. Nadeem's patience was wearing thin. He did not want to spend the next two hours waiting. It was only a matter of minutes before he started making a fuss. He yelled and hollered at the head constable, said he had contacts in the department that could strip off all their uniforms in a heartbeat. He claimed to be personally acquainted with the Additional Commissioner of Andheri police station. Finally, Dilip came out of Inspector Nagpal's office to silence him. He told Nadeem that if he continued his bellyaching, he would spend the night in remand. But Nadeem was adamant. Eventually, it came to a point where he had to be physically restrained by two constables.

When Warren was called in for questioning, the two constables took Nadeem back to his seat, trying to calm him down. After a couple of deep breaths and reconsideration,

Nadeem realized that it was best to just toe the line and wait for however long he had to. He didn't want to dig himself any deeper into the hole he seemed to have got himself into. He asked the constables if they could escort him out for a cigarette, which they refused. He pleaded with them, begged even, but they had orders to keep an eye on him and not to let him leave the confines of the waiting room until further notice.

As the chaiwaala came by on his rounds, Nadeem summoned him with a whistle. He trotted up to him grumpily, yet dutifully. He didn't like being whistled at, especially by people who were there not by choice, and he made his dislike quite apparent. He raised his eyebrow at Nadeem, asking him what he wanted.

'Make it one cup!' He grumbled. 'Actually . . . no, wait. Make it two.'

'That'll be ten bucks.'

Nadeem looked towards the hawaldars assigned to him and asked if this was their idea of a joke.

'What kind of police station makes you pay for tea?' he scoffed.

'This one does,' said the chaiwaala under his breath. 'Do you want it or not? I don't have all day.'

'Thanks, but no thanks!' Nadeem snickered, 'Cheapskate!'

'Keep quiet!' The hawaldar barked at him.

Just as the chaiwaala was about to walk away, he called him back and told him to pour him a cup.

'How many? One or two?'

'Make it one,' said Nadeem, handing him a five-rupee coin.

The Widow in White

As the chaiwaala walked off, offering the others tea, making a sound under his teeth, he nearly collided with Senior Inspector Chetan Raane who charged in from the main entrance. A convoy of senior constables followed him, escorting a rather timid-looking lady. Nadeem glanced at her, as did everyone else in the waiting room. She pretty much fit the description Warren had given him earlier of Makhija's wife.

She sported a white salwar, had a yellow dupatta draped around her shoulders, a gaudy purple bindi plastered on her forehead, a silver chain around her neck—which she wore like a dog collar—and enough grief in her carriage to let the world know that she had just walked out of a Fabindia sale. Each move she made sounded like a wind chime. Every time she swept the hair off the side of her forehead, her bangles, earrings and other paraphernalia would jingle. She had a pair of dark glasses on, so it was difficult to tell whether or not she had spent the last two hours crying. But there was something about the delicacy with which the police treated her, which hinted that she had displayed some emotion in one form or the other. She seemed stoic, however, with a resolute grimace that ran across her tightened jaw. The constables asked her to sit outside the inspector's cabin, as Senior Inspector Raane entered, shutting the door behind him. A female constable sat beside her.

Nadeem kept a firm eye pointed in the direction of the door. In a couple of seconds, it opened and Warren came out. Srikant then asked the woman to come inside.

'What did they ask you?' Nadeem asked Warren frantically as he sat down next to him.

'Nothing. Just a couple of questions about Makhija, and also about you.'

'What did they say about me?'

'They asked if you associated with any questionable characters. I, of course, said no . . .'

'And what else?'

'Also, if you had any personal quarrel with Makhija. They asked why you had called up the secretary to complain about him. Was it about the water? Apparently, the tap had been left on at the scene of the crime.'

'This is ridiculous . . .'

'Again, I said that I didn't know anything about that, and that we've never really had any water problems except day before yesterday . . . but I don't know, man . . . this sucks! The last thing I wanted was to get myself mixed up in a murder investigation. Today, out of all days, when

Mortal Kombat: Annihilation is coming on Star Movies at 9 o'clock.'

'Well, we're gonna miss it.'

'They should be out there questioning the watchman and that stupid landlord of ours! What the heck have they brought us here for?' Warren shook his head in bewilderment, adjusting his spectacles. 'That Nagpal's got something on his mind,' he whispered, 'I don't know what it is.'

Now, Nadeem was really tense. He was hoping that he wouldn't be counted as a suspect, given the circumstantial nature of the case. He thought that his being the person who discovered the body was enough of an alibi in his favour, but despite that he could be certain of absolutely nothing. He felt that Inspector Nagpal was conducting his investigation in the most unorthodox manner imaginable and was presenting and evaluating the facts with the least objectivity possible. To accuse the very person who brought the incident to light went beyond common sense. It went beyond stupidity. Just because he didn't like Nadeem wasn't enough of a reason for him to hang the case on him.

Ever since he was a kid, Nadeem Khatib would constantly be beaten up for things he didn't do—being punished for crimes he didn't commit and paying prices that were far beyond his means. But this was different, this meant getting mixed up in something that smelt of twenty years to life. He didn't like the look of this and he didn't like the direction in which the investigation was headed either. He thought it would be better if he got a whiff of the conversation taking place inside. He asked the hawaldars seated on either side if he could shift to the chair near the inspector's cabin, the one Rohini Makhija had just vacated. They saw no reason to refuse his request. He settled himself on the chair right outside the closed door. He could faintly hear what was going on inside. He first leaned his head against the wall, pretending that he was trying to get some shut-eye, and then discreetly, when no one was watching, turned his head sideways to stick his ear to the door. He could hear bits of what was being said. He closed his eyes as he listened. No one noticed that he had put his ear to the glass and was eavesdropping. They thought he had dozed off.

'How long have you known Chintan Makhija?' Senior Inspector Raane asked Mrs Makhija who was seated on the opposite end of Nagpal's desk.

'Two and a half years. We had met at Inorbit Mall through a mutual friend who was a broker and was helping me find a flat.'

'What kind of man was Mr Makhija? Was he a particularly possessive sort of husband?'

'No.'

'Was he a big spender?'

'Not really. He couldn't handle his affairs. I used to take care of his finances for him. When he got himself fired from HSBC, he moved to the cheapest accommodation he could find.'

'Which he found in Little Heights,' said Inspector Nagpal.

'Where do you currently reside?' asked Senior Inspector Raane.

'Shakuntala Building. Block number three, B-Wing, Juhu Tara Road. I stay there alone. I had a flatmate, my friend from college, but she left Bombay and went back to her home town.'

There was a long pause as Senior Inspector Raane got up from his chair and began to pace up and down the room. Nagpal asked her if she would like any tea or water. Srikant then opened one of the files and started noting down some facts and information that seemed relevant to the case. After having put up a sufficient display of protocol, Inspector Nagpal leaned back in his chair, breathed heavily and asked with a hint of informality in his strained voice. 'Why would anyone want to kill your husband?'

'Plenty of reasons,' she sighed. 'He owed a lot of money around town. He wasn't an agreeable sort of fellow. Got into a lot of altercations and conflicts. Was a bit of an antisocial element.'

'Is that why he used to visit a psychiatrist?'

'I don't know anything about that.'

Srikant pulled out the prescription from his chest pocket and flashed it before her. It said: Dr G.D. Vengsarkar, Healthy Mind Clinic, Dadar (East), next to King's Circle.

'We've sent our men to look over the place. We have reason to believe,' said Nagpal, 'that your ex-husband was receiving counselling and therapy from a shrink by the name of Dr G.D. Vengsarkar. We found this medical prescription in his pant pocket.'

'I wasn't aware of that. Chintan always opened up to me about his problems. Even after our separation, we were on good terms.'

'I see,' Inspector Nagpal smiled.

'Would you by any chance,' asked Senior Inspector Raane, scratching his forehead, 'happen to have any idea why your deceased husband was visiting a psychiatrist?'

'For sleeping pills, I suppose. He used to have trouble going to sleep at night.'

'Was that one of the causes of your separation?' asked Inspector Nagpal.

'I'm sorry,' she muttered.

'Are you a sound sleeper?' asked Inspector Nagpal, again in the same tone of militant formality, yet there was a note of insincerity in his voice.

'I don't see what that has to do with the case?'

'I do apologize, Ma'am,' he laughed. 'I'm simply trying to comprehend the circumstances of your marriage. I mean, Mr Makhija was not exactly the kind of person who could knock you off your feet. Not exactly a matinee idol, if you know what I mean. He was an overweight, middle-aged man with enough debts to keep his forehead permanently creased.'

'He was a good man,' she added.

'I'm sure your divorce counsellor would gladly corroborate that statement.'

'Ahh!' She smacked her hand in the air, turning away from the inspector to look outside the window. There wasn't much to look at.

Inspector Nagpal had every reason to detect some rudeness in her manner and clamp down upon it, yet he used his discretion. Her face started contorting into a righteous frown. She hadn't said a word out of place as far as she was concerned. There was silence in the room. The wind blew a couple of dried up gulmohar tendrils in through the window. By now, Nadeem had silently crept into the conversation by pushing the door slightly ajar, so he could hear more clearly. Srikant noticed this and whistled at him under his teeth to back off. He slammed the door shut and locked it.

'Mrs Makhija,' Inspector Nagpal began. 'I'm sure you don't mind if I refer to you as Mrs Makhija, do you? After all, you seem to have had a change of heart regarding your husband.'

'You can call me Rohini,' she snapped, having lost all patience and civility by now.

'I'm not exactly on a first name basis with you as yet, Ma'am,' said Inspector Nagpal, as politely as he could. 'That, however, is completely up to you. As you know, I can either be a friend and confidant or an adversary. Whatever you wish. I would advise you to avoid the latter, given the circumstances.'

'Would you like us to call your parents?' asked Senior Inspector Raane.

'No.'

'Then I'm afraid you must cooperate with us and answer a few questions,' said Inspector Nagpal. 'When was the last time you got in touch with him?'

'I didn't get in touch with him. He got in touch with me.'

'Your name was first in the call log on his mobile phone.'

'He had called to ask if he could keep my deck.'

'Your what?'

'Music system. I objected saying that I wanted it back.'

'That's right,' said Inspector Nagpal. 'According to one of my men, on your visit to the house prior to this, you had asked if you could collect certain articles and objects of value which you claimed belong to you. Isn't that a little insensitive considering the tragedy that has just occurred?'

'Those things are my property and I have the legal right to their possession,' she said. 'Plus, I don't know when I'm ever going to get to see them again. It was my first visit to his house, and I hope it was my last.'

'What was the reason for your divorce, Ma'am?' asked Senior Inspector Raane after a long, deliberate pause.

She didn't say a word.

'Why did you get married to him?' asked Inspector Nagpal, breaking the awkward silence.

'I would like it, Inspector Nagpal,' she snarled, 'if you could keep your curiosity out of this conversation.'

'It is merely my curiosity as a police officer, Ma'am, that leads me to inquire why you divorced him.'

'And your curiosity as a man that leads you to ask why I married him.'

'There is a certain curiosity even men cannot explain and certain actions even women cannot justify.'

'Look around you, Inspector,' she thundered. 'What kind of men do you see? Studs, Greek gods, frog princes, poster boys, Adonis', eligible bachelors?'

'The kind of men I come across in my line of work hardly fit the bill for model husbands!'

'What makes you a think that a woman has a choice for anything other than the bottom of the barrel as far as finding a suitable partner is concerned?'

'I wouldn't go as far as to say that, Ma'am,' said Inspector Nagpal. 'There are plenty of good, honest hard-working men out there. You just haven't found the right one.'

She couldn't take any more of Inspector Nagpal's badgering. She trembled, reached for her handkerchief, and before Srikant could even lift a finger to get her a glass of water, burst into tears.

'There, there, now, Ma'am!' Senior Inspector Raane consoled her. 'This is no way to display your concerns. We expect you to be in as much control of your faculties as we are. If we were to let our emotions get the better of us, I dare say we'd scarcely make it through a day's work.'

Srikant got her a glass of water, which she sipped thoughtfully. She asked if she could step out for a smoke. Senior Inspector Raane did not approve of a woman smoking in his presence, but Inspector Nagpal was of the opinion that it might get her to open up a bit. They escorted her out to the entrance of the police station where the jeeps were parked.

She seated herself on one of the steps while the female constable sat on the one just above her. Inspectors Raane and Nagpal stood attentively, waiting for her to speak, hanging on her every puff, but all they got in response was a deep disconcerting sigh.

'We are ready to talk whenever you are, Ma'am!' said Inspector Nagpal.

The Lizard

After signing their statements, Nadeem and Warren were allowed to leave the claustrophobic confines of Malad (West) police station. Rohini, however, was detained, held in police custody for further questioning. The autopsy report was due in the morning, and until then they had a watch planted outside the building to monitor the movement of all residents. A hawaldar was spending the night outside flat no. 502. The beat patrols had been notified to circle the area at intervals of fifteen to twenty minutes. Dilip and Srikant split up with a squad of four men in two jeeps and began to go to each and every chemist, pharmacy and hospital in the entire Andheri (West) region, all the way from Juhu Circle to Madh Island. They were still trying to trace and locate the two unidentified visitors who had signed in the register with fake names. They had put out a notice of the descriptions Kishorie Lal had given.

At the building, the secretary's congregation had disbanded for the night and was due to report in the lobby first thing in the morning for a summation of the night's proceedings. Two men in plainclothes sat in a white Maruti Gypsy parked right outside the compound. One of them kept dozing off, while the other kept busy unscrewing the green cap of his white tube to pour the *chuna* out into the tambakoo-laden palm of his hand. The hawaldar upstairs kept doing rounds of the fourth and fifth floors, checking if the terrace was still locked. The likelihood of it having been a possible entry point was considered practically negligible, according to the investigation. The watchman was going door to door, personally questioning every resident if they had had any visitors at all during the past few days. The secretary was not pleased with this. A slip-up of this sort was liable to cost the watchman his job. That was what they were paying him for, to keep a firm eye on everything and not let anyone slip by on his watch. They couldn't afford a CCTV camera.

It was late at night when Nadeem and Warren returned home. Warren immediately leapt on to the sofa and switched on the television. Nadeem dragged out the dustbin and placed it next to the doorway for the garbage man to collect in the morning. After closing the door, he turned the circular lever behind the latch twice, adjusting the lock in place. Even though it wouldn't rotate any more, he still kept turning it just to be sure. He didn't want to go to sleep with an unlocked door that night, not after what had happened.

'I have to say,' said Warren, 'I'm surprised that neither Makhija's landlord nor the watchman has been called down to the station for questioning.'

'They did their questioning on them in the compound premises,' said Nadeem.

'Then what makes us so special?' grunted Warren, as he fumbled with the remote control.

Nadeem too wondered why Machhiwaala and Kishorie Lal had been spared the painful ordeal that the two of them had endured.

'Hell! You know, Warren,' said Nadeem. 'Paranoia's a funny thing.'

'Why is that? Can't say I've ever suffered from it.'

'Gets so that you start thinking that the whole world is conspiring against you. That the walls are closing in. You see, the more I think about this whole situation, the less I like it.'

Warren put the television on mute to try and comprehend what Nadeem was blathering about.

'You see, I'm trying to think that things will be all right, you know, hope for the best and what not, keep the fingers crossed. I answer each of your questions the way I hope the law will answer mine. But when you start asking me certain things that even I don't have an answer to, it gets me thinking.'

Warren looked at him in numb silence. The night insects could be heard rattling about in the distance. They were getting a good breeze at that hour of the night. Nadeem always did say that at least the place had good ventilation. He liked to focus on the good things of life, the little things that made all the difference, but unfortunately, Warren couldn't see things his way. His chief concern was making it through the day in one piece so that he could be in front of the television for the graveyard shift.

'It gets me thinking about things, Warren.'

''Bout what?'

''Bout a lot of things, things that actually matter. You see, if the law only thought about things that truly mattered, we would have a lot less crime. The only problem with them is that they only think about things that look good on paper. It doesn't work like that on the ground level. Things that look good on paper don't necessarily look too good when you see them in front of your own eyes. Like, take the two of them for instance, the watchman and the landlord. Right now, I'm beginning to wonder why I had been sent up there by Mr Machhiwaala in the first place, and why it wasn't a task that he could have accomplished himself.'

'Well, I don't know. I suppose it's because you were a . . . uh . . .' Warren didn't know how to put it in words, and the words that were coming to his head, he didn't want to use in front of Nadeem.

'If it were for the sole reason that I have a background of being an underworld collector or a messenger of doom to people who do not want to face the facts, then it does seem reasonable that Mr Machhiwaala should call upon my services for such an endeavour.'

'Hmm . . .' contemplated Warren.

'But the very fact that he was aware of my background brings up another disconcerting question altogether.'

Warren sat up, literally upright, in attention. His droopy eyes were suddenly enlivened and things were beginning to make sense to him.

'How did he come to know that one of his tenants . . .'

' . . . who had submitted to him only one photocopy of his PAN card and driver's licence . . .'

' . . . had previously been under the employment of Taufiq Ahmed Sheikh?' Warren completed Nadeem's sentence.

'From whom did he find out, and what would be the first step he would take in such a situation?'

'Would he eject his tenant?' Warren looked around to make sure he was still sitting in the same flat.

'Or go to the authorities as any decent, respectable, law-abiding citizen and landlord would?'

Nadeem highly doubted that his landlord would have informed the police, for the sake of his own interest.

'Taking a name like that to the police tends to get a person mixed up in something he should have never got mixed up in, in the first place,' he said. 'If he would have taken Taufiq Maharaj's name, he would have been the one being investigated, not me.'

'Well, we're going to need funds if we're to get a lawyer.'

'We can't afford a lawyer. I'll have to take care of this myself.'

'We can take a loan.'

'Forget about that. I still owe Taufiq and co. twelve lakhs. Don't forget that. And any one of these days I'm sure they are going to send someone around to collect it.'

'I'd say one of those days has already passed by.'

'Well . . . I don't know . . .' Nadeem mumbled, studying the dotted patterns on the tiles, his mind wandering off to thoughts of the inevitable. 'Anyone could have sneaked into the apartment from the wall at the back. It's not impossible to scale. There's no broken glass on top of it.'

'What do you think Kishorie Lal told them?'

'God knows,' exhaled Nadeem, as he untied his shoelaces. He didn't want to think about it. He didn't have anyone to turn to but Warren, who wasn't exactly being much of a help in the anxiety department. He had no funds for legal assistance, no friends he could ask a favour from at such short notice. Not even a relative that would vouch for him.

After being released from prison, Nadeem had been banished from his home and set free to roam the streets, to live in perpetual fear of coming across one of Taufiq Bhai's shooters while crossing the road or in some back alley while taking a leak on a dark night. The word on the street was that Taufiq Maharaj had put out a *supaari* on his head. He had acquired this information, or khabar as people on the street liked to call it, at the risk of his own life by going to one of Taufiq Maharaj's sites, despite having been strictly instructed by the police to cut off all relations and keep a safe distance until they needed some more information.

Eventually, he had to go back to the Byculla police station, where he had originally been apprehended, and look for Inspector V.M. Gaekwad, who was the apprehending officer and DCP Kaambli's subordinate. Since DCP Kaambli was not exactly approachable, he had to count on Inspector Gaekwad's complete assurance that no harm would come to him under any circumstance.

Which is why, as time passed, he earned the nickname of 'khabri', which means tipper. He would wander the streets at night, arm in arm with the patrolling jeeps that paraded the area, circling the activity they beheld before them at all odd hours. Many a time, Nadeem would go to sleep on the benches of the waiting room at the Byculla police station, and as the approaching dawn would bring with it a grumpy hawaldar who gave him the lathi (stick), he would invariably be on his way.

He came to be known as Nadeem Chipkali, meaning the lizard, an appropriate name considering his ability to change colours like a chameleon at the drop of a hat. He was one of those rare birds who were on comfortable terms with those on either side of the fence.

'The way it looks,' Warren concluded, 'we got two options. Either we go to Byculla or to Bandra. It's either the cops or the company.'

'The company's not an option. Taufiq Bhai's family lawyer, Razzaq, won't even designate one of his underlings to me. And if they do agree to help us out, it'll only be because they have other plans for me, and then, they'll be the ones standing trial for murder.'

'I think we should just wait it out and hope to God that we don't get summoned again, or else we make arrangements for what we do if we do get summoned. If you're going to be doing a murder stretch, I'm gonna need someone else to split the rent with. I can't afford twelve-three-seventy-five a month.'

'WARREN! I am NOT going to be doing a murder stretch! For God's sake! I didn't do it!'

'I know you didn't, man,' Warren jittered, possibly exhibiting some genuine apprehension for the first time. 'You think it was him?'

'Who? Taufiq?'

'No . . . I mean, as in . . . him . . .'

'Who?'

'The little guy?' Warren murmured, his eyes shying away.

Nadeem froze. He slowly turned his head towards Warren, as it dawned on him. 'He called on your phone today afternoon.'

'I know,' said Warren. 'I got like a hundred missed calls. Why don't you just tell him to call on your number? By the way, do you know what happened to my phone? There seems to be a scratch on the corner,' he said, examining his phone with the keenest precision.

'I don't know . . .' Nadeem mumbled. 'I think it fell or something.'

Just then, Warren's phone lit up, glowing into a silent ring. It vibrated even though it had been put on silent mode. Warren glanced at the number in reflex and looked at Nadeem. 'What do you wanna do?' he asked, his mouth open wide and his face evidently stricken by what he had just seen.

'Who is it?'

'Who do you think!' He spoke from the corner of his mouth, holding the screen up for Nadeem to take a good look.

'Oh!' The number had been stored as 'IGNORE' in the contact list, in big, bold capital letters that were tough enough to ignore when they appeared on the screen in the first place. There were barely any contacts in Warren's phone, as it had recently been purchased at a discounted rate from a sardar who ran a second-hand mobile repair shop on Fifteenth Road, but Nadeem's phone had been his weary companion through all his sordid years—long enough to list everyone who had had the misfortune of having encountered him. His contact list was practically a black book. It contained the names and numbers of every crooked, thieving, conniving scumbag in the city. So being, the mobile phone had acquired a position of karmic significance—a source of income, as well as a faint cosmic promise to peace of mind. If he received a call from anyone out there in the universe, it meant that he had more than himself to fend for in the passing moment. And just so long as it didn't ring, what went on outside the enclosure of those four walls didn't matter, one way or another.

The Little Guy

As far as he could remember, Nadeem Chipkali had always been known to keep the wrong kind of company. He was constantly hanging around with the wrong kind of people and making the wrong kind of friends, friends his parents never approved of but who could always spare a quick buck, such as Taufiq Maharaj's son, Irshaad Ahmed Sheikh, alias Irshaad Batla.

'Batla' was a name Irshaad particularly resented, as it meant short or small. Most of his adversaries revelled in calling him just that, but over time he had learnt to laugh at it. After all, he had carried that nickname since he was a kid. He had had enough time to get used to it. But, somehow, it was always a matter of considerable uncertainty as to how he would react to being called 'Batla'. Nadeem was one of those select few who had a long-standing acquaintance with him and had been granted the privilege of referring to him as Irshaad 'Batla'. Otherwise, Irshaad 'Bhai' was the name he generally preferred.

He had been apprehended once under the charge of half murder. He and his cronies had tailed an A7 that had overtaken them in a rash manner on the Eastern Freeway. They caught up with the car, made the driver pull over, smashed the windscreen, removed the bumper, tore down both the side view mirrors and left the person in the passenger seat with a dislocated collarbone.

Naturally, he was the kind of person Nadeem's parents didn't want him to associate with. Given Irshaad's family's involvement in nefarious activities, he had acquired the reputation of being an intimidating presence in affluent society. Although Nadeem had only known him socially before going to work for Taufiq Bhai, he was acquainted with him well enough to engage in real estate brokerage. Apparently, his old man was thinking of moving into the building and construction business, and Nadeem helped facilitate a few transactions of land purchase in the Navi Mumbai region. Having impressed Taufiq Bhai with his resourcefulness, Nadeem was put to work first as a sales manager for property dealings and later in the book keeping department. Invariably, due to his proficiency with the financial side of things, he went to work on their accounts and the loans that they gave to those unfortunate enough to require them. Eventually, his job entailed collecting overdue payments and tracking parties that were absconding. No one ever took a rupee from Taufiq Maharaj and didn't pay it back, especially as long as Nadeem made sure of it. He could find out where a person ate, slept, walked, hung out and parked his rear end sooner than the person himself knew where he was going. Tracking people was something of a specialty, and when put to use in service of his former employer, always yielded consistent monetary output. Little did he know that one day he would find himself at the receiving end of those strong-arm tactics he himself had once employed to such effect.

'Don't pick up!' Nadeem instructed Warren.

'Okay . . . You gonna go on dodging his phone calls forever?'

'I can get a new number,' he said, rolling up his shirt to scratch his belly like a baboon.

'Maybe you should just keep my phone. Whaddaya say we exchange phones?'

'No thanks. I have no intention of exchanging identities with you of all people. I'd prefer someone loaded, with a house on Marine Drive and a platinum membership at CCI.'

'I'm loaded!'

'Yeah, with lice,' Nadeem stuck his hand into Warren's formidable locks and plucked out a handful of hair. Warren pushed his hand away.

'Don't touch my hair!'

Nadeem smirked. 'Like it's the prime property of Sunsilk or Pantene Pro-V.' He reached for an unopened Pepsi can from the fridge and plonked himself on the couch, taking his shoes off. He had had a long day. He popped open the can, spilling the froth that fizzed out of it on to the floor. He got up to wipe it with a cloth and took a couple of newspapers out to soak up the soda.

'There's gonna be ants crawling all over the place by the morning,' Warren yawned.

Nadeem took off his shirt and sat back on the couch in his vest, snatching the remote control from Warren and taking a swig from the can. Just as he had settled and was beginning to feel at ease, his phone began to ring. It was Inspector Gaekwad. He sat upright and promptly answered it, with a trace of sycophancy in his voice.

'Hello.

'How on earth did you manage to get yourself into this mess, Chipkali?' boomed the voice on the other end of the line. 'We've had enough trouble trying to keep you off the radar.'

'I was sent up by my landlord to collect his rent.'

'Apparently, Inspector Nagpal checked your police record and came across my name in your files.'

'How did you find that out?'

'That's immaterial. I have my sources. Apparently, the son of a bitch had the audacity to ask if I was a crooked cop.'

'You? Crooked?' Nadeem giggled. 'That's a laugh! I suppose you're about as straight as a Philips screwdriver.'

'You better get down to the headquarters, pronto. I have a couple of questions I want to ask you.'

'What? Now? It's 1 a.m.'

'If you hurry to the station, you'll make it in time for the last local.

Nadeem slid his shoes back on, put on his T-shirt and threw the can into the dustbin.

'Where you going?' asked Warren, as Nadeem opened the door.

'Out. Hopefully, I'll be back before dawn.'

Downstairs, he asked Kishorie Lal about what he had told the police.

'Nothing,' he replied, puzzled. 'I just told them that you had some guests over the other day. What's wrong with that?'

'You said they were hoodlums.'

'Well,' he winked, 'weren't they?'

'I don't know who they were or what they had to do with me. I don't know anything about them.'

'They came here the day before yesterday, didn't they?'

'I don't know. You tell me! I wasn't here. You're the one who keeps track of whoever enters and exits the building.'

'I was lucky enough to get a look at the body,' he smirked. 'Judging by the condition, I'd say he had been lying that way for about one or two days, not more! That means the day before yesterday.'

'So?' Nadeem stuttered. 'What about it?'

'The day before yesterday is the day those two came here, the day you weren't here. And the day before that, you were the last one to come back to the building. Around 2:30 a.m., wasn't it?'

'That's none of your business.'

'Everything that passes through this lobby is my business, Nadeem. It is my duty as an honest, law-abiding citizen to supply the authorities with whatever facts

I am aware of. As I told them before, no resident of this building, with the notable exception of yourself, has had any visitors over the last few days, and no one else has been known to be awake at this hour of the night. At least as far as I know, not taking into account the tossings and turnings of our various strained marriages.'

'So, I fit all the characteristics.'

'Of course you do. Unemployed, bachelor, criminal record. You ought to take a look at yourself in the mirror every once in a while, Nadeem, and groom yourself better. The way you present yourself makes a hell of a difference where I come from. I'm telling you for your own good. The way you look to a person is bound to affect the way he talks to you. I bet Inspector Nagpal didn't talk to you the way he spoke to Mr Machhiwaala, did he? Or for that matter, the way he spoke to me? You know you ought to talk to me every once in a while, I could tell you a couple of things.'

Nadeem flicked his fingers at the watchman, telling him to shut his trap. He had heard enough. He stormed off towards the gate, which was locked and which Kishorie Lal would have to open for him. He stood there silently, trying to ignore his presence. There wasn't a soul in sight except the Gypsy parked outside, and they weren't going to give him a ride. The streets were empty and there wasn't much likelihood of finding an auto rickshaw anywhere around the building at this hour. Nadeem's tired eyes wandered all about the compound, as Kishorie Lal fumbled with the keys, searching for the right one. To the left of the gate, behind the watchman's cabin, along a brick margin, was a column of shrubbery and vegetation that the mali would tend to on a daily basis. Often, the children would clamber through it in pursuit of a lost cricket ball, stamping over half the saplings and ruining his day's work. The plants were swaying wildly in the escalating night breeze. It was their time to play now. The bushes rattled vigorously, the leaves quivered into their corners and the uneven grass danced in the wind. It was almost as though they were alive, in rebuke to the stillness of the night.

Nadeem's gaze lingered on the plants. Suddenly, his eyes froze and his mouth curved downwards in disbelief. His ears perked up, scanning the area around him. He could vaguely perceive a presence lurking about in the vicinity. The crumpling of dry leaves was followed by the shake of a branch. Whatever the night concealed could be found out only by way of instinct. Prowling about the premises at this time was not a wise idea, given the circumstances. So, he paid no further attention to it and turned away from the momentary distraction. But just as Kishorie Lal managed to yank open the front lock, Nadeem's neck snapped back towards it. He was certain that he heard something rustling within the shrubs.

'What's that?' Nadeem whispered, pointing towards the plants.

'What?' The watchman did a swift about-turn, brandishing his torch almost instantaneously. He shone it into the shrubs, trying in vain to detect a presence in the darkness.

'Probably a cat,' he said.

Nadeem continued looking at the plants as he stepped outside the gate. Even after Kishorie Lal had closed and locked it from the inside, Nadeem stuck his chin in through the spokes on top. He couldn't see much over the gate, despite him standing on his toes. It was at a height of six and a half feet and not easy to scale from the outside. He wondered why they even locked the damn thing. 'Who would want to rob this building anyway?' he asked himself, as Kishorie Lal trotted off towards the lobby.

Nadeem strutted down the empty streets, annoyed and exhausted. He was not in the mood for a trip to town. It was a long way from Malad and he had had enough of police stations for one day.

He managed to make it just in time for the last Churchgate slow train that was crossing Malad. A couple of bums, beggars and hobos lay along the floor of the second-class compartment. For once, he felt as if he was alone on the train and had it practically to himself. The seats were weathered because of the daily commotion and crowd that inhabited the compartment during the day. An empty local train, he thought, was like a horse carriage with no one to steer it. The wheels kept moving, but for whom and for what no one knew.

He got off at Mahalakshmi and hopped on to a bus bound for Byculla. It, too, was empty. One stray eunuch sat in one of the front seats, gazing out of the window in a tired stupor. His hair was dishevelled, his make-up smudged. He didn't even have the energy to clap his hands and ask Nadeem for a tenner. He probably thought Nadeem was broker than he was, by the looks of him.

Midnight Summons

The Byculla police station was unusually up and about at so unearthly an hour. It was almost as if it was used to being fully functional in the wee hours. All kinds of lowlifes hung around the railings of the front porches and a drowsy hawaldar was shaking his head in the form of a 'no' quite furiously at arbid requests. Nadeem was on a first-name basis with almost all the staff at the police station. After all, he had spent more time there than he had at Little Heights. It was like a second home, an orphanage of sorts for lost souls—a place with room and board free of cost. Inspector Gaekwad's deputy, Hiren, escorted him into the former's secluded office on the first floor, next to the interrogation room. A polished nameplate on the left side of the doorway proudly proclaimed: Inspector V.M. Gaekwad, Crime Branch.

Inspector Gaekwad was wide awake and on the phone. He smiled at Nadeem as he entered, gesturing him to sit down and signalling Hiren to leave. Hiren exited, shutting the door purposefully after asking Nadeem if he wanted tea. Nadeem graciously refused the offer and turned around to face the inspector who, after saying many goodbyes and laughing in falsetto, cut the call he was so strenuously engaged in.

'Alright, Chipkali! What have we got?'

'Homicide by the looks of it.'

Inspector Gaekwad opened a large brown file on his desk and flipped through the pages. Nadeem eyed it closely before finally mustering up the courage to ask.

'What's that?'

'Autopsy report.'

'So soon? How did you manage to get your hands on it?'

'It just came in. I had my people go to the morgue and go over the matter personally.'

'Even Nagpal hasn't gotten the forensic report yet and he is the officer in charge of the case.'

'No case goes by his desk without me laying a finger on it.'

Inspector Gaekwad licked his fingers as he turned the pages, reading out the report.

'We have got an entire chart of the chemical reports, blood tests, DNA samples and iodine levels. According to Dr Laabru's preliminary examination, there are signs of chemical imbalance in the bloodstream. The drugs detected in the autopsy were not any of the ones mentioned in the prescription, which till now is their only conclusive lead. Instead, 12 mg of Mandrax and 25 mg of Dexadrine were found in the blood samples.'

He handed the files over to Nadeem for him to take a good look. After going through the files, Nadeem was astonished at what he took to be a case of criminal negligence.

'It says overdose!'

'I know.'

'I'm not quite sure, sir. It didn't look like an overdose, there were multiple neck wounds!'

'Ah! Flush that old overdose story down the toilet. Forensic scientists! What do they know? For them, looking at a dead body is like sitting on the shit pot with a cup of coffee and reading the morning paper. Here's the medical report.'

He tossed another set of files, which landed on Nadeem's side of the table with a thud.

'Cause of death,' Nadeem read out, 'Overdose resulting in paralysis and collapse of the central nervous system. Sounds a bit far-fetched, doesn't it?'

'Nonetheless,' sighed Gaekwad, 'it is the official statement for the press. We can't argue with that. It'll be in the morning papers by day after tomorrow. And if the officer in charge of the case decides to conduct his own investigation and arrive at his own set of conclusions as to how the overdose occurred, it might not be so good for you. After all, you are the only one in the building known to have questionable guests over. It's right there in the register. Every name, time, phone number, address and detail. They even clock your time of entry and what time you come home at night. If they start to run a check on some of your pals, they're bound to wind up with something or the other . . .'

'I don't call my friends over. The only one that's been to our place is Warren's cousin brother, Howard.'

'But what about your personal conduct? Once they find out about your underworld connections, it won't be long before they put two and two together. Mandrax is one of the primary drug-running operations of the Mumbai underworld. They ship it wholesale and sell it to peddlers and smackies off Colaba Causeway and Grant Road, to hookers on Falkland Road, and to beggars, freaks, cripples and ragpickers in Churchgate. The whole city's infested with addicts—every kind, from the two-rupee variety to the rich kids in SUVs. The Dexedrine he could have easily obtained from any shady chemist or quack in town. If I was in charge of this case, the first thing I would do is to check your apartment for drugs. I would turn the entire place upside down, even plant something if I had to.'

'A man's record goes a long way, doesn't it?'

'In this case, it does. A senseless crime. You don't know how it is for us. We have to answer to superiors who are far less sympathetic to us than we are to you. If I've learnt one thing from all my years in the force, it's this. The mechanics of law and order, especially on a small scale, tend to be governed by convenience. If something looks right, it ought to be. All it takes is a hunch.'

'One I wish I had!'

Inspector Gaekwad looked at him sternly. 'This Nagpal fellow's got his eye on you.'

'That's what it looks like.'

'That's bad news. Means you'll need an alibi. And that's going to have to be me. Means we'll have to let you off the hook. You'll be no good to us out there, not once the whole Malad police force knows you are our tipper.'

'Oh, come on! You're not going to let go of me. Not after all that I've been through.'

'What you've been through is your cross to bear, not ours. We've carried you long enough. We still haven't got a damn thing on Taufiq Maharaj, or even his stupid son. We can't just keep spending the taxpayer's money for your welfare. You can't expect us to be held accountable for your safety for as long as you live. What about after I retire? What will you do then?'

'Look, just give me another week. Let me take a crack at this case.'

'A week? By then, they'll be taking a crack at you.'

'Maybe it has something to do with the medication he was taking,' suggested Nadeem. 'Did you check his medical history?'

'He was admitted once to Cooper Hospital for diarrhoea, once to K.L. Hospital for dengue and malaria. He suffered from high blood pressure, diabetes and asthma. They found an inhaler next to the bedside table.'

'Incidentally,' said Nadeem, 'there's just one more piece of circumstantial evidence which I haven't disclosed to the Malad authorities, which could make them tear up the entire report and change the entire complexion of the investigation.'

'And what's that?' Inspector Gaekwad asked, leaning in over the table towards him.

'The fact that the bathroom door was latched from the outside.'

Inspector Gaekwad scratched his chin, looked up at the wall, his forehead wrinkled in thought. 'That obviously means there was another presence in the house,' he nodded. 'Did they find any footprints?'

'I don't think so. The fingerprints expert did not detect anyone else's prints on the glass panel of the sliding door as well. It isn't impossible that the assailant wore gloves.'

'What makes you think there was just one?'

'Have you made a trip down to the morgue to have a look for yourself?'

'I had my boys do that. They don't seem to be convinced with the report, judging by the characteristics of the corpse. There definitely are traces of external force. It would require the strength of one or more persons to inflict the kind of wounds that were found on his neck. His collarbone has been practically dislocated. There were nail marks around the back of the cervical spine, substantial swelling on the double chin.'

'It wasn't a pretty sight, I can assure you!'

'Well . . . from the expression on his face, it seems possible that he died in the middle of a seizure or an epileptic fit of sorts. But the possibilities are endless. And I'm afraid that all this is mere conjecture. The fact of the matter remains that there is no concrete proof substantiating any of this. Even after conducting a more thorough inspection, they were able to come across nothing more conclusive than what the blood tests offered. The presence of those drugs in the bloodstream rules out all possibilities of a murder attempt. Even the watchman's testimony suggests that no one entered or exited the house, including Makhija himself. So, the only possible solution before the authorities is that the wounds were self-inflicted and could have been caused by any object ranging from a jute rope to a belt, and that he was of unsound mind. Either that, or you and everyone else in the building must be investigated. Those are the only suspects. The building residents.'

'Hah!' laughed Nadeem. 'I'd like to see our secretary, Mrs Miranda, in the interrogation room.'

'You're the only one who would like to see that. No one else wants to waste the detection unit's time to go around looking for some murder weapon from God knows where, for God knows what and God knows why. No one except the people involved with the post-mortem are even going to get a look at the corpse, so it doesn't matter whether he was strangled or choked or even throttled to death. They just want to get it over with and close the files. No one has to know in microscopic detail exactly what happened to him. No one cares. All the public wants is the big picture, not the sordid details. Anyway, an overdose sounds better in the newspapers and makes for a better story than an unsolved murder case without any clues, motive and reason for anyone to give a damn about the victim.'

'I know for sure that it was something that happened in the building when no one was aware of it,' said Nadeem. 'It is not possible to watch each and every corner of a building with just one watchman, no matter how small a building is. Perhaps it happened in the middle of the night when the watchman was asleep. For all we know, the murderer could have escaped from the balcony by jumping on to the terrace of the next building, which is not as high as Little Heights. The sliding door of the terrace balcony was jammed shut, but it could have been closed from the outside. None of the rooms were in any apparent disorder, the switches had all been left on and the tap in the bathroom was running. That's about it. There was no furniture out of place. Nothing stolen, no motive. None of this evidence seems to be having the slightest bit of bearing on their investigation. Instead, all that they are choosing to focus on is the fact that I discovered the body. So, I am a potential suspect.'

Inspector Gaekwad got up from his chair and stretched his neck left and right. He looked outside his mosquito-gauzed window and began pacing up and down the room, taking each step with deliberate precision.

'Don't worry,' he exhaled. 'As long as I'm around to vouch for you, Nagpal can't pin a thing on you. I suggest you let me handle it and forget about the whole thing. You don't want to go on this wild goose chase. For all we know, the murderer might be considerably deranged, perhaps mentally disturbed.'

Nadeem looked out with him, his gaze trying to follow the inspector's train of thought. 'Speaking of which,' Nadeem blurted out in a sudden change of tone. 'Irshaad Batla tried getting in touch with me today. He called today morning on Warren's phone.'

'I know. I've got his number tapped. Apparently, he has had two of his men tailing you for the last two weeks.'

'Apparently, they even came by to the building.'

'I have had my men watching them for the past few days. They are driving a dark green Ford Ikon, licence number MH-02-NA-0425. They seem to be making a lot of trips to the ATM.'

'You think they could have had anything to do with it?'

'That's what you ought to find out. If I was you, I would go and have a word with this Rohini lady.'

'You seem to be spending a lot of time wondering what it would be like to be in someone else's shoes. You ever tried wondering what it would be like to be yourself?'

'I have enough troubles where I sit. The only reason I'm stretching my arm out is to save your neck. What do I want with a stupid murder case that doesn't concern me?'

'What if I manage to find something that links this to Irshaad Batla? Then it does concern you, doesn't it?'

'I got a call from his lawyer today.'

'Razzaq Bhai?'

'No, some other guy. Younger fellow. Can't remember his name. He wanted to meet me. I, of course, told him to go to hell.'

'Probably wanted to cut some kind of a deal.'

'It's going to be tough to nail them. If you want my advice, I suggest you go through all of Makhija's postal records for starters. All mails and couriers he received in the last month.'

'Now we're talking . . .' Nadeem's eyes lit up. 'Go on, I'm listening.'

'Go to the bank with his account details. Take that Nagpal idiot with you, make him check Makhija's bank statement, balance sheet, all transactions and transfers made by him or to him in the last year or so. Trace the flow of his expenditure. See if you can trace anything back to Taufiq and company, Irshaad, Razzaq, Naved 'Pathla'. We did a background check on this Makhija character.'

Inspector Gaekwad opened another file, which contained Makhija's Vodafone bill, his receipts and his registration form.

'We have got all the information on this guy from his mobile phone customer care service provider,' said Inspector Gaekwad, as he handed over the file to Nadeem. 'Apparently, he moved to Bombay in 2004, worked as a teller at Hong Kong Bank first, then went on to become a Prudential Fund salesman for HSBC. He was fired and apprehended for embezzlement last year. He spent two nights in custody. Shifted houses constantly, never managed to stay put in one place, at least not long enough to make friends. And by the look of his call records, it seems he had been looking for a new place for quite a while.'

Nadeem glanced through his application forms. He had changed four SIM cards and was denied verification for the fifth one. Vodafone had deactivated his service because his phone bills were overdue for over three months. He was currently unemployed and had no visible means of support, no source of income. His wife had filed for a divorce.

'His spouse was registered under the name of Rohini Makhija in the bank records,' said Inspector Gaekwad, 'but her actual name is Soniya Karamchand, daughter of advocate Hans Anand Karamchand. She changed her name after running away from home and is currently estranged from her family.'

'According to the testimony I heard her give Inspectors Raane and Nagpal a couple of hours ago, she claims to have married Chintan Makhija for the money and had filed for divorce due to irreconcilable differences.'

In one of the envelopes was a printout of all of Makhija's mobile phone messages and notifications from the bank. One of the messages contained all his bank details: account number, CVV code and debit card number. There was a record of all the transactions made by him and his wife. They held a joint account. They had been living separately for the past year and she had maintained virtually no contact with him since their alleged separation.

'Which bank does Makhija have an account in?'

'Punjab National Bank, Andheri (East) branch, next to Shopper's Stop.'

Inspector Gaekwad's phone rang. He picked it up and spoke into it as if it were a loudspeaker. He could be heard till the opposite wing of the headquarters.

'Well,' he sighed after finishing the call, 'I guess you will be taking a taxi back home. I'll pay your cab fare, unless you want to spend the night in the detention centre and wait for the first local out of Churchgate at 5:30 a.m. We've got a comfortable bench and it would save the taxpayers 350 bucks.'

'400,' Nadeem corrected, 'Midnight charge.'

'Knowing you,' Inspector Gaekwad laughed, 'you'd probably pocket the 400 and take a train back anyway.'

'I guess I don't have much of a choice, do I? Being on your payroll, I guess I won't get to sleep much.'

'Being on my payroll, you'll be lucky to sleep at all.'

The Naked Dawn

Warren was fast asleep when Nadeem returned home at 6 a.m. The television was still on and the curtains were open, carelessly letting in the sunlight that trickled in through the grill. The newspaper was folded and stuck into the door handle. The night watchman from the neighbouring building, who worked part-time cleaning cars in Little Heights, had taken note of Nadeem's inappropriate entry into the building at so earnest an hour. He dutifully informed Kishorie Lal, who was in the staff bathroom, that the guy from the third floor had returned. The sweeper, meanwhile, minded his own business, emptying dustbin after dustbin and polishing the floors of the compound with his broom, blowing dirt and dust into the windows of the ground and first floors.

Nadeem glanced through the narrow slits in the bathroom window, watching the particles of dust rise and settle on the glass. He could see the entire drainage system of the building descending into a network of pipelines

converging and burying themselves into the plaster above
the parapet of the ground floor, eventually spilling out
into the shielded sewer holes at the base of the structure.
Another narrower set of pipelines that ran along the walls
disseminated into a network of capillaries that fed into the
kitchen and bathroom water supply.

Right above their flat, in 403, lived the Goyales, a
rambunctious family of four who were known to be
quite generous with their use of water. They sometimes
even used up the water supply from Nadeem's tank, by
having the kids go up to the terrace where they played
and steal water from the nearest tank (which happened to
be 303) and empty it out into theirs. As a result, Nadeem
and Warren often ran out of water when they needed
it the most, while taking a shower or while brushing
their teeth. They had complained to the secretary but
to no avail. At night, they could often hear Mr and Mrs
Goyale quarrelling through the ceiling, the kids' footsteps
thumping, tennis balls bouncing and the washing machine
rumbling in the morning. Every now and then, bits of
laundry would drop accidentally into their balcony. At
any given time, the railings could literally be strewn with
children's underwear, banyans and coloured socks. Like
any good God-fearing neighbours, they lacked civic sense
and revelled in the discomfort of others.

Flat no. 403 also happened to be the one below
Chintan Makhija's apartment. Obviously, they hadn't
stolen from his tank as it was presumably full. After all,
the water had been running out of the bathroom tap
for quite a while before depleting the supply. Nadeem's

thoughts immediately went to the water. Why was it on? Who left it on? And whose fingerprints would show up on the knob of the bathroom tap? If it was an overdose, then it was possible that his first response would be to turn on the tap and try to reach for water, but if the tank had been running for a day and a half, as common speculation suggested, then the water that had filled up should have been considerably more. If it wasn't, then that meant that it hadn't been flowing for quite as long as was suggested. That meant it was highly probable that the body was not more than a day old.

The intercom rang, causing Warren to toss and turn as his slumbering face broke into an irritable frown. He did not even consider waking up to answer it; he just covered himself with the blanket, as if it were soundproof. Nadeem got out of the bathroom to answer it. It was Kishorie Lal.

'What happened?' Nadeem barked into the intercom.

'All residents and service staff are to report in the ground floor lobby at 1 p.m. for a society meeting.'

'I won't be able to make it. I have to step out for some work.'

'You better make it.'

'Or else?'

'Or else I'll be forced to inform the secretary that you were the only one who was absent from the building the night before Mr Makhija was found dead, and the last one to return to the building the night before that. Is that clear, Nadeem?'

'Would you also be kind enough to inform her that I was the one to discover Mr Makhija in the first place?

Had it not been for me, God knows how much longer he would have been sitting there in that condition before we came to know about him.'

Nadeem slammed the intercom down. It began to ring again. He finally took it off the hook, and when it continued to ring despite that, he pulled out the wire and disconnected it. He checked his mobile phone as he climbed into bed, an act he was habitually reduced to from time to time. It was as empty as a cornerstore on a Sunday afternoon, with neither a visitor nor a patron in sight. He browsed through it compulsively, aimlessly wandering past empty WhatsApp corridors, scrolling down the vacant column that was his inbox, as if searching for some answer to all that ailed him. Just a gentle reassurance that he had left his imprints on some corner of the rotten earth. There were no replies to any of the messages he had sent out to his potential clients. As he closed his eyes, he wondered whether anyone would reply. No one seemed to need a house, at least not the kind of houses that he offered. Everyone was too busy trying to find accommodation in the more fashionable areas such as Bandra, Versova and Juhu. Students stayed mostly in town as that was where most of the colleges were located. That left him with the dregs of humanity. The ones who had been kicked out of their flats by stern landlords and desperately sought accommodation elsewhere, or even those who had spent months sleeping on the living room couches of random friends. Unfortunately, the only people who called him were the ones who were as broke and unemployed as he was. The only missed call he had was from Irshaad

Batla, and the only message he had in his inbox was from a sarcastic Inspector Gaekwad, which said, 'Goodnight sweetypie! Sweet dreams'. It was replete with emoticons of an infinite variety from the hugging and kissing kind to the hearts and flowers. Inspector Gaekwad had just purchased a new phone and was probably testing it out.

Investigation at the Building

At 1:30 p.m., the painstakingly reassembled alarm clock went off. It kept beeping persistently until Nadeem was awake and hit the button on top to make it stop. He kicked himself upon noticing the time. The bank would be closed by now and he would have to wait another day to get any information on Makhija's financial situation. He checked his phone. There was still no response from any of his clients.

Downstairs, Feroz Machhiwaala, with the help of the watchman, Kishorie Lal, Mr Paritosh Sahoo and Mrs Miranda, had managed to round up the morning newspaper man, the milkman, the garbage man, the sweeper, the car cleaner, the dhobi, the mali, the bhaajiwaali, the kabaadiwaala, the electrician, the plumber, the postman and even the courier delivery boy to conduct an investigation of their own.

Nadeem buttoned his shirt as he descended the stairs to take a look at the congregation that had assembled outside the lobby. They were all lined up like students outside a principal's office. Mrs Miranda walked up and down like a policewoman, with her hands behind her back, looking them over from head to toe and flaunting her authority to intimidate them. Machhiwaala stood at the head of the line, sporting an expression of immense seriousness and gravity, with his eyebrows knotted in thought.

'What's all the fuss about?' asked Nadeem, as he walked out of the lobby in his shorts and slippers.

'As you can see,' began Mrs Miranda, 'we, the residents of this society, have taken it upon ourselves to explore all possible facets of the situation and come to a satisfactory conclusion so that we may judge for ourselves who the culprit was.'

'Isn't this the police's job?' asked Nadeem.

'There are certain things that we would like to know for ourselves,' said Mrs Miranda, with her hands folded.

'And will you submit this information to the police?'

'If we think it necessary.'

'Who is "we"? Is there a committee that is going to sit on it? Do I have a say as a society member?'

'If you pay your last month's rent, you do!' shouted Machhiwaala.

'Otherwise,' continued Mrs Miranda, 'you can come along on our investigation as a casual observer. We, however, cannot take your opinions into consideration.'

The Courier Delivery Boy

The courier boy, Suresh, was the first to be questioned.

'I never deliver personal mail,' he began. 'Strictly bank notices, phone bills, circulars and a hell of a lot of official paperwork. Sometimes, I come for long-distance packaging. Once or twice he [Makhija] was even kind enough to let me in because it was very hot. He offered me a drink of water. Sometimes, when he was in a bad mood and I disturbed him in the middle of his afternoon nap, he would scribble his sign and refuse to share his phone number.'

'When did you make the last delivery?' asked Mrs Miranda.

'The last two times that I came, he did not answer the door. He did not seem to have employed a cook or maid. He took care of the apartment pretty much all by himself. So there was no one there to receive his mails. I ended up leaving them in his rusted postbox which probably hadn't been used for centuries.'

'When was the last time he received his mail personally?' she asked.

'A week before the last. There was a package for him from some hospital, I forget which . . .'

'What was it?' asked Machhiwaala.

'I have no idea. I will have to check the records at my branch. I think the hospital's postal address was somewhere in Malad, near Inorbit mall if I'm not mistaken. The courier envelope was so big that I can't be sure what it contained. Once, I had fallen sick and was unable to go on deliveries, so my colleague, who works for the same agency and was new on the job, delivered a parcel for me to 502. Since I pretty much handle this entire road, I had

to instruct him where to deliver which courier so that he
didn't go to the wrong address by mistake. I personally
supervised the transfer of those couriers. There was
nothing suspicious about them.'

The Plumber

Mrs Miranda, Machhiwaala and Nadeem took the
plumber up to the terrace to have a look at the water tank
connected to flat no. 502. They climbed the stepladder
over the elevator control room (where the lift wires
converged into a pulley system) to where the tanks were
placed.

Once all four of them were on the raised area of the
terrace, they were able to locate Makhija's tank. The
plumber opened the lid to peer inside. It was completely
empty.

'This tank has a capacity of about 300 litres,' he said.

'How long would it take to drain that much water?'
asked Nadeem.

'Depends on how fast the water was flowing out of
the tap. If it had been left running at full speed, it would
finish within a day, but if it was dripping, then maybe up
to two days, sometimes three, depending on the speed of
circulation.'

'Was there any water shortage on the day he was found
dead?' asked Mrs Miranda.

'No,' he affirmed. 'There had been a water shortage
two days before that. There was no water in the entire
area that day.'

'When was the last time you were called to the building?' asked the secretary.

'Day before yesterday in the morning. There was a leakage in Mr Goyale's bathroom. The whole place was flooded, so I went to fix it. It was just a minor geyser implosion. Nothing big. All the water had spurted out. No one got hurt.'

'If you're not telling the truth, you know what's in store for you, don't you?' said Mrs Miranda.

'Why wouldn't I be telling the truth?'

'The mali said he saw you fixing the pipes on the fifth floor, outside Mr Makhija's house,' said Mr Machhiwaala.

'That's not true. I was on the fourth floor, inside the bathroom. I may have popped my hand out of the window to reattach the pipe from the geyser, but I certainly wasn't outside fixing the main pipeline.'

'That's not what the mali had to say. He said you spent quite a bit of time fixing the pipes on the outside, not the inside.'

The Mali

The mali was busy watering the plants with the irrigation tube connected to a pipe, which in turn was connected to the tap in the staff bathroom.

'I think I was watering these plants,' he recollected, 'when all of a sudden I saw somebody on the side of the parapet of the fifth floor. He must have made his way down there from the terrace.'

'The terrace door is locked at all times,' said Nadeem.
'The only one who has the keys is Kishorie Lal. There
is no way he could have gone up to the terrace without
Kishorie Lal knowing. I've tried to go up to the terrace a
few times myself.'

'He claims he was working on the fourth floor in Mr
Goyale's bathroom,' said Mrs Miranda. 'We'll have to
cross-check that with Mr Goyale.'

'He could have climbed up the pipes to the fifth floor
parapet from a window on the fourth floor,' the mali
suggested.

'It seems highly improbable,' remarked Nadeem.
'He'd have to be an acrobat to pull that kind of stunt off.'

'Not so,' insisted the mali. 'It is an easy feat often
accomplished by labourers who work on the bamboos
during renovation jobs in multi-storeyed buildings. I
clearly remember that I saw him hanging off the railings,
fixing the pipes to Mr Makhija's house. A rather dangerous
job! He must have got paid a lot of money to do it. What
was strange was that I saw him open the valve of the main
pipeline which hangs off the side of his bathroom.'

The secretary looked at Machhiwaala, who in turn
looked at Nadeem.

'Are you suggesting that the plumber contaminated
his water supply?' asked Nadeem.

'Didn't you mention that the taps had been left on
when you discovered the body?' he asked.

'How does that have anything to do with the plumber?
The taps could have only been turned on by someone
who was inside the house.'

'There is a way to turn on the tap by adjusting the lever on the connecting pipeline. I do it all the time when my irrigation pipe needs water and the staff bathroom is occupied. I can turn the water on from the inside as well as the outside,' said the mali.

The Electrician

Next to the garage, in the farthest corner of the building, lay the meter room.

'You said one entire phase had gone. When were you last called in?' asked Mrs Miranda.

'Well, madam,' said the electrician, 'as you know, the good folks of this building only call upon my services where there is something urgent. I don't go loitering about the building premises when I'm not required. I was called in two nights before the tragedy. Mr Goyale had been having some trouble with his extension board. It was an eight-plug board. Too much load on his . . . uh . . . main circuit. I went to open the panel of the switchboard, and as I turned one of the switches off, an entire phase went off like a *phool jhadi* [a sparkler]! It was scary, madam! I nearly burnt my hand, but then again, these hands are used to it. They've taken more voltage and electrical shocks than any generator in the world!'

'Was there anything wrong with the geyser in Mr Goyale's house?' she asked.

'Oh, yes! I heard it blew up the following day. You know how it is; the children must have left it switched on for a long time.'

'So, how long do you think the lights were gone in Makhija's flat?' asked Nadeem.

'It would be difficult to say. Often, when the circuit blows in one house, the neighbouring apartments too suffer the repercussions—those on the same phase—till however long it takes them to muster up the courage to open the switchboard and turn the main switch on.'

'Perhaps that's why all the lights and fans were running when I entered the apartment,' said Nadeem.

'Mr Makhija must have put the switches on and waited for the electricity to come back, not realizing that it was just a phase that had blown.'

The Bhaajiwaali

The bhaajiwaali sat on the floor near the lobby with all her vegetables laid out on a mat. She emptied her basket to show Mrs Miranda and Machhiwaala that she was carrying nothing that she wished to hide from the authorities.

She was an elderly lady who spoke in a shrill, piercing voice, like that of a mechanized drill. She protested vehemently at being questioned, maintaining that she had always considered Makhija to be a peculiar fellow. She was always suspicious of anyone who ate their vegetables out of an MTR packet and never spent a buck on the real stuff.

'Perhaps he died of malnutrition,' she speculated. 'In today's day and age, all doctors stress the importance of a healthy and balanced diet. Anyone who prefers synthetic food for the sake of saving a little money is penny-wise and pound-foolish. They don't realize what they are missing out in the long run. God didn't create the good green earth simply for an old lady like me to squat on day in and day out. The packets and plastic wrappers are depleting its goodness and nourishment.'

'What about non-vegetarians?' asked Nadeem.

'There's a special place in heaven for them,' she said. 'Or maybe a place in hell. To deprive one of God's creatures of life to fill one's own stomach is as good as murder.'

The Dhobi

The dhobi, a wiry and morose-looking man who wore his blank face like a passport-sized photograph, unravelled his bundles to show what they contained. By now, Nadeem was beginning to wonder how futile and moronic the investigation had become. It had degenerated into a worn-out ego trip for the secretary and Machhiwaala to assert their authority on those beneath them in the economic food chain. If it carried on like this, they would probably get the garbage man to empty the building dustbin just to prove his innocence, thought Nadeem.

According to the dhobi, the late Mr Makhija did not own a washing machine and seldom sent his clothes for washing. He wore the same clothes often and was never home to receive his laundry. The dhobi even informed him that he came once at 11 a.m. and then at 7 p.m., and that he could not alter his daily routine for the sake of one man's convenience. It finally came to a point where he began leaving Makhija's bundle of clothes with the watchman.

There was one occasion, however, that he had stumbled upon a slip of paper in one of Makhija's trouser pockets, while folding and ironing his clothes. He handed it back to him when he delivered the laundry and Makhija clutched at it protectively as if he were embarrassed to reveal it. There was a number written on it in fairly illegible handwriting, and as the dhobi tried to decipher whether or not it was an article of any importance, he ended up looking at the paper a number of times, thereby having memorized the number by heart.

'Do you remember the number?' asked the secretary.

'Yes. It was 09820241675.'

Nadeem immediately dialled it on his phone. The phone rang but no one picked it up. He tried again and was cut off just as it began to ring. In two minutes, there was a call from the same number.

'Hello!' Nadeem spoke softly into his phone. 'Who's speaking?'

'You tell me who's speaking,' the voice answered in unfriendly haste. 'You were the one who called!'

'I got this number from Chintan Makhija! I'm calling with regard to his death!'

'Oh! I'm sorry to hear that!' The man's initial curtness gradually dissolving into courtesy. 'When did he die?'

'He was found yesterday.'

'I wasn't aware.'

'What business did you have with him?'

'He owed me a considerable sum of money!'

'What for, if I may ask?'

'It's a little complicated. He didn't exactly owe me money per se, he actually owed a client of mine who owed me. My client had asked me to collect the money from him . . . wait a minute! Who am I talking to?'

Nadeem immediately cut the call. The man called back without missing a beat. He didn't want to be left hanging mid-sentence, but Nadeem reckoned it wouldn't be wise to communicate with someone whose identity he wasn't as yet certain of. He didn't answer the call, instead, he stored the number in his contacts under the name 'MAKHIJA CREDITOR'. He would look into the matter at ease.

The Kabaadiwaala

The kabaadiwaala was one of the select few who had been granted the privilege of entering Makhija's humble abode just three days prior to the day he was found dead. He remembered the house being in quite a mess. It did not look like it had been cleaned for a while. The plaster was beginning to peel off the walls, the tiling was getting weathered, there was a pile of clothes on the bathroom floor, dishes were piled up in the kitchen sink and the bed had not been made. The only thing that seemed to be functional was the television, which was perennially switched on, whether or not anyone was sitting in front of it. He happened to vaguely remember that the fans were not working and that he sweated profusely as he gathered objects and dismantled hardware from the cupboards and cabinets, such as broken mugs, shredded wires, aluminium foils, cardboard cartons, glass bottles of Duke's lemonade, phenyl, sprays, toiletries, mosquito repellents, tin cans, tiffin boxes and containers. He remembered Makhija bargained for quite a few hours before he could leave with all the stuff. He finally settled on a measly sum of a hundred and forty rupees for a truckload of unusable household supplies.

Before leaving the house, after having wrapped up and parcelled the items and articles that he had purchased, the kabaadiwaala had noticed a half-empty bottle of Phensedyl cough syrup next to the medicine cabinet. He picked it up to take a look and, seeing that it was half-empty, asked whether Makhija would be interested in parting with it. But Makhija took it as a moral affront and aggressively refused, showing him the door and asking him how he had dared to take the liberty to look around his house. He said he had not opened up a store for people to come and pick up and buy whatever they liked and that there were certain things money could not buy.

It was just a bottle of cough syrup and the kabaadiwaala had wondered why Makhija got so upset. According to Machhiwaala, when he inspected the house, the bottle was still lying next to the medicine cabinet. It was also one of the few objects that Rohini had claimed as her own on her brief yet thorough visit to the house. She, however, was not allowed by the police to pick it up as it was considered a piece of evidence.

Dr Vengsarkar

After having wrapped up the interrogation with the building staff, Nadeem went back to his apartment to change into presentable clothes so that he could step out.

There was something peculiar about both the plumber's and the electrician's statements. It seemed as though they were either withholding information or covering up for each other. The mali was the only eyewitness to their activities. They could have been doing anything. No one, not even the watchman, notices in detail what a plumber and an electrician are doing all day long. If the switches had been left on and the phase had blown, then the electricity would have come back only if someone went to Mr Makhija's switchboard and turned on his inverter. If he had done so himself, then perhaps the lights, fans and television in the living room wouldn't have been left switched on considering how stingy he was known to be. Nadeem was certain that the electricity and water had been turned on by

whoever had committed this vile atrocity. Perhaps to give
the impression that all was well inside the house. He had
the number that the dhobi had mentioned stored on his
mobile phone, and he planned to check on it as soon as he
could. Then, there was the irregularly large package that he
had received from the courier boy, but all along it was the
kabaadiwaala's mention of the cough syrup which seemed
to play on his mind and occupy utmost importance on his
list of concerns. As Warren awoke, he shared his findings
with him. Warren did not seem particularly interested
at first, but after having washed his face and woken up
properly, he walked up to the balcony and looked out of it
in deep thought.

'What it looks like, Nadeem, is that there are five
distinct possibilities of a freak occurrence or mishap
within the day-to-day routine and daily scheme of things.
One is that he was electrocuted by someone who had
control over the voltage in his house.'

'How's that possible?'

'You send a current through a zinc wire and you can
zap anyone who has got his or her hands or feet anywhere
near it.'

'Two?'

'Two is that he received a parcel that directly or
indirectly had something to do with his demise.'

'Highly unlikely.'

'Three is that his water source was contaminated.'

'He would need to drink copious amounts of tap
water for that to happen, which might be possible. Bisleri
has started costing twenty bucks a bottle.'

'Four is that the kabaadiwaala was involved in some way, as he is the only one to be heard of officially entering Makhija's house.'

'I doubt it.'

'And the fifth is that our two visitors unlawfully gained entry into his house and are responsible for the acts of violence perpetrated against him. The last six people to have open access to his house were the courier guy, the plumber, the electrician, the kabaadiwaala and our two visitors, as the watchman claims Makhija hadn't stepped out in weeks and had had no visitors of his own save for the daily denizens and frequenters of the building.'

'The fifth possibility seems to be the most likely one. I think the drugs detected in Makhija's bloodstream are incidental. He was brutally murdered. His neck was mutilated. I saw it with my own two eyes. I'm not stupid. I know what a murder looks like. I have a bad feeling that the two people who came by the other day to pay us a visit went to the wrong flat.'

'You think that maybe we should come clean about the two men to Inspector Nagpal?' suggested Warren. 'Tell him what that was all about, who they were and why they came here. I'm sure he would understand, after all, you can tell him that it was you that they were after, and that technically even your life is at risk.'

'I'd be putting my life even further at risk if I told Inspector Nagpal anything about it.'

'I don't know, Nadeem. Maybe they're right. People often do funny things to themselves when they're on medication.'

'Don't be daft, Warren. If he wanted to knock himself off, he would have picked a more painless way to go about it.'

'Well, man. I suppose you better go down and have a word with his psychiatrist to figure out what kind of dose he was on. I had a friend whose uncle was manic-depressive and heavily into these hyper anxiety pills. Every time he would run out of them, he would go off his rocker. He wasn't allowed to leave the house, so he jumped off the balcony.'

'Did he land on his feet?'

'I wish!'

'I don't know what to make of it, man,' sighed Nadeem. 'It's a funny world. Anything is possible. I had an uncle who was paraplegic. They put him on all kinds of painkillers. He used to act funny. He would insist on walking his dog in the evenings, even though he was on a wheelchair. One day, I was out buying groceries at Sakari Bhandar when nearby, on the pavement, I saw him trying to walk the dog. I could see that he was having some difficulty, so I went up to help him, when all of a sudden, the Pomeranian saw a female German shepherd and got excited and charged towards it. My uncle cried out for help as he was going out of control and tried to let go of the leash, only to realize that it was tied to the wheelchair. He was dragged across the road by the Pomeranian and got hit by an SUV. He's still in the ICU in critical condition.'

'I think you better go visit the psychiatrist,' said Warren. 'You need it!'

Nadeem decided to go and pay a visit to Dr G.D. Vengsarkar to see what he could find out. He got down from the building and caught the number 241, which was headed to Dadar, from the nearby bus stop.

He got off in Matunga and walked from there. Dr Vengsarkar's clinic was a discreet, rundown little place in Dadar. A hard-headed receptionist sat behind the desk and asked Nadeem if he had an appointment. Nadeem told him that he was just there to look around. He glanced at the magazine rack next to the sofa in the waiting room. Dr Vengsarkar's degree and practising licence hung on the wall in a glass frame. While Nadeem was examining it, the door to the psychiatrist's office opened and an elderly man walked out. He avoided eye contact with Nadeem and was presumably ashamed at being seen at the clinic. Dr Vengsarkar stepped out with him and halted on noticing Nadeem.

'What can I do for you?' he asked courteously.

'I was friends with Mr Chintan Makhija.'

Dr Vengsarkar looked at the receptionist and then asked Nadeem to step inside his office.

Nadeem took a seat on the opposite side of his desk. There were drawings and posters all over the room. A bookshelf in one corner was filled from top to bottom with an array of books ranging from the abnormal to the subnormal realms of human behaviour.

'Paranormal psychopathology! The psychopathic neurosis of the subnormal strata! You've got an interesting library out here, if I may say so,' said Nadeem, browsing through the bookshelf.

'These books are my only escape,' said Dr Vengsarkar, dropping himself on his swivel chair. 'They give the illusion of space. That is why I surround myself with them.'

He wheeled himself a foot and a half back to shut a rust-coloured steel cupboard that stood beside a teak-wood cabinet of drawers. All kinds of documents were spilling out of the cupboard. After arranging all the files in their allotted compartments, the doctor closed it shut with a clang and pulled up the handle to adjust the lock in place. Checking once more, just to be doubly sure, he turned back towards Nadeem who was still busily going over the contents of the bookshelf from his chair. On noticing that he had the doctor's undivided attention, Nadeem leaned forward to face him, hesitantly abandoning the bookshelf.

'This where you conduct your proceedings?' he asked, glancing about the room.

'I barely step out of this room,' the doctor told him.

'I see . . .'

'I am prone to the terrors of confinement. A chronic case of claustrophobia. But . . . little by little, one learns to cope with their surroundings. As you can see . . . uh . . . comfort is never a factor taken into account in my profession.'

'Nor mine, doctor.'

'I take it that you are some kind of a private investigator.'

He handed Dr Vengsarkar his card, a routine exercise in his daily line of duty, but here it seemed almost out of place. It was a neat little synthetic cardboard cut-out he had printed himself. A floral design was embedded along the margins of the red and yellow lettering hewn in fantastic obligation.

'Nadeem Sayed Khatib, Realty and Property Consultant,' Dr Vengsarkar read from it.

It was crisp and to the point, with nothing declamatory about it, just like the gash on top of Nadeem's left eyebrow which hadn't as yet healed. It was just that prominent enough to be assertive, yet it never announced itself. Nadeem always felt that you could tell a lot about a man's practice by the look of the card he handed out. He had dozens of them lying around all over the place. If he reached for his pant pocket, he would probably fish out a cartload. He could afford to lose one.

'I was Mr Makhija's broker,' Nadeem informed him. 'More of a confidant, really. A sort of helping hand . . . I was supposed to help him pack his things and find a place to move to.'

'You said you were a friend.'

'If a person like Chintan Makhija could be said to have any friends.'

'Then I take it that you were intimately acquainted with him?'

'About as intimately acquainted as a person like Makhija would allow himself to be with another individual. Did he tell you about his marriage?'

'He did mention it occasionally, from time to time.'

'Was he undergoing any form of stress?'

'Well, he was a relatively new patient! He had started his treatment a year ago for what he claimed was a routine case of nervous exhaustion. He said he was suffering from stress due to the excessive workload at his office, but I could sense something simmering beneath that blank expression he wore to such effect. My eyes are trained to penetrate even the most rigid surfaces. I could even tell you a couple of things about yourself!'

'Thank you, doctor. I appreciate it, but perhaps right now you'd better tell me a couple of things about your patient.'

'I had put him on some mild anti-anxiety medication. After a couple of months or so of medication, his condition started to deteriorate, so I had to increase his dose. It took a while before I got him to open up about what truly ailed him.'

'When was the last time you saw him?'

'About a month or so back. He had abruptly ceased his counselling and was absent for most of his appointments. In the last couple of sessions, though, he neglected to discuss his personal difficulties and seemed inquisitive about one of my other clients who suffered from a similar condition. He insisted on taking a look at some of his files out of idle curiosity, or perhaps, I suppose, to be sure of my credentials and working methods. I, of course, refused and told him it was out of the question, that I'd be putting myself into a great deal of legal trouble if I did so.'

'If I may ask . . . are you a practising psychiatrist?' asked Nadeem, nonchalantly.

'Well, I have my degree,' Dr Vengsarkar said, pointing towards the wall. 'As you can see, I have spent the last fifteen or more years with the Nandlal Pramod Functionality Centre. Counselling isn't exactly my area of expertise. My field is more inclined towards cognitive disabilities and emotionally debilitating disorders.'

'Have you been a practising clinical psychiatrist in the past?'

'Well, yes, I'm a practising clinical psychiatrist now. I have my licence.'

'I'm afraid this licence only applies to the Nandlal Pramod Functionality Centre, as you call it. It only applies to the patients of the institution.'

'It's not an institution. It's a reform centre.'

'In which case, you have no medical background in the field of clinical psychiatry?'

'I . . . well have been practising here for the last couple of . . .'

'In which case, you are not authorized to prescribe any sort of medication to any of your patients! You can only offer them your infinite wisdom and hope to enlighten them with counselling, or advice in this case.'

Dr Vengsarkar was growing increasingly alarmed at Nadeem's insinuations, and as he took out his folded handkerchief from his chest pocket to wipe the sweat off his forehead, he practically broke down.

'Look,' he pleaded. 'He couldn't sleep for months! I had to do something for him!'

'Don't worry, doc. You are not on trial here. You don't have to start getting all melodramatic about it. I would prefer it if you remained strictly clinical. That's the way I like to operate. I haven't seen any of your victims alive enough to make a comment, but I'm sure you function fine that way.'

'What do you want to know?'

'I must confess that the nature of this case baffles me. No clues, no fingerprints, nothing to go on except the coroner's report.'

'There's nothing unusual about what happened. Mr Makhija was just a difficult person and exhibited all the symptoms of the terminally troubled. What happened to him was bound to happen sooner or later. I couldn't figure what it was that truly ailed him, and it's not my job too either. My job is to provide help, not an answer. For all you know, he may have used my services for ulterior purposes, such as to procure pharmaceutical drugs to ease the pain.'

'What pain?'

Dr Vengsarkar leaned back in his chair, involuntarily swivelling around until it came to a halt. He looked at Nadeem with a wry chuckle and answered, 'The pain of existence. You see, when a person's moral compass collapses, there is no turning back from the point of no return. He had committed a crime, stolen money, embezzled, lied to his wife and purchased a stolen automobile for half its market rate. After a point, there's not much help I can provide to lighten the burden of that on one's soul. Thereby, it's only logical that he took his own life, given the odd behaviour he had been exhibiting over the past month.'

'Or so it may seem, doctor. To enhance our effectiveness, we must take into account the unseen—the inadmissible: the certain degrees of temperament which do not lie within the realm of human behaviour!'

'In order to do that you would be asking me to refer to something that I have kept under a strict oath of confidentiality.'

'Confidentiality to what? A piece of paper on an office wall?'

'Look, I have already had a word with the police. I have told them everything they needed to know about him. My job is thoroughly thankless, as I presume yours is, which is why you are here with a psychiatrist who spends his whole life trying to solve the misery of others. I do all the dirty work while the others sit back and send the kids to school! It is only those that ride the bus that learn to live happily. Not the bus conductor.'

Nadeem didn't understand his double talk. He looked around the office trying to make sense of the doctor.

'Are you?' he asked Nadeem.

'Happy?'

'Yes.'

'I don't know, doc. It's really difficult to say.'

'Isn't that what sets us apart from them then?'

'From whom?' asked Nadeem, getting progressively more puzzled.

'From the happy!' replied Dr Vengsarkar. 'The ones who sit in the bus and enjoy the leg space! But who repairs the bus when things go wrong? Who changes the wheels when the bus has a flat tyre.'

'When was the last time he visited you?'

'I'll have to check in the files. You can come visit me tomorrow any time. By then, I will have all the details of Mr Makhija's previous visit for you.'

Nadeem could sense that Dr Vengsarkar was trying to brush him off.

'At the moment, I am afraid you are going to have to excuse me. I'm extremely busy. I'm sure you can understand,' he said to Nadeem.

'What did the police ask you?'

'I'm not privileged to lend out that information to you, sir. I run an honest man's business. I help people with their problems, and we try and keep things nice and quiet so no one finds out. Least of all the police.'

Dr Vengsarkar was sweating profusely, even though the AC was on full blast.

'Please excuse me. I cannot help you. I'm extremely sorry.'

He suddenly got up from his chair, showing Nadeem the way out.

'I come to you for help to try and understand one of your patients and you show me the door,' said Nadeem, dead serious, like he really meant it.

'I'm sorry, but you are going to have to leave. I have an appointment for 4 p.m. and my patient must be waiting outside.'

'Doc,' Nadeem whispered, 'I need Makhija's files. Only if I find out what was bothering him will I be able to make some sense of what happened to him.'

'It is my life's most important and meaningful principle to maintain complete confidentiality in whatever my clients tell me. I can't say a word to anyone!' said Dr Vengsarkar animatedly, as he opened the door.

'You're going to regret this, doctor,' said Nadeem, as he stepped out.

'Thank you! Goodbye!'

Dr Vengsarkar closed the door and locked it from the inside. Nadeem turned his head away in disappointment, stepping into the waiting room. The receptionist still sat in the same position, his face buried in a Marathi newspaper, trying to solve the crossword puzzle on the back pages. Nadeem tried smiling at him in an attempt to make some kind of contact and interact with him on a human level, but it was of no use. He tried to get him to open up with a couple of friendly questions, but the only replies he got were monosyllabic. He finally turned to exit the clinic with a defeated smile. Just as he waved goodbye to the receptionist, he noticed a man seated on the sofa. He was covered by a newspaper and did not look like he was reading it, but instead, using it to conceal his identity. He glanced up by mistake, or perhaps out of curiosity to take a quick look at who had come out, when he noticed Nadeem. He threw the newspaper to the side and got up.

'Nadeem!'

Nadeem stopped dead in his tracks as he registered the face behind the newspaper. It was Irshaad Batla.

Irshaad Batla

Irshaad literally jumped at Nadeem and grabbed him, hugging him in a brotherly embrace. He rejoiced at the sight of his old friend and made a big display of his affection. Two of his cronies who had been waiting outside entered the clinic on hearing their boss's loud voice. They too recognized Nadeem, but did not say a word.

'How are you doing, buddy?' Irshaad yelled.

'I'm good, man!' Nadeem replied.

'How've you been, brother?'

'I've been okay, brother.'

Nadeem looked at Irshaad's cronies, who looked back. Nadeem looked away as soon as they made eye contact. The receptionist was intrigued by the familiarity with which Irshaad Batla had greeted Nadeem.

'Where you been, man?' Irshaad asked Nadeem. 'I have been trying to call you since God knows how long. You don't pick up your phone!'

'I was waiting to get in touch with you once the heat blew over. My phone was tapped. I didn't want to get you into any trouble.'

Irshaad burst into uproarious laughter. He nearly choked as he bent down trying to control himself.

'Me? Into trouble? You would never do a thing like that, would you, Nadeem?'

'No, Irshaad. I wouldn't.'

'Of course, you wouldn't.'

There was an excruciatingly long pause. Irshaad signalled to one of his cronies to check the area outside.

'So,' Irshaad broke the silence, 'you came here alone?'

'Yes, all by myself.'

'What brings you here? You all right? Anything troubling you? You know if you ever need anyone to talk to about anything, I'm always there for you. Feel free to call up anytime if you need to talk.'

'Of course, Irshaad.'

'You know you've always been like a brother. You're like a little brother to me.'

'Of course, Irshaad. I consider you my elder brother.'

Irshaad hugged him a little tighter than normal and showered him with more affection than what Nadeem was accustomed to from him. He then pulled his cheeks a little too hard, patting him on the back, going on about how he was like a younger brother and how he should not hesitate to give him a call if he ever needed anything. He didn't even mention anything about the cops or Nadeem getting busted. He just went on cackling at the top of his voice and bringing up old times. The receptionist asked them to be silent. After all, it was a doctor's clinic, not a nightclub.

'I'm extremely sorry,' said Irshaad, with a phony politeness that bordered on sarcasm. 'I'm very, very sorry. I didn't mean to create a racket, it's just that I'm meeting my friend after so long that I couldn't help myself.'

'It's okay,' said the receptionist, 'I understand.'

'There are certain rules and regulations here,' Irshaad giggled, 'and we wouldn't want to violate any of those, would we, Nadeem?'

'Oh no,' Nadeem stuttered, 'we wouldn't.'

'After all,' continued Irshaad, with an exceedingly wide grin, 'this is a delicate, sensitive place and we wouldn't want to draw too much attention to it, would we?'

'Absolutely not!'

Irshaad's smile was now beginning to crack at the seams, and as Nadeem looked down at the floor to avoid eye contact, it turned almost instantaneously into a grimace.

'You wouldn't tell anybody about this place, would you, Nadeem?'

'Me? No, of course not.'

'You wouldn't tell anybody that you saw me here, would you, Nadeem? It's not the kind of place I'd like to be seen at, if you know what I mean.'

'You can count on me, Irshaad.'

'Because if you do tell anybody that you ran into me here, and I find out about it, you know what that means, don't you, Nadeem?'

'Yes, I do.'

'I'm here for my counselling session. I have to come once a week. My hearing is coming up. The doc from Nandlal Pramod Functionality Centre sent me here, so you see, I'm not here out of my own choice.'

'I understand.'

Irshaad Batla looked into the mirror, studying his own reflection. He then tilted his head sideways to get a good clear look at Nadeem. He was trembling and was about to break into a sweat. He tried calming his nerves down by turning his attention to the receptionist who was engrossed in a sheet of paper. A magazine lay next to him on the table, which Irshaad had probably just read. Nadeem tried to reach for it when, all of a sudden, Irshaad pounced on him, grabbing him by the scruff of his neck and pinning him against the notice board, which had a poster on it saying: 'Behavioural Symptoms of Schizophrenia and How to Cure Them'.

'You listen to me, Chipkali. If you so much as open your mouth to your flatmate or tell anybody you saw me here, I'm going to have to take precautionary measures to ensure you never talk again.'

'You have my oath on it. I give my word that I will not tell a soul about this.'

'You think it's funny? Me needing to go for therapy to a psychiatrist.'

'No, Irshaad, I don't!'

'I wasn't born yesterday. Don't think that I don't know that you snitched on me!'

'No, Irshaad, I swear I didn't!' cried Nadeem, practically bending down on his knees.

'You're a rat!' screamed Irshaad. 'You're a grade-A stool pigeon. The lowest form of humanity. The scum of the earth.'

'Look, Irshaad, I can explain!'

'Explain it to this,' Irshaad brandished an automatic pistol which he pulled out of his pant pocket.

'Irshaad! Please! Don't do anything stupid, Irshaad. You don't want to go to jail for shooting a worthless piece of shit like me! Come on, Irshaad, please calm down!'

Irshaad stuck the gun into Nadeem's mouth. Nadeem nearly gagged on it as the receptionist got up to reach for the intercom. One of Irshaad's cronies prevented him from doing so. The bell on his desk rang, which meant that Dr Vengsarkar was calling his patient into his office. Irshaad slowly turned towards Dr Vengsarkar's door as he heard the bell. He removed the gun from Nadeem's mouth and kicked the doctor's office door open.

'Doctor, would you kindly step outside your office for a moment?'

Dr Vengsarkar got up from his desk, visibly agitated, and came out of his office into the waiting room. Irshaad held the gun up for him to take a good clear look at.

'Today, I'd like to ask some questions,' he smirked, pointing the gun at Dr Vengsarkar's stomach, 'and this will be doing the counselling.'

'Irshaad, please put the gun down!' Dr Vengsarkar stammered.

'What's the matter, doctor? Are you afraid of me?'

'Irshaad, son, please put the gun down,' Dr Vengsarkar begged him. 'Whatever it is that's troubling you, we can talk it through. You're an unstable person, you're clinically diagnosed.'

'What is this guy doing here?' he asked the doctor about Nadeem.

'I don't know who he is,' the doctor assured Irshaad. 'I've never met him before.'

'I came here to ask the doctor about one of his patients,' said Nadeem.

'Which patient?' Irshaad sneered.

'A man who lived in my building. He was brutally murdered.'

Irshaad's eyes lit up. He lowered the gun and went up to Nadeem, grabbing hold of him fiercely.

'How did you find out about this place?'

'They found a medical prescription slip in his pocket which was traced to this clinic. That's why I came here.'

'Don't lie! Who told you I was coming here for counselling?'

'No one! I swear!'

Irshaad put the gun down and shoved it into his back pocket. He looked at Nadeem with a blank stare and picked up the phone book and the register from the counter where the receptionist sat. The receptionist was stunned and had frozen in mid-sentence. He looked towards his employer who told him to remain calm and that everything was under control. Irshaad Batla shrugged his shoulders a couple of times, adjusted his shirt and looked at himself in the mirror again. He fixed his hair and buttoned his sleeves, turning back to Dr Vengsarkar and following him into his office. Dr Vengsarkar shut the door gently.

Harbour Line

Nadeem caught his breath as he exited the clinic. Irshaad's maroon Honda Civic was standing outside. Nadeem asked the driver, Kaashif Bhai, to give him a lift till Dadar station, which was only five minutes away.

'What are you doing here, Chipkali?' he snickered, as Nadeem got into the car.

'Getting treatment for anger management.'

'Irshaad could do with some of that,' he laughed.

'How often does he come here?'

'Once a week.'

'Ever see a white Indica parked outside the clinic?'

'Once, if I remember correctly. There were scratches all over, the mudguard had some damage on it. Nothing serious.'

'How long do his sessions go on for?'

'Depends. Sometimes they take hours.'

'Can't be too much fun for you, I imagine.'

'I'm used to it. A good driver has to have patience.'

'What about a good getaway driver?'

'I wouldn't know about that.'

'What's Irshaad been up to lately?'

'Nothing, just laying low. Heading to Singapore next week. They're moving into construction.'

Kaashif pulled over next to Dadar station. It was swarming with hordes of passengers. The ticket counter had lines stretching all the way out to the main road. Nadeem requested Kaashif to drop him to King's Circle instead. He thought it made more sense to take the harbour line.

Once he boarded the train and was certain that no one had followed him, he took out his phone and dialled Warren's number. The whole compartment was smelling of fish and was relatively empty compared to the Western or Central Railway line. Nadeem was on the train bound for Byculla. As usual, Warren didn't pick up the phone and Nadeem had to try three more times before he got a response.

'Hello,' he mumbled into the phone as the train started moving. 'You won't believe who I ran into at Dr Vengsarkar's clinic.'

'NADEEM! Get your ass here right now, this instant!'

'What happened?'

'I can't explain, just hurry up and come here,' whispered Warren, cutting the call.

Nadeem decided to change trains in order to head back to Malad immediately. He wondered what the matter was and why Warren wouldn't speak, as he got off at Cotton Green and caught a train for Wadala. He changed trains there and got back on to the Western line.

Home Invasion

By the time he reached home, Inspector Nagpal and his deputy, Srikant, were seated on the couch, watching television after having conducted a painstaking and arduous search of the house, which was not an easy task considering how messy it was. They had made themselves at home and were enjoying the various facilities and amenities of their humble abode.

'Come in,' Nagpal called out to Nadeem, as soon as he noticed him get out of the lift.

The flat had been literally ripped apart inch by inch. There were all sorts of files and documents, which had been collected from the flat upstairs, scattered all about the place. There were four empty cups of tea, which hadn't been cleared, and Srikant was busy going through a series of papers, crumpling pages out of them and tossing them into the dustbin.

Srikant asked Nadeem to take a seat.

'Let him stand,' Inspector Nagpal muttered.

'It's my house,' Nadeem reminded him, 'and I'm going to take a seat.'

Warren stood morosely in a corner, playing host to the two policemen, certainly looking like he was not in the best of moods.

'We ran a check on the white Indica,' said Inspector Nagpal. 'The number plates had been changed and it was registered under the name of one H.S. Mehta—Harry Suketu Mehta, a restaurant owner from Lokhandwala, who had filed for a missing car back in 2016.'

'We also checked with all the chemists and pharmacies in the area,' said Srikant. 'The only one that had a record of Makhija as a patient was the pharmacy in K.L. Hospital in Malad, just off the flyover, next to Inorbit Mall. It's not a very good hospital.'

'Why would he go all the way there?' asked Nadeem. 'He could easily have obtained the prescribed medication from any chemist or pharmacy in this area.'

'We checked the hospital records,' said Srikant. 'He was admitted there for dengue and malaria a couple of years ago. It was the only place he could afford. Apparently, he's even donated blood in the same hospital for money. Used to get paid per gallon.'

'Did you check his bank details?' asked Nadeem.

'There was a cash transfer made from his account to an unverified one. We have all the account details, but apparently, the account holder registered under a fake name. The mobile number, however, is genuine and we are trying to trace it.'

'Is this the number?' Nadeem showed him the number he had noted down from the dhobi.

'How did you get hold of it?' asked Inspector Nagpal, inquisitively.

'The dhobi found the number in Makhija's pant pockets.'

'If you find anything else in there, let us know,' Inspector Nagpal laughed, telling Srikant to go and make some more tea. Nadeem checked with Warren whether they even had any tea leaves or teabags and was told that there were still some dregs in one of the containers.

'We've already had four cups,' Inspector Nagpal told Nadeem.

'I'll go and make some more,' Nadeem said, heading towards the kitchen.

'That's all right,' Srikant stopped him before he could leave the living room. 'I'll go and make it; I made the last two rounds.'

Srikant went into the kitchen and opened the cabinet over the sink, which contained indiscriminate objects of household value like cups, glasses, plates, forks and spoons, fetching the sugar and a year-old packet of Taj Mahal tea. He washed the vessel which had been used to make the previous cups, got rid of the milk powder dust and proceeded to make the tea as if it was his own kitchen. After having searched and ransacked the apartment, he was reasonably aware of where things were kept.

'Looks like you guys have made yourself at home,' sneered Nadeem.

'Srikant makes a hell of a cup of tea. You ought to try it.'

'If it's any better than what you serve at the police station, it'll do,' said Nadeem. 'You think you could send him over to make breakfast in the mornings?'

'Shut up and sit down, Khatib,' Inspector Nagpal snapped. 'I have some pertinent information I want to share with you.'

'Are they facts or is it information?'

'What's the difference?'

'There's plenty of difference, Inspector. You're talking to a person who deals in information. You could say that's how I make my living. You ever heard of Inspector V.M. Gaekwad?'

'Which area?' Inspector Nagpal seemed slightly offended by his referring to another officer.

'Byculla. Call him up and have a word with him. Take my name and ask him who I am.'

'Don't try and be smart with me, Khatib. You're a two-bit broker and nothing else. You try and pull any stunts with me, taking officer's names, and I'll take you down to the station with me and give you such a thrashing that you'll forget your own name. Then, you can take all the names you like. Who do you think you are? Taking big names! It may work with the traffic police or the RTO cops, but not with me. Is that clear?'

'Crystal clear,' laughed Nadeem.

'Sit down and listen to this. You wanted to know his financial records. Here they are. According to his widow, he had been caught trying to embezzle a sum of

Rs 7 lakh when he was a prudential fund salesman for HSBC. He was fired immediately and the bank manager filed an FIR against him. Although he was broke at the time of his separation from his wife, he had stashed away enough money in a fixed deposit, which he had made on his commissions, to put up in a terrace flat in Malad. Apparently, even Machhiwaala didn't know his financial history until he was due to vacate. That's why he sent you to collect the rent. I guess he figured that the less he had to do with him, the better it was for whomsoever concerned. Little did he know that his tenant wouldn't make it beyond his lease. Now, he's stuck with all the paperwork. He isn't going to be able to find a buyer for that flat even if he gives it out for free.'

'I can find him a buyer with my eyes closed,' Nadeem boasted.

'That's what you think. No one wants to live in a flat where the previous tenant never made it past his tenure.'

Srikant entered with a tray on which three cups of tea were placed neatly in a single file. He handed a cup to Nadeem.

'Thanks,' he said, taking a sip. 'What about Warren? Didn't you make him a cup?'

'We asked him for the last two rounds, but he didn't want any,' said Srikant.

Nadeem took a sip slowly, blowing a ripple into it to cool it down. It tasted sour and bitter, as if the tea leaves had gone bad. There was probably fungus on them by now.

'We got a simple clear-cut case out here, gentlemen,' Inspector Nagpal stated, turning towards Warren who had maintained a dead silence all this while. 'It's not an overdose as the post-mortem claims, but a case of pre-meditated murder with the motive to usurp his financial assets.'

'What financial assets?' Warren wailed.

'You keep out of this,' Srikant instructed him.

'I'd recommend you to not get involved,' Inspector Nagpal seconded him.

Nadeem studied the bills and receipts the pharmacy had provided them.

'Who was his physician?' asked Nadeem, sipping on his tea. 'Did he visit a general practitioner or a specialist?'

'Dr Harish Dang of K.L. Hospital. But he's nowhere to be found,' sighed Srikant. 'We tried calling his residence. He's quit his practice and is apparently out of town for a medical convention.'

'Was he known to be so liberal in prescribing medication to his patients?' asked Nadeem, sarcastically, as he browsed through the pile of Makhija's prescriptions. There was one page which caught his attention and it looked like it had been forged. The signature did not match the one by Dr Vengsarkar, which was found at the scene of the crime. He showed it to Warren who took one glance at the prescription and stated without missing a beat, 'I've seen this handwriting in the watchman's register.'

'What do you mean?' asked Inspector Nagpal.

'It's identical to the handwriting in the register. The one the two unknown men had signed with,' Warren remarked. 'They wrote their names as Ganpat Shukla and

Jasmeet Zhaveri. You can tell by the way he's stressed the 'G' and by the cursive that conjoins the two words.'

'I suggest you go and flip through the watchman's register and try to match the lettering,' said Nadeem. 'What are you doing here, anyway? This is private property.'

'I've got news for you, Khatib,' Inspector Nagpal scowled. 'In the eyes of the law, you are the primary suspect.'

'I thought the case was closed. The post-mortem report said overdose.'

'We went through his flat again before paying you a visit. We conducted another inspection of the house and this time, we found an empty bottle of Phensedyl next to the medicine cabinet.'

Srikant produced a zip-lock packet from his pocket, which contained the empty bottle, and waved it for Nadeem and Warren to get a good look at.

'It was drained completely, sucked dry, not even a drop was left,' said Inspector Nagpal. 'The receipt sticker on the bottom of the bottle says the date of purchase was six days ago and the expiry date is 2 March 2020, manufactured a month ago. It is obviously new stock. As you know, it takes more than two and a half months for any healthy, normal person in his right mind to go through a bottle of cough syrup, even with the sorest throat imaginable.'

'Even if he had tonsillitis,' added Srikant, 'or tuberculosis or coronary thrombosis, he still wouldn't be able to finish a bottle of cough syrup in five days, unless . . .'

'Unless,' continued Inspector Nagpal, 'it was stuffed down his throat. A case of poisoning. We are having the bottle sent down to the lab for a fingerprint test.'

Inspector Nagpal and Srikant got up to head towards the door.

'You better hope your fingerprints don't show up on that bottle, Khatib.'

Down with the Sickness

'What do you make of all this?' asked Warren, after the two cops left the house, slamming the door shut extremely hard as if it were a display of hostility .

'I don't know what to make of it,' sighed Nadeem. 'The bottle hasn't moved an inch from its original position in six days and yet it seems to have been consumed. When the kabaadiwaala saw it last four days ago, it was half-empty.'

'What? How is that possible? He said it was bought six days ago. If he finished half a bottle of Phensedyl in two days, he'd be on the floor when the kabaadiwaala showed up.'

'And if the person who used it was smart enough not to let his fingerprints show up on it, as he was with the glass on the balcony door, then . . .'

'Then the only prints that'll show up on the bottle are the kabaadiwaala's!'

Nadeem looked out of the window distraught and perplexed to the point of disorientation. He wasn't able to think straight. His faculties of judgment weren't in the best shape. He was feeling jittery and unwell.

From the window he could see Inspector Nagpal and Srikant get into the police jeep, after having a few words with the watchman. He cleared the empty cups they had left and went into the kitchen to wash them. Srikant had spilt some of the tea on the kitchen slab while pouring it into the cups. Nadeem wiped it with the cloth that hung by the washbasin and washed the seven cups. He threw the remains of the tea leaves from the strainer into the dustbin and checked the packet of tea. He smelt it. It definitely smelt bad, but the two cops still enjoyed it enough to go through six cups.

'They must have a cast-iron stomach,' he thought, as his stomach began to grumble. He fished out a thermometer. He was pretty sure he had a fever. The reading said 101 degrees. His throat was drying up, he had a splitting headache, his sinuses were clogged and he hadn't eaten anything all day. He looked frantically for the first-aid kit. The whole house was in disarray. Things were lying everywhere. Nagpal and Srikant hadn't had the courtesy to put things back in their rightful place. Nadeem popped a Crocin, thinking it would do the job.

'You better get some rest, Nadeem. You look sick.'

'Is there anything to eat in the house?'

'I doubt it.'

Nadeem rushed out to the neighbourhood bania. It was shut. He checked every department store in the area, but could not come across even one that was open. Finally, he decided to take an auto up to DMart. That was his only chance.

DMART

Nadeem strolled aimlessly about DMart, looking for anything that would even half satisfy his growing starvation. He felt no need to pick up a shopping basket. He rarely visited DMart since the need for him to do so seldom arose. They purchased everything from detergent to naphthalene balls from the neighbourhood department store.

He stumbled past the drinks trays, picking up a bottle of soya milk from the fridge. He then put it back on noticing a tetrapack of chocolate milk, which he settled for instead. He didn't wait to pay for it, he just stuck the straw inside and began sipping away as he walked on, keeping an eye on anything reasonably affordable that caught his fancy.

The section stocked with chips, biscuits and Maggi noodles occupied the corner shelves. All those fancy, new imported products had taken up the centre aisle. He browsed through them with no intention of laying a finger on any item. He just looked at them with an amused scorn, as if they were the real enemies.

It was the kind of section Irshaad Batla would have probably felt at home in. He seldom drank anything out a bottle that hadn't been flown in specially from Hong Kong. Just then, Nadeem remembered Irshaad's indulgences. All those leather suitcases and imported belts and shoes, all that fancy cologne, and all those duty-free plastic bags that smelt of another candy-coated land! All those platinum and gold standard inextinguishable credit cards. They had all sort of acquired a foothold in Nadeem's existence, although he was at a comfortable distance from them. They still provoked their lure towards him ever so often. He often thought of the so-called upgrading of one's livelihood, but it never seemed to divert him enough to turn his stool around. He, every now and then, even resented this other life but observed it with glaring eyes, knowing that although deprived of its privileges, he did in some degree have access to it. He never thought of himself as one of them. Those robust young men from Bandra who paraded restaurants, arriving in souped-up fancy cars with rims and 1.8-turbo charge engines that could be heard all across the neighbourhood, nursing their whiskey sodas with a plastic stirrer at the smoker's corner, talking shop with their hands in their pockets with that expression of seriousness and certainty giving gravity to their contentment, their overtly amplified laughter, which sometimes sounded like a war cry, a mating call, or an exclamation of understanding in their varied wandering concentration spans, their thoughts and ears all about the places they inhabited—looking over and ahead, replying to someone on their immediate left—greeting each other with militant affection and familiarity.

The very thought of them made Nadeem feel even more ill. He let the thought linger as he looked about the place, hoping to chance upon a familiar face. He was beginning to feel weak and desperately needed to have a bite. The chocolate milk made his stomach feel even worse. He felt like he was about to heave, his guts were churning and he desperately needed to go to the bathroom. He grabbed a bottle of room-temperature Bisleri water and cracking the seal open, drained the entire bottle in one go. That made him regain his bearings. He walked on further to the chips section, which he avoided. He needed some real food and got his hands on a packet of cashew nuts. Just as he tore open the packet, he noticed a lady in front of him going through the shelves on his immediate left. She wheeled a trolley cart and was having a tough time reaching for something on one of the top shelves. Nadeem went over to help her, when he noticed that it was none other than Rohini. She was dressed in black and looked preoccupied, like she was there on an errand and not to take in the scenery.

'A bit late for mourning, isn't it?' Nadeem joked, as he reached for a jar of Szechuan sauce for her.

'Thank you. But I'm wearing the colour because I feel like it, not because I have to.'

'I'm in a bit of a black mood myself. Nadeem Khatib, pleased to meet you,' he shook her hand, introducing himself proudly. 'And your good name?'

'Call me whatever you like.'

'It's sad to see a woman with your redeeming characteristics so cynical about things. I'd say you have a lot to look forward to.'

'Like what?'

'Like a good, strong man in the pipeline. Someone with strong shoulders and a heart of gold. Not some loser like Makhija. You can do better than him with your eyes closed.'

'It's too late in the day for flattery. Do I know you?'

'I saw you at the police station. You see, I knew your husband.'

'Oh!

She started fidgeting in her purse, going through it like she was trying to unearth a buried treasure. Nadeem was mildly amused at her nervous manner and wondered if it was an act or whether she was genuinely neurotic. She seemed to put on a plain face in front of the police, but out there in the public sphere of DMart, she was a bumbling wreck. Nadeem smiled at her. She couldn't be bothered.

'Can I help you with that?' asked Nadeem, gesturing towards the trolley cart she was wheeling.

She shook her head, not paying attention, preoccupied with her purse. 'What?' she said, getting her nose out of the purse.

'I asked if I can help you with your groceries?'

'Look. Whatever the hell you want, just save it! Because right now, I really haven't got the time. I'm trying to look for my wallet. I can't seem to find it. It's got all my cards, my driver's licence, my PAN card, debit card, credit card.'

'Let me help you with that.' said Nadeem, grabbing hold of her purse. 'Here, let me check for you.'

She snatched the purse from him before he had the chance to go through it.

'How dare you!' she fumed.

'I was just trying to be chivalrous.'

'Chivalry is one thing and stupidity's another.'

'I'm sorry! I was just trying to help. I didn't mean to go through your purse.'

'But nonetheless you did.'

She shuffled her belongings into the purse and, after zipping it up, dumped it into the trolley cart. She looked towards Nadeem with her face bearing the promise of a faint smile.

'Did you see anything of interest?' she asked.

'I barely saw anything at all.'

He followed her trolley cart past the racks of Huggies and Cerelac.

'Do you have anything to hide?' he asked.

'I don't. The police have already gone through my purse.'

'Look. I don't mean to be impertinent or anything but would you like to go out for a cup of coffee with me?'

'Are you out of your mind!'

'I'm not making a play at you or anything. It's just that there's a couple of things I'd like to know about your late husband.'

'Right now?'

'There's a Café Coffee Day next door. If you like, we could grab a bite. They do a pretty good chicken samosa or veg puff in case you're not a carnivore like myself.'

Rohini looked around and dumped her last item of grocery shopping into the trolley.

'I don't know. I barely know you.'

'Well,' he smiled, 'we could change that in a heartbeat.'

Rohini looked him over, studying him from head to toe.

'Okay,' she said. 'Just let me pay first.'

Café Coffee Day

They managed to get a corner table at Café Coffee Day. There wasn't a single waiter in sight. They wondered whether the place was open or not, but since the lights were on and the kitchen seemed active, they figured they had a chance of getting something. Thankfully, they didn't have to share a table with the swarming crowds. The place was practically empty, save for a few couples and business conferences with laptops attached to the plug points. A bespectacled lone man, who wore a synthetic shirt and creased trousers, sat by the glass window looking out towards the neon-lit main road with hoardings hovering over the decrepit, crumbling renovated buildings. The road was being dug up from Malad all the way up to Goregaon. Cement rollers, road excavation bulldozers and JCBs stood in the middle of the road near the dividers, like the empty shops and showrooms, all shut down for the day, or like the drifting mongrels sleeping on the sidewalks. From the distance could be heard the blaring of some horn or the shrieking of the haggard madman picking up rubbish from the floors. The lone man, who sat by the window, sighed and looked down at his empty cup of coffee. He took the last sip before calling for the bill. After paying up, he put the receipt into his back pocket, picked up his motorcycle helmet from the table and went out into the neon-lit wilderness.

Finally, a waiter did come up to the table where Nadeem and Rohini sat, almost as if he was doing them a favour. He had a nameplate on his chest which read 'Mehul'. After Nadeem placed his order, he tried to ask Rohini about her deceased husband, but she still studied the menu as if that was more important.

'Would you like anything to drink?' he asked.

She called for a pineapple milkshake but was disappointed on being told by the waiter that it was not available. She settled for a fresh lime soda.

'They do a pretty good iced tea too,' Nadeem remarked. 'But I think I'll settle for a good old frappuccino.'

His stomach was beginning to grumble again. For a moment he pulled his guts together, trying not to let the turmoil show on his face. He cringed, squirming in agony, camouflaging it with an over-friendly smile.

'How come I've never seen you around the building?' he asked, trying to take his mind away from his worries.

'Because I've never been around the building. We split after he was caught for embezzlement.'

'Is that why he used to visit a psychiatrist?'

'I don't know anything about that.'

'You ever felt the need to talk to one of those shrinks?'

'I can't say I have. What about you?'

'Well, I have my moments of self-doubt. My flatmate tells me that I have a reduced concentration span as a result of excessive channel surfing. I guess he'd know because he suffers from a chronic condition of attention deficit hyperactivity disorder. Some people say he's a vegetable, doesn't possess the capability for abstract thought. His family members call him a zombie. But he used to be a smart aleck when he was young. The overconfident cocky type who got his brains squashed in by consistent defeat. Probably a bit like your husband in that regard.'

'We all have our problems.'

'I guess we do, but some less than others. And only when it reaches an extreme do people take extraordinary measures to stop their suffering. Your husband struck me as a very depressed man. He never got out of the house much. Never spent any money, never fraternized with any of the other building members. Kept to himself, was aloof. Did he have any family?'

'Everyone's got a family. They were notified by Senior Inspector Chetan Raane. I don't think Inspector Nagpal has it in him to do anything that noble.'

'They shown up yet?'

'Apparently, his sister is on her way from Nagpur.'

The fresh lime soda arrived later than they had expected. The waiter pointed towards the counter, implying that the grilled chicken sandwich and frappuccino Nadeem had ordered were light years away from being prepared.

'What's your interest in all of this?' she asked Nadeem, taking a sip of her fresh lime soda.

'I was the one who discovered your husband.'

'Oh!' she said, draining the entire glass till it reached the bottom.

'I also happen to live in the same building as him.'

'What do you do?'

'Broker.'

'Could you find me a place?'

'Sure. What's your budget?'

'About 25,000.'

She kept making the irritating slurping sound that a straw makes at the end of a drink.

'I'd have to look into it,' said Nadeem, trying to ignore the sound. 'Any particular preference with regard to areas?'

'Anywhere.'

'There's a good offer on a one-BHK in Goregaon (East). If you'd like, I could show you the flat.'

Rohini contemplated the proposition and wondered whether Nadeem looked like a trustworthy sort of fellow. Nadeem kept looking towards the counter in anticipation of his order arriving. He was famished. His stomach was beginning to make peculiar noises, which he tried to prevent Rohini from hearing by continuously talking as fast as he could. Finally, it reached a point where he could not take it any longer. He slammed the table in anger, almost falling off the side of his chair.

'Waiter!' he yelled.

'Are you okay?' Rohini asked, out of polite concern. 'What's the matter?'

Nadeem was trying to be as courteous as was humanly possible under the circumstances, but when the waiter showed up asking if he was all right, he nearly grabbed him by the neck demanding his food. The waiter looked at him strangely as Nadeem got up and ran towards the washroom.

The Café Coffee Day washroom was under maintenance and not functional. It had a yellow sign standing on the floor saying, 'Caution, wet floor, slippery', but Nadeem did not care and barged in, breaking the door open. He got inside and locked the door before the waiter had the chance to knock and say, 'Excuse me, sir! Kindly vacate the bathroom. It is out of order.'

Nadeem threw up all over the bathroom, practically tearing the place apart as he reeled and fell head first into the urinal.

'Excuse me, sir,' the waiter knocked again. 'Excuse me, sir, is everything alright?'

By now, Rohini too had got up to see what the matter was. When there was no response from the bathroom, the waiter called his supervisor who had a skeleton key for the bathroom. When they opened it, they found Nadeem on the floor without the slightest sign or indication of movement. He had evidently lost consciousness and fainted. The broken-down urinal lay next to him with bits of ceramic scattered all over the slippery floor.

Rohini gasped in mortal terror as she beheld the sight before her. The two Café Coffee Day personnel picked Nadeem up and put him on a sofa, calling an ambulance.

Hospital

They immediately rushed him to the nearest hospital. Rohini had the good sense of checking his phone and calling the last dialled number, which happened to be Warren's, and informed him of Nadeem's condition. Warren, for the first time in his life, was propelled out of his lethargy on registering the gravity of the situation. He leapt out of the couch with fierce urgency and put on a pair of trackpants with much difficulty in order to rush to the hospital.

Nadeem was lying on a stretcher when Warren arrived. The doctor was examining him thoroughly. He checked his pulse, respiration and blood pressure. He also took a blood sample.

A couple of hours later, after having revived him with ammonia, they were able to get him back to his senses. He was still heavily disoriented though. Rohini and Warren sat in the waiting room while the doctor had a word with Nadeem.

'How are you feeling now, son?' he asked as Nadeem opened his eyes.

'Weak. I've got a bit of a body ache and my stomach is still hurting.'

'I'm not surprised. I would like you to answer a question, and I would like you to answer it honestly and truthfully. Needless to say, this is for your own good that I ask, not out of any morbid curiosity of your habits.'

'Sure, doctor. What's the matter?'

'Do you take drugs? Any kind of injections from a syringe? Morphine, ketamine or heroin of any kind?'

'Hell, no! What makes you think that, doctor?'

'Well, I conducted a blood test while you were asleep. Now since you are awake, I would like to do a urine test if it is not too much of a problem.'

'Not at all,' Nadeem said, gallantly. 'I'd be only too glad to provide you with my urine!'

Nadeem suddenly got up but the doctor stopped him, reminding him to take his time and to get up slowly when he felt sufficiently recuperated. He called out to the nurse to help Nadeem.

'Well,' the doctor sighed, 'as per the reports of your blood test, the sample indicates traces of Phensedyl.'

Nadeem's heart skipped a beat. He froze and lay back on the bed without moving a limb.

'Are you sure?'

'Yes. And the traces are fresh, indicating that it was ingested into the blood stream not too long ago. Now tell me the truth, son. Have you been ingesting cough syrup?'

'Heavens, no, doctor. I don't even drink alcohol, I'm a teetotaller. I'm Muslim! I'm not allowed to drink.'

The nurse got him some water and Electrol, which he downed in an instant.

'What did you last have to eat or drink?' asked the doctor.

'A cup of tea,' said Nadeem, as it dawned on him.

The doctor asked the nurse to fetch a tray of hospital food. He had been told by Warren that Nadeem had not eaten anything all day. Warren and Rohini entered the room, with Mehul following them inside out of concern.

'Is everything all right, sir?' he asked timidly.

'Yes, thank you, Mehul,' said Nadeem, as he sat upright.

'I have to return to the shop. It's closing time and I have to pull down the shutters and lock the cash register.'

'Yes, Mehul, you may leave. Thank you very much,' said Rohini.

'I'm extremely sorry,' he said. 'I hope you understand.'

'I understand,' said Nadeem.

As Mehul left, Warren and Rohini went up to Nadeem's bed. She sat beside him, checking his forehead and his chin for bruises. There was an ice tray next to the bed on a table stand. Warren stood still, not knowing what to do or say.

The hospital food did not in the least look appetizing, and the elaborate procedure with which it was served to him only succeeded in making it appear all the more uninviting. The nurse turned the lever to incline the bed so Nadeem could sit up straight. Warren looked sullenly at the food. Its morose characteristics seemed a matter of fascination for him.

'How are you feeling?' asked Rohini.

'Slightly better,' said Nadeem. 'I'm extremely sorry. I hope you will forgive me for this.'

'Don't be silly.'

'I didn't mean to ruin our date.'

'It wasn't a date. Plus, if I knew I was going out with a sick man, I probably would have turned the other way and run, but I'm glad I was there to catch you when you fell. It's times like these that a stranger comes in handy. You would have done the same for me.'

'I'm eternally grateful to you for that.'

'I've saved my number on your phone,' she said, handing him his phone. 'You take care of yourself and if you need anything, give me a call.'

'I was hoping to use that line on you.'

'You're the one who needs help, Nadeem, not me,' she said, getting up from the bed and swinging her purse as she turned to walk out the door.

'You want Warren to drop you home?' asked Nadeem, chivalrously.

'Na,' she said, turning aside. 'Thanks, anyway! I'll get home safe.'

'How are you going to get back to Juhu at this time?'

'I'll go by rickshaw.'

'Message me when you reach home,'

'That was one line I was hoping you wouldn't use on me.'

'Nevertheless.'

'If you insist.'

As she left the room, Warren sat down beside Nadeem, leaning in towards him to ask what the matter was.

'I've been poisoned,' said Nadeem.

'By whom?' asked Warren.

'By Inspector Nagpal.'

Warren's eyebrow rose, taking the shape of a question mark.

'Call Machhiwaala,' said Nadeem tossing the phone to Warren. 'Ask him whether the bottle of cough syrup was empty or half-full when he last saw it.'

'How does that make any difference?'

'If it was empty, then all of it was poured down Makhija's throat, and if it was half-full then it was like that when it was in the possession of the police, and it's empty now. That's why Srikant insisted on making tea.'

'Why the hell would they spike you with it?'

'That's what I want to find out.'

Nadeem pushed aside the tray that obstructed his way and adjusting the recliner, jumped out of the bed, much to the nurse's protest. He informed the doctor that he had some urgent business to attend to and, after much persuasion, was permitted to be discharged. When he asked how much the total bill came to, he was astonished to find out how reasonable it was.

'Well, good thing she brought me here,' he realized.

'It was the Café Coffee Day guy's idea,' Warren told him. 'She didn't know what to do. Told me she had never been in such a situation before.'

'Ya?'

'Ya . . .'

'She tell you anything else about herself?'

'Na . . .'

'You spent two hours with her in the waiting room. After a point, you run out of magazines to read.'

'She was on her phone the whole time. A bit too preoccupied in it, if you ask me.'

'Well, sounds like someone else I know,' he clicked his tongue at Warren, slinking off to the bathroom to unleash a urine sample into a canister the doctor had given him.

While exiting the hospital after settling the bill, he persisted to marvel at how accommodating and affordable it seemed to be. He assured Warren that the next time anything happened to him, it was their services he would be using.

'What's the name of this hospital?' he asked.

Warren turned back to look at the board above the main entrance, that stood beside a red cross.

'K.L. Hospital,' he read from it.

Nadeem stopped, turned back slowly and reading the board himself just to be certain, darted back across the foyer into the main entrance. He asked the night clerk the way to the pharmacy but was told that it was shut. He still insisted on being shown where it was and was told that it was behind the hospital and had a separate entrance. Warren followed him all the way around the perimeter of the hospital to the pharmacy, which lay in the corner of the compound towards the back. The shutter was pulled up, but Nadeem was sure he could perceive a faint glow emanating from the inside. Warren too detected it and proceeded to bang on the shutter as Nadeem called out into the grills through which he climbed high enough to peep inside. There was a presence shuffling about the racks and shelves. Nadeem tried to call out to whoever it was, but no one responded. He quickly crept into the hospital through the back entrance near the lavatory and, winding his way through a corridor, which was in absolute darkness, reached the entrance to the pharmacy. The door had a sign on it saying 'Closed' but it was not locked. He pushed the door open to enter when he heard the sound of a carton falling from a height, followed by the sound of Warren banging on the shutters from the outside. He could not see anyone immediately as he looked through the shelves and behind the counter. The pharmacy was apparently empty. There was a stepladder next to one of the shelves, near the farthest corner of the pharmacy. It seemed to lead to an attic, which opened through a trapdoor to a concealed chamber. Nadeem climbed the ladder to gaze inside the attic. He spotted a small, timid-looking man hiding behind one of the shelves. He wore an unusually thick-framed pair of spectacles and the collar of his shirt was worn out and stood upright. His expression was alarmingly uncertain, his eyes were large and magnified in the lenses through which they appeared. Nadeem puzzled over his nose that had about it the distinctive flare of a beak, admiring the growth of hair that sprung out from his ears and trespassed on to the hair that ran around the corners of his head, fortifying the top into a bald patch.

'May I help you?' the man asked.

'What are you frightened about?'

'Are you a patient?'

'Are you the pharmacist?'

The little man's head began to shudder vigorously, as if extremely agitated. He fumbled with the crates and cartons that he was handling, and adjusting his spectacles spoke in a most indiscriminating tone.

'If you are not admitted to the hospital,' he began, 'I'm afraid I must ask you to leave otherwise I will be forced to call the authorities.'

'I advise you to do nothing of the kind,' said Nadeem, as he shot a glance at the telephone that hung near the calendar. 'For if you do not comply with my requests, I am afraid it is I who will be forced to call upon the authorities.'

'What do you want? Who told you about this place?'

'I was brought here on account of a sudden and unaccountable illness that upset my prior condition. For I can assure you that I have always been in the pink of health and have never needed the urgent medical attention that I was forced to endure over the past few hours.'

Nadeem always liked the smell of a pharmacy, the bland synthetic flavour of its fragrance. Like the smell of the plastic coating over a Becosule capsule. A sort of indefinite quantity, difficult to put one's finger on, but sufficient enough for the acutest sense to grasp. He glanced over the strips and boxes that lay stacked in the compartments of the shelves. Beneath the shelves lay a column of drawers, all labelled with names, each more complex than the other.

'New stock?' Nadeem asked.

The little man dropped one of the cartons as if in affirmation.

'I would like a bottle of Phensedyl,' said Nadeem.

'We're closed,' the man insisted.

'There's a patient registered in your records under the name of Chintan Makhija.'

The little man's face shrank on hearing that name.

'I was sorry to hear about him,' he sighed. 'The police have already been here.'

'I know, which is why I'm here. You see, one of the prescription slips that the late Mr Makhija had used to purchase medication from you was forged.'

'Forged?'

'Yes. When was the last time Mr Makhija had come down here to procure his medication?'

'I don't remember.'

Nadeem browsed through the drawers and compartments, much to the little man's dismay. He tore apart the entire attic looking for their stock of Phensedyl. On finding a bottle, he immediately turned it around in order to check the bottom. It said, 'Best Before 2/3/2020'.

'Did he buy a bottle of this from you?' Nadeem asked.

'Yes . . . but . . . uh . . .'

'What about the Dexedrine?' Nadeem stopped him mid-stride, grabbing him by the scruff of his neck with the inquiry.

'The what?'

'And all the other nonsense the doctor prescribed for him. I don't think you realize the gravity of the situation . . . Mr . . .'

'Nair.'

'Nair. In the entire area, your pharmacy is the only one the police have zeroed in on. It's bound to be investigated in relation to his death. Dr Kang has conveniently taken off for his medical convention, leaving you here to face the music.'

Just then, the little man's phone burst into activity. A deafeningly banal tune played out as his caller tune, loud and clear for everyone within a five-mile radius to hear. He literally jumped upon hearing it in his pocket and tried to reach for it to shut it up, but by the time he managed to get a hold of it to put an end to the incessant noise, Nadeem had already vacated the attic and was making his way down the stepladder. He had satisfied his curiosity and, having put two and two together, made for the door with the intention of acting upon his recent findings. He wondered whether to first inform the doctor upstairs or Inspector Gaekwad. He decided to go with the latter and started dialling Inspector Gaekwad's number as he reached for the front door. The little man tried to hurry down the attic in pursuit of Nadeem but stumbled over a fallen carton and got entangled in a mess of cardboard at the stepladder. Nadeem turned to look back towards the attic as he put his hand out to push open the door. As the door slid open and his neck turned back in place, he floundered at the exit. Outside the door stood a person whose features, on account of the darkness, were not clearly perceptible. It was apparent from his demeanour that he was eager to get in, but all that was distinguishable from his silhouette was that the man held a phone to his ear, not who he was or what he was doing there. On noticing the presence outside, Nadeem immediately retreated into the pharmacy and closed the door shut from the inside, putting his phone away. The ringing of the little man's phone could be faintly heard from the attic, almost as if the phone itself were growing anxious from not being answered. By now, Warren's knocking too had ceased. Nadeem quickly hid behind one of the shelves, concealing himself from the sight of the encroaching party. Through the gaps between the shelves, he had a clear view of the entrance. The front door to the pharmacy creaked open as the figure emerged from the darkness of the corridor behind him. It was the eminent Dr Vengsarkar himself, in person. He was accompanied by one of Inspector Nagpal's deputies, Dilip, who stepped back and slowly tilted his eyes up to the attic.

'Mr Nair,' Dilip called out. Mr Nair promptly popped his head out, greeting the doctor and the policeman with a good deal of reverence and business-like haste. He first looked at Dr Vengsarkar cautiously, then at Dilip, nodding with a firm yet polite air of casual sincerity. He then went on looking about the place, preoccupied in trying to find Nadeem, as he descended the stepladder. Dilip held out the forged prescription. 'You know it's illegal in the state of Maharashtra to facilitate the unauthorized sale or purchase of any kind of pharmaceutical prescription drug,' said Dilip with the knowing air of a supposed expert on all matters concerning the law. 'The penalty for breaking this law is two years, sometimes two and a half, depending on the nature of the dosage and medication. And what we have here isn't exactly child's play. It's enough to send a man to the point of no return.'

'Look,' began Mr Nair, 'how was I supposed to know that it was a forged prescription?'

'You can read, can't you? Or are you illiterate?' Dilip barked. 'One could say that you indirectly engineered his death by giving him the medication without a legitimate prescription.'

Dr Vengsarkar nodded. He was trying to cover his own rear end and had to put up a straight face, acting all high and mighty like he had done the right thing by refusing to prescribe Makhija the drugs. 'There was a reason I hadn't allowed him any more medication,' he insisted in as earnest a tone as he could muster. 'You really shouldn't have given it to him. It could have been fatal.'

There wasn't a grain of truth in what he was saying, but he dished it out like it was wholegrain, gleefully passing on the nourishment of blame. Mr Nair's eyes kept fluttering about the place like fireflies, his neck turning back and forth in irregular postures.

'What's the matter?' Dilip asked, his attention suddenly alerted. 'Is there someone in here?'

'Oh no . . . No one at all. Just a rat or a lizard, I think.'

Nadeem lowered his head, glancing through a rack of Huggies and Cerelac. It was significantly darker where he had crouched. Only his eyes glowed through the narrow slit between the shelves. Dilip slowly turned towards the shelves, his eyeballs shiftlessly scanning the vicinity with the veracity of a bloodhound. 'I think I heard something,' he said softly.

Dr Vengsarkar stood absolutely still, not moving a limb. He looked around and then at himself. 'What is it?' he asked Mr Nair. 'What are you looking at?'

'Shhh . . . silent,' Dilip ordered.

Nadeem bent even lower, practically on all fours to avoid being seen, slowly crawling away into as distant a corner he could creep towards. All of a sudden, there came the pounding of the shutters, breaking the stillness of his posture. 'Hello!' Warren called out.

'Who's out there?' Dr Vengsarkar turned. Dilip ran out of the entrance in response to check who was banging on the shutters. Nadeem took the opportunity to make a swift exit. He dashed past the doctor and the chemist, who were standing baffled at the counter, and before they could call out, he ran past the dark corridor that led to the back entrance of the hospital. As he made his way out to where Warren was standing in front of the closed shutter, he noticed through the grills that the lights were being switched off suddenly from the inside. He quickly redialled Inspector Gaekwad's number and made for the exit of the hospital, as Warren swiftly followed him out. By the time they reached the main road, Inspector Gaekwad had answered the call.

'Hello,' Nadeem shouted into the phone, panting profusely. 'Can you hear me?'

'Loud and clear, Chipkali. Go ahead, what's on your mind?'

'I have just survived a poisoning attempt.'

'When was this?'

'Just a few hours ago, sitting at my own home, drinking out of my own mug.'

'By whom?'

'Inspector Nagpal!'

'Where are you right now?'

'Outside K.L. Hospital.'

Nadeem felt a gentle tap on his shoulder. Preoccupied in looking into the other direction, he had failed to notice that there was a police jeep parked right outside the entrance. It was a night patrol jeep that belonged to Nagpal's subordinate, Dilip.

Dilip politely asked Nadeem to get into the jeep. Nadeem hesitated at first, then turned to Warren and handed him his phone.

'Look,' said Dilip, smiling uninhibitedly. 'Get into the jeep and don't make any trouble; that goes for you too!' he said, pointing at Warren and promptly confiscating the phone. He snatched it away from Warren and told the two constables in the jeep to grab hold of them and put them in handcuffs. They dragged Nadeem into the back of the jeep, with much resistance from him. He made quite a spectacle of himself in the middle of the road, right outside K.L. Hospital. Onlookers were drawn out of their closed shops and sheds to behold the commotion. The neighbouring watchman, the parked autorickshaw driver, the lost pedestrian and the ragpicker crossing the road, all watched with equal interest and curiosity. Nadeem and Warren were forcefully shoved into the police jeep. The constables tried to drive off the onlookers by yelling at them and waving their arms, but no one budged. On noticing an ambulance arrive at the hospital, the police jeep skidded off as the doors slammed shut.

Interrogation Room

By the time Nadeem and Warren were brought to Malad police station, Inspector Nagpal was already seated in his office, sipping on another cup of tea.

'Come in,' he called out to Nadeem, as soon as he noticed them enter the police station.

Nadeem walked past the head constable's desk with his nose in the air.

'Don't have to wait in line today to meet your sahib,' he sneered at the head constable.

Inspector Nagpal had some files stacked on his desk. He pulled out a pen that was clipped to his chest pocket. He had a pair of reading glasses on, which he took off to greet Nadeem and Warren, as they entered his office.

'How are you feeling, Nadeem?' asked Inspector Nagpal.

'Fine, thank you, inspector,' Nadeem replied, courteously.

'I'd like to have a word with you.'

'Another cup of tea? No, thank you! I take mine without sugar and certainly without cough syrup.'

Srikant closed the door and quickly turned towards his sahib, looking at him with questioning eyes. Inspector Nagpal signalled something to him with his customary flick of the fingers, as if implying serious business.

'What do you want to do with the other one?' asked Dilip, gesturing towards Warren.

'Lock him up,' ordered Inspector Nagpal. 'Put him in solitary confinement till further notice.'

Dilip and Srikant pulled Nadeem and Warren out of Inspector Nagpal's cabin. Warren was relegated to the junior constables, but Nadeem was given the special treatment. Dilip and Srikant led him through a dark corridor to the dreaded chamber. Inspector Nagpal followed them in, folding his sleeves ominously.

The interrogation room was sealed shut after they entered. A single ceiling lamp provided all the light in the dingy room, which was musty with the smell of countless thrashings and beatings that must have taken place within its hallowed walls.

Nadeem sat on a stool while Srikant stood beside him in a corner. Inspector Nagpal turned a chair around and settled himself on it, pointing the lamp in Nadeem's direction to get a better look at him.

'You ever heard of an officer by the name of Sumant Rao Kaambli?' he asked Nadeem.

'I've had the pleasure of gathering his acquaintance.'

'Then you must be fully aware that he has set quite a standard for this side of the police force to live up to. He has raised the bar, so to speak. Sometimes I wish I had his resolve, and sometimes, when I come face-to-face with guys like you, I wish I had his scruples. Compared to him, I'm soft. They say he sold his conscience when he was a kid and has been looking for it ever since in every frightened face he had the displeasure of having to work on.'

Srikant switched on the ceiling fan. It came on at its own leisurely pace, rotating slowly and creaking into the stillness of the dense air that filled the room. Inspector Nagpal stretched his palm out for Dilip to put something into it. Dilip searched his pockets for Nadeem's mobile phone, tapping his chest, hips and back pocket. Once he got hold of it, he placed it neatly in the inspector's hands. Inspector Nagpal unfolded his reading glasses and went through it thoroughly, as though it were his birthright as a police officer. There was a new message in the inbox. He opened it and his eyes glowed with mischievous delight as he read it.

'Just reached home,' he read. 'Take care and get well soon. From Rohini.'

Nadeem looked down in absolute silence. He didn't say a word.

'Who is Rohini?'

Nadeem still remained silent.

'I thought you said you never had anything to do with Makhija.'

'I didn't!'

'Then how do you have his wife's mobile number stored in your contacts, and why is she messaging you at this time of the night?'

Just then, the sound of a car screeching to a halt
tore across the police station. The thud of the car door
slamming preceded the growling of the engine as it
revved off.

Irshaad Batla, followed by two of his flunkies, walked
into the police station like they owned the place. Their
demeanour suggested contempt for authority and also
an amusement at the circumstances at hand. The head
constable showed them into the interrogation room,
where Inspector Nagpal was seated with Nadeem.

Nadeem glowered at Irshaad as he entered the
chamber. Inspector Nagpal offered Irshaad his chair,
but he refused and insisted that he preferred to stand.
He instructed his henchmen to exit the room and keep a
watch outside. Nadeem looked at Irshaad with melancholy
eyes, hoping to inspire empathy. He was trying to get the
waterworks going, but ended up putting on a sloppy act.
He barely even caught Irshaad's attention, with his moist
eye lashes, as he kept running his fingers through his hair
like it was a sign of utter despair.

'How do you want to do this?' Irshaad asked Inspector
Nagpal.

'We can take him out tonight for a round.'

'Where?'

'Madh Island,' said Inspector Nagpal, looking at
Srikant. 'We can do an encounter on him and close the
books.'

Srikant's smug expression was suddenly overcome by
an approaching anxiety. Irshaad looked up at the ceiling
fan and took a long deep breath. Just then Nadeem's

phone, which currently lay in Inspector Nagpal's pocket, started to ring. Irshaad asked to take a look at it.

'Who is it?' he asked.

'Gaekwad!' said Inspector Nagpal, as he handed the phone to him.

After it stopped ringing, Irshaad pressed the top button on the phone, switching it off. He then gently removed the SIM card after sliding open the battery cover. After having put it into his pocket, he placed the phone down on the floor and smashed it with prodigious force.

'Look,' Nadeem pleaded. 'Please, Irshaad, listen to me, we can work this out! Let's talk this through with a cool head . . .'

Before Nadeem could utter another syllable, Irshaad pulled Inspector Nagpal's chair out from under him and swung it at Nadeem. Nadeem was pushed towards the wall as he ducked, missing it narrowly. Irshaad smacked him across the face with three consecutive strokes till he collapsed on the floor. Once he was down, Irshaad took the opportunity to kick him in the stomach, his heels digging firmly into Nadeem's abdomen, producing a variety of raucous and squawking sounds that sounded increasingly pitiful and undignified as they grew more vigorous. He flung the stool Nadeem had been sitting on at one of the windows, smashing it for the sole purpose of demonstrating his wrath. Irshaad's body was convulsing with a simmering rage. He started banging his clenched fists on his thighs. He shrivelled up like a petulant child in the midst of a tantrum and began shrieking and screaming at the top of his voice. Nadeem knew he was having one of his outbursts and, as he looked towards Inspector Nagpal, he sensed an uncertainty in his ability to cope with the situation.

'Take it easy, Irshaad,' Nadeem spoke like a matador trying to tame a charging bull. 'Please, I beg you, listen to me.'

Nadeem knew how to handle Irshaad in these situations as he had had the opportunity of having done so before. He tried beckoning to him with his reasoning tone, tried to make him see sense, but nothing succeeded in preventing him from going out of control.

Nadeem received a terrible beating. Inspector Nagpal and Srikant stood by solemnly and watched. It was almost as though the matter was not in their hands, or outside their jurisdiction, left solely to the discretion of the aggressor. Irshaad had paid handsomely for their confidence and it seemed only reasonable to let him have his money's worth.

The Mac

An hour and a half later, Warren was called in for questioning into the interrogation room. Bits and pieces of Nadeem's phone were scattered all about the floor.

Nadeem sat in a corner looking considerably roughed up. His hair was dishevelled, he had a bruise under his chin, a black eye and a swollen upper lip. Srikant was caressing his hair, promising him it would be all right and that he didn't have a thing in the world to be worried about. He ordered one of the hawaldars to bring some ice wrapped in a handkerchief.

Irshaad was standing near one of the windows talking on the phone in a sort of code language like the 'p' language, only he replaced the 'p' with an 'ant'.

'Mantalad Puntolice stintation!' he said into the phone.

Inspector Nagpal asked Warren to sit on the only chair that stood in the room. Warren sat on it, tilting left and right since it was unsteady, as it had been thrown at the wall and at Nadeem. Inspector Nagpal studied Warren from head to toe and looked at his locks with abject disdain and disapproval.

'Does the name Rohini Makhija mean anything to you?' asked Inspector Nagpal.

'No,' replied Warren.

'What relation does your friend have with her?'

'I don't know.'

Warren looked at Nadeem, who avoided eye contact.

'I got a call from his phone,' said Warren, 'and was told by her to come to the hospital. I was told it was an emergency.'

Irshaad Batla cut the call that he was so strenuously engaged in and turned his attention towards Warren.

'How much, does he know?' he asked Nagpal.

'Not much, by the looks of him,' said Inspector Nagpal.

'Anyway,' said Irshaad, 'I'm not taking any chances. Naved Bhai and Adnan Bhai are on their way here right now. They've got two of our Behram Bagh shooters; they'll take care of it. Just close the files and say they're absconding.'

'Where are you going to dispose of the bodies?'

'We'll take them to the creek in Ghodbunder and dump them in the mangroves. No one will find them there.'

'Listen,' said Inspector Nagpal, visibly alarmed. 'Maybe you'd better let me handle this. I'll take them to Madh Island, into the jungle, and do an encounter on them, say they were trying to escape. We'll plant a revolver in his hand. He's known to carry firearms, after all, he used to work for your dad.'

'This Chipkali never worked for my dad. He worked for me. He was my pet. My right hand man, you could say. In those days, he marched to my beat. Isn't that right, Nadeem?'

Nadeem wasn't in a condition to talk.

'Look,' trembled Warren. 'Whatever it is, I am sure we can work this out. How much do you want? I can arrange some money. My cousin, Howard, works in the merchant navy. He'll have some money lying in his flat.'

'Your friend's in deeper than you think,' said Irshaad. 'Needless to say, if it was anything that money could buy, I wouldn't be out here wasting Inspector Nagpal's time.'

Irshaad took a long pause, wondering whether or not to waste his time on Warren.

'As of now,' he began, 'your buddy is twelve lakhs short in our books. Twelve and a half, plus interest. That's how much he owes me.'

'I am sure it can be arranged,' suggested Warren, naively.

Irshaad looked at Inspector Nagpal, who smiled back at him.

'What's your name, Paolie [Christian]?' asked Irshaad.

'Warren.'

'I used to know a guy like you once, Warren. His name was Flavian. Flavours they used to call him. He didn't make it past the third grade. He used to sit in front of me in class and never let me concentrate. Kept stealing my pens and pencils. One day, he got more of my pencil than he bargained for.'

There was a long pause as Warren looked around, thinking of a comment that would be worth his while.

'Which school did you go to, Paolia? I'll bet it was a macapao school!' said Irshaad.

'St Stanishlaus,' replied Warren.

'I thought as much. You see, I went to St Teresa's. First to St Anne's and then to St Teresa's. I quite liked St Anne's, but the unfortunate incident with my classmate prevented me from continuing my schooling there. But I always say that it's what I learnt outside the classroom that made me what I am today. Tell me, Warren, you ever knew a guy called Valen? Little guy. In St Stanish? I think he would have been your batch.'

'No.'

'Your friend Nadeem knows him. I only mention it because that's how I know Nadeem. Through Valen.'

Warren was not getting the drift of this conversation.

'I just thought you might know him, the world's smaller than you think. I only mention it to remind you that Nadeem knows certain people who I know. I don't know about you, but Nadeem certainly does know them. And you see, his squealing to the cops about my dad's operations is one thing. That I can take, but what I can't take is him spreading shit about me to people I know.'

'Look,' interrupted Nadeem from the farthest corner of the room.

'Shut up!' barked Irshaad.

Nadeem got up from the floor and took two unsteady steps in Irshaad Batla's direction. Irshaad turned his attention back to Warren.

'Tell me, Warren,' he continued, 'by any chance did Nadeem mention anything about running into me today?'

'IRSHAAAAD,' screamed Nadeem, trying to distract his attention from Warren.

Warren looked at Nadeem, who was trying to say something to him fiercely with his eyes.

'Tell me, Warren,' said Irshaad. 'Tell me the truth. If you lie, I have ways of finding out.'

'He mentioned,' began Warren, 'that . . .'

'WARREN!' yelled Nadeem, trying to shut him up.

All of a sudden, Irshaad charged at Nadeem and belted him one in the eye. One of his cut's opened up and started flowing uncontrollably. Inspector Nagpal disgustedly told Dilip to fetch some cotton wool.

'He mentioned,' continued Warren, stammering and stuttering, 'that he met you at a psychiatrist's clinic.'

Irshaad sighed in satisfaction. He had heard what he wanted to hear all along. He paid Warren no further heed and proceeded towards Nadeem.

'Now, Nadeem,' he breathed heavily, 'when we met earlier in the day, hadn't I specifically told you not to tell anyone under any circumstances that you saw me there, including your roommate?'

'Look, Irshaad,' pleaded Nadeem, 'I can explain.'

'Now,' Irshaad cut him off before he could utter another word, 'how am I to take your word that you will not tell anyone about this? You are the only one who has seen me there. I cannot take any chances.'

'Listen, Irshaad. If you pop either one of us, Gaekwad is going to be on your ass sooner than you think. In fact, he's on his way here right now.'

'Then shouldn't he have reached by now?'

'I'm sorry, Irshaad, but I got held up,' said a voice from outside the interrogation room. 'I had to bring along a witness.'

From the shadows of the corridor, like a guardian angel, emerged Inspector Gaekwad, followed by Dr Vengsarkar, whom he led into the interrogation room.

Saved by the Bell

'Yes?' asked Inspector Nagpal, as he stood up in attention.

'Inspector V.M. Gaekwad, Byculla police station,' proclaimed Inspector Gaekwad, as he flashed his badge before Inspector Nagpal.

'You're a bit out of your jurisdiction, aren't you, inspector?' asked Inspector Nagpal.

'It isn't for nothing that I've made this long trip to Malad in the middle of the night, Nagpal. I've only heard of you before, I'm glad to finally meet you in person.'

'I'm afraid I can't say the same,' said Inspector Nagpal, shooting a discreet glance at the doctor. 'What do you want here, Inspector Gaekwad?'

'The man you've held in custody works for me. His name is Nadeem Khatib. I can gladly vouch for him, show you his police record, his dossier, whatever you require.'

'This man is held here as a suspect,' stated Inspector Nagpal. 'He's not in judicial custody as yet. He's going to spend the night in the lock-up.'

'He didn't do it,' said Inspector Gaekwad. 'You have my word.'

'Your word doesn't count for much here, Inspector. How can you be so sure?'

'Because I know who did it.'

'Who?'

'Him,' he smirked, pointing at Irshaad Batla.

Inspector Nagpal turned his neck to look at Batla, as if for the first time. 'Him?' he laughed. 'Not possible. He's here as a witness. The deceased Mr Makhija owed him money. He's the last person who would want to see Makhija dead.'

'Why don't you let me handle this three-stripe paandu!' spat Irshaad Batla. 'He's a piece of cake.'

'No, Irshaad,' Inspector Nagpal quivered. 'Don't! Let me handle this.'

'I've heard all about you, Gaekwad,' growled Irshaad, closing in on him. 'You're the one who's been on to us since this worm got himself arrested. Let me tell you something!'

'What?' Inspector Gaekwad raised his nose in the air, glancing down at him through his nostrils.

'You carry on like that and you might find yourself transferred sooner than you know it!'

Inspector Gaekwad looked aside, rolling his eyes in disbelief. He had heard worse. He didn't even bother to look him straight in the eyes. He, instead, turned to Inspector Nagpal and addressed his line of inquiry to him.

'You haven't made much headway in this case, have you?'

'That, right there,' said Inspector Nagpal, pointing at Nadeem, 'is all the headway I need to make.'

'What do you want with this?' Inspector Gaekwad asked, suddenly dead serious. 'I thought they shut the case. What are you getting out of this? How much is he paying you to pin this on Nadeem?'

'As I said before, Mr Sheikh is merely here as a witness.'

'Then what's he doing here at this time of the night?'

'As I said before, the late Mr Makhija was in debt with him. He owed him money.'

'You didn't say all that much before, but let me tell you something I haven't said as yet. Your Mr Sheikh out here owes some money too.'

'What nonsense!' Irshaad protested. 'I don't know what you're talking about!'

Nadeem got up from the ground in an instant and, wiping his wounds fiercely, began to pace up and down the room.

'I don't owe anyone jackshit!' yelled Irshaad. 'I don't even know who the hell you're talking about. This is all rubbish!'

'Take it easy!' ordered Inspector Nagpal. 'I'm afraid I'm going to have to ask you to leave, Inspector Gaekwad. This is my case and I don't want anyone else getting involved. If you have inquiries to make about a separate case, then it can wait till tomorrow morning.'

'Maybe you'd like to have a word with DCP Kaambli,' Inspector Gaekwad told him.

At the mere mention of Kaambli's name, the blood drained from Inspector Nagpal's face. He froze, absolutely still.

'I can buy out a cop like that, blindfolded, with both hands tied behind my back,' spat Irshaad. 'That goes for you too, Gaekwad, make no mistake. If this is your idea of a threat, just remember I've brought along four shooters with me who are outside in the car. All they need to do is make one phone call to my cousins and they'll be here with officers who are Kaambli's superiors.'

'It's not a threat,' said Inspector Gaekwad. 'I only mentioned Kaambli to convince you that I mean business.'

'It'll take more than a conversation to convince me about that.'

'Yup, it'll take some pretty hard and fast measures, which I'd be glad to take, provided everything's insured and you have someone to pick up the broken pieces of whatever's left once they hit the floor.'

'They employ sweepers for that.'

'Not in my line of work. In my profession, you've got to do your own dirty work. You don't have fifteen flunkies that'll jump every time you reach for the newspaper. I know you're the kind of person who wouldn't even go to the toilet without a republic day parade giving the urinals a heads-up.'

'You haven't got anything on me, Gaekwad, nothing that will stick in court.'

'Well, I have something,' Inspector Gaekwad winked at Nadeem, who was standing quietly in the corner.

Questioning

Inspector Gaekwad introduced everyone to Dr Vengsarkar, and mentioned that he was Irshaad's counsellor.

'What the hell is he doing here?' yelled Irshaad. 'Take him out of here this instant. I won't stand for this.'

Irshaad rose from his seat, visibly agitated, and made for the door, but Inspector Gaekwad stopped him.

'Take it easy, Irshaad,' said Inspector Gaekwad, under his breath. 'Don't shout here. This is a police station. Not your private bathroom.'

Irshaad glowered down at him, a scowl erupting on his tightly wound face. Inspector Gaekwad asked him to be seated on the stool beneath the overhead lamp. He looked towards Nadeem, who still stood motionless in the corner. He offered Nadeem his chair, which Nadeem, of course, politely refused, but Inspector Gaekwad insisted. Nadeem sat down awkwardly, knowing fully well that he was depriving the police officer of the comfortable seat.

Inspector Gaekwad took the opportunity to pace up and down—perhaps it made him think clearer.

'I have a couple of questions of my own I'd like to ask you, Irshaad,' he said. 'If that's okay with you, Inspector Nagpal?'

Inspector Nagpal looked at Irshaad tensely, fidgeting his eyebrows as if in alarm. Irshaad calmly nodded at him, implying it was all right.

'Sit down, Irshaad,' sighed Inspector Gaekwad. 'Would you like anything to drink? Tea, coffee, water, Coke, Pepsi, Sprite, 7 Up?'

'Cut to the chase!' Irshaad spat. 'I'm getting hiccups waiting for the buildup.'

'That's cause your PA is remembering you,' Inspector Gaekwad laughed.

'He's in jail!' said Irshaad, not finding it quite as funny.

'That's exactly why. No doing of yours, of course. Just one of those miscellaneous accidents that tend to happen just about as often as they are seldom.'

'You can't blame anyone for them.'

'You can't do anything about them either.'

'Sure you can. If you spread money in the right places, there isn't a thing in the world you can't do.'

'Except live. There's no price tag on that.'

'Yup, but there is a warranty.'

'First and foremost,' said Inspector Gaekwad shrewdly, ignoring his remark, 'what are you doing here, Irshaad?'

'I heard my name popped up in the investigation, so I thought I'd better come down to give my statement.'

'Where did you hear that?' asked Inspector Gaekwad, evidently sterner than before.

'You're not the only one with tippers out on the street, Gaekwad. If you could have nailed me, you would have done so ages ago, with or without providing protection to your informers. If I wanted to cut this lizard's tail off, what makes you think I wouldn't have done it by now?'

'You're not stupid.'

'And neither is he. He knows how to play his cards right. Isn't that right, Nadeem?'

'I don't know what you're talking about!' said Nadeem. 'All I know is that you've had two guys tailing me ever since I got out of the clink.'

'I didn't have anyone tailing you. I've got better things to be concerned about than a two-bit stool pigeon.'

Nadeem first looked at Warren and then at Inspector Gaekwad. 'You mean to say,' he said, 'that those two men who came by to pay me a visit were not sent by you?'

'If they were sent by me, you wouldn't have made it out of the building in one piece.'

'Does the name Rohini Makhija mean anything to you?' asked Inspector Gaekwad, suddenly changing the subject.

'Rinki?' asked Irshaad, bursting into a visible smile. 'Of course I know her.'

'Who the heck is Rinki?' asked Nadeem.

'Never mind,' continued Inspector Gaekwad. 'What was your relationship with her?'

'We had been going steady for a couple of years.'

'Was she your item?'

'Oh, she was much more than that, inspector. As a matter of fact, I was at one point engaged to be married to her.'

'What broke off the arrangement?'

'She found out about my background.'

'Have you had any contact with Rohini since?'

'She stopped picking up my calls. I got word some time later that she had married some guy. So I got in touch with him and had a little man-to-man talk. I thought maybe he was the guy who had filled her head with second-hand information about me, but he didn't look the type. He had met her at Inorbit Mall, through a mutual friend who was a broker, and was helping her find a flat. I guess he gave her the impression that he was some kind of real estate tycoon and had flats all over the place. He told her that he was the chief financial adviser at HSBC. But when I met him, it turned out he was broke and in dire straits. He had embezzled certain sums of money from the workplace in order to sustain his wife's monthly expenditure, which was way beyond their means. After a year and a half of living with him, she eventually found out that he was actually a mere prudential funds clerk and threatened to leave him. Now I found all of this pretty funny at first, but on second thought, I didn't find the guy's plight funny. He was in a shambles and needed my help. So, I gave him a loan.'

'How much?' smirked Inspector Gaekwad.

'One peti [lakh] with 25 per cent interest,' said Irshaad.

'When was the last time you spoke to him?'

'We transferred the money to his account in four monthly instalments. I got a call one day from Rinki, when she found out where the money was coming from. She said she would pay it back to me with interest. I told her it was okay and that she didn't have to worry about it. I tried sweet-talking her, even asking her out to see if she wanted to catch a movie or go out for dinner. But she just had her mind on the money. She was only interested in talking shop. Finally, I told her that she didn't have to worry about the loan, after all, it was Makhija's headache not hers. It was his responsibility to pay back the loan whenever he could afford to. Next thing I heard, she withdrew the cash and left him.'

'That's bullshit,' hollered Nadeem, leaping out of the chair. 'That's a filthy lie! She'd never do a thing like that. I know her. She saved my life.'

Inspector Nagpal told Inspector Gaekwad to calm Nadeem down and that he would not stand for aggressive behaviour in his police station. This was his jurisdiction and not Byculla. He was doing Inspector Gaekwad a favour by letting him sit in on this investigation in the first place, even though by now he had figured out that Inspector Gaekwad had an agenda as far as Irshaad was concerned.

'At least, that was Makhija's side of the story,' said Irshaad. 'I don't know whether she actually milked him or not. But that was the sob story he used on me the last time I caught him trying to dodge my phone calls. He started crying on the phone, telling me he was ruined, that everything was going to hell for him in a handbag.

I couldn't be much of a consolation to him, so I decided to extend my sympathy a little bit and told him he had another month to cough up the dough. If not, then, first his flat and then maybe even his car. I found out who his landlord was and got in touch with him. Man by the name of Feroz Machhiwaala, claims to know my uncles. Bit of a smart alec, if you know what I mean, was a bit overfamiliar. Anyway, he told me that Makhija's lease was coming to an end and that he had a month's notice period in which to vacate. He mentioned that he had some lucrative offers coming in, thanks to a tenant of his who also happened to be a part-time broker.'

Irshaad looked at Nadeem, who sat down on the chair, pondering hopelessly over the khaki broken tiles spread across the floor. Warren had nearly fallen asleep, but Nadeem listened with a fierce attentiveness. Dr Vengsarkar stood awkwardly in the corner, surrounded by Dilip and Srikant.

'Anyway,' continued Irshaad, 'he said he had to kick Makhija out and get the flat cleared out in time in order to show it to potential clients. I realized there was no point in pursuing the situation with the flat, so I ran a little check on the car. Turns out that it was a stolen vehicle. So, again I tried getting in touch with Makhija to get some assurance that he possessed some assets I could rely on. But he didn't pick up my calls for days on end. Finally, one day I got a call from Rinki, who claimed he had been calling her up persistently, begging her to talk me into extending the time period. I told her not to get involved in the matter and that I would come to a settlement and sort it out. I promised her that no harm would come to him under any circumstances. I sensibly, however, left out any mention of his claim that she had withdrawn the money. I spoke of old times instead, reassuring her that her ex-husband would be fine. Next thing I know, the son of a bitch went to the police. First to Inspector Nagpal, who immediately notified me that he was filing an FIR for threat and extortion.'

'That's right,' Inspector Nagpal affirmed. 'Makhija didn't get any help in this police station . . .'

'. . . so he went straight to the Anti-Extortion Cell in Kalbadevi and took my name there,' continued Irshaad.

'And that's when he was transferred to me,' broke in Inspector Gaekwad.

Nadeem sat upright in his chair and looked at Inspector Gaekwad, who avoided eye contact. Warren too snapped to attention and took note of the inspector's claim.

'I was notified by DCP Panth of EOW Unit V,' said Inspector Gaekwad. 'According to him, Chintan Makhija claimed he was being pursued by Irshaad Ahmed Sheikh's men and that he had been receiving threatening phone calls.'

'Why didn't you tell me all of this in the first place?' asked Nadeem, in a hollow voice.

'I told you that I had his records, his Vodafone application form with all his bank details, address, PAN card number and a photocopy of his driver's licence,' said Inspector Gaekwad. 'I just happened to leave out how I knew he was connected to Irshaad Batla.'

Diagnosis

'Look,' said Irshaad, 'I don't know what any of this has to do with me. I've told you everything I know about this man. Why am I being questioned with regard to his murder? I even have an alibi for where I was yesterday.'

'Well,' Inspector Gaekwad cringed. 'That's the thing. No one knows the exact date when he was killed. The post-mortem report said he had been lying in that condition for over twenty-four hours, judging by the disintegration. All we know is when he was found.'

'Why have you brought him here?' asked Irshaad, pointing at Dr Vengsarkar.

'Because, Irshaad,' began Dr Vengsarkar, 'as your counsellor, it is my duty to clarify certain facts to the authorities before we conclude our treatment. I daresay your bills for therapy are still pending.'

Irshaad jumped up from his stool and sprang on Dr Vengsarkar. Nadeem pulled him back as Dilip and Inspector Nagpal restrained him, shoving him back on the stool. Inspector Gaekwad was as cool as a cucumber and hadn't budged an inch, having anticipated the volatile reaction from Irshaad.

'I thought, doctor,' laughed Nadeem. 'That you did not share information about your clients?'

'Given the circumstances,' said Dr Vengsarkar. 'I think I can take the liberty to do so.'

'Keep your trap zipped, Nadeem,' ordered Inspector Gaekwad.

'Why?' asked Nadeem. 'I have the right to talk when I want to. It's a free country.'

'And it'll be a free funeral for you if you carry on that way.'

'I wouldn't want to wind up like Makhija,' said Nadeem, looking the inspector straight in the eye.

'Look, Nadeem,' said Inspector Gaekwad, with a sudden change of tone. 'You're like a son to me. Once I have given my word to one of my boys, I stand by them to keep them in the clean.'

'What about Makhija? What was he like to you? A brother or an uncle, or maybe a stepson even?'

'Shut up, Nadeem! Don't talk back to me!'

Nadeem looked down at the floor again, dead silent. He held his head down low, as if in shame, and waited for what the inspector had to say. Inspector Gaekwad didn't have much in way of an explanation, so he decided to give a clinical history of his relation with Makhija.

'When he came to me,' began Inspector Gaekwad, 'I didn't know what to do for him. I told him that I had been trying to nail Irshaad Batla but hadn't succeeded so far, and that it was no good coming to me with a stupid extortion case. But he insisted I do something about it. I told him the only thing I could do was put him in protective custody, but he was desperate. He looked haggard and worn out, like a man on the brink of a nervous breakdown. He was ready to do anything to ensure his safety. So, I put two plainclothesmen with him and offered to repay his loan in exchange for his services. I decided to execute a little plan I had been harbouring for quite some time.'

'What plan?' asked Irshaad.

'I had a copy of your files for the half-murder case on the Eastern freeway. It said that due to certain outbursts when in the custody of the police and three acts of vandalism, including two chairs in the interrogation room and the registrar's desk, you were immediately restrained by two hawaldars and confined to the nearest cell. After having observed your uncontrollable behaviour, while in the lock-up, the authorities decided to have you transferred to the special ward for an examination by the psychiatric authorities. It also mentioned that your bail had been set at Rs 1,28,000, and that you had to undergo mandatory counselling and therapy from a psychiatrist.'

Dr Vengsarkar stepped forward in order to corroborate that statement.

'Well,' he began, 'according to the authorities at the Nandlal Pramod Functionality Centre, the preliminary evaluation determined that you have complete and total possession of your mental faculties. You were, however, diagnosed with advanced neurosis, pathological hysteria and occasional instability. You had been exhibiting recurrent trends of psychotic behaviour and violent homicidal tendencies. One prognosis did predetermine that the asylum is no place for you and that a person like you belongs in the penitentiary. However, we at Healthy Mind Clinic beg to differ. Instability is a common problem and we aim to do whatever we can to correct it.'

'You mean cure him?' asked Nadeem.

'Same thing,' said Dr Vengsarkar.

'Look,' Irshaad broke in agitatedly, looking towards Nadeem but addressing Dr Vengsarkar. 'All I ever wanted from you was a clean bill of health so that I was certified stable and could apply for immunity from the case.'

'Are you sure, Irshaad?' asked Dr Vengsarkar, with the cunning command of a clairvoyant. 'Is that all you came to me for?'

'Well, of course,' he laughed nervously, looking at Nadeem. 'Why else do you think I'd go to a psychiatrist?'

Nadeem nodded silently in agreement.

'I had tried getting in a word earlier with Dr Vengsarkar, but to no avail,' said Inspector Gaekwad. 'So, I decided to send Makhija to him as a decoy patient. To pretend as if he was suffering from work-related stress in order to undergo therapy, so that he may be able to fish for some information regarding your case history, and to try and get hold of your files if possible.'

'Little did we know,' added Dr Vengsarkar, 'that his condition was far more grave than he had presented.'

Irshaad looked at Dr Vengsarkar in utter bewilderment, with impatient eyes that had by now grown agitated.

'He suffered from the same condition as you, Irshaad,' said Dr Vengsarkar. 'Only worse. I can spot a paranoid-schizophrenic from a mile away. You see, when there begin to appear certain physiological manifestations of the psychic state, the matter goes outside the realm of my jurisdiction and into the field of a physician. I have only to add that were it not for me, they would have probably put him away in a sanatorium.'

'That is one way of putting it,' broke in Nadeem. 'But yet another way of putting it is that he was made that way by you. By becoming one of your patients and taking your prescribed dosage.'

'He used to ask me all kinds of questions about you, Irshaad,' continued Dr Vengsarkar, ignoring Nadeem's remark. 'But I never told him a word.'

'You don't mean to tell me,' gasped Irshaad, 'that that son of a bitch stole my files from the clinic?'

'I must confess,' sighed Dr Vengsarkar, 'that, at the moment, certain files of yours do appear to be missing. When I found out from the receptionist that Makhija had once been in my office during my absence, I immediately demanded the files back from him but he claimed to have no idea what I was talking about. I told him that I'd cancel his prescription until the files were returned. I didn't see him after that. I had no word from him. My receptionist used to try his number on a daily basis every morning at 11 o'clock. But he'd never answer.'

'How much do you want for the files, Gaekwad?' trembled Irshaad.

'I don't have them, Irshaad,' frowned Inspector Gaekwad. 'If I did, I wouldn't be here. I've had two of my men tear up his entire place to search for them, but there was no sign of them. If Dr Vengsarkar would have told me about this earlier, I could have done something. Little did I know that it would take Makhija's death to get Dr Vengsarkar to open up the books.'

Dr Vengsarkar handed Inspector Gaekwad a large and imposing-looking file, which he opened and read from.

'In one of your sessions,' read Inspector Gaekwad, 'you had opened up about certain things that had been troubling you.'

'This is none of your business,' yelled Irshaad. 'How dare you divulge this information!'

'Apparently you confessed to owing more than forty-two lakhs to various friends and associates of yours all over town. And that it had been weighing you down. Eating away at your peace of mind. You were worried your father would find out about it.'

Irshaad didn't like where this was going, especially with Nadeem sitting in. Nadeem shrivelled up, turning his face away, his upper torso in position. He looked outside the window trying to shift his attention, but he couldn't get the sound of this conversation out of his mind, not even if it took a brain surgeon to drill it out. He had that look on him like he wasn't listening, but Irshaad wasn't stupid. He knew Nadeem was stuck in a soft spot and tried to do the best he could to make him feel comfortable in his chair. He didn't for a second let Nadeem in on it that he didn't want him there, for he had always generously endowed him with his confidences. But Nadeem knew that this was different. This was a different matter altogether that went beyond the personal domain. This had to do with the account you kept not in any safety deposit box but deep down in your own soul. That's where all the deductions, interest and debts finally land up. Irshaad didn't want Nadeem to see this side of him, and Nadeem didn't want to know either. But he hoped Nadeem would understand. He had always thought of Nadeem Khatib as a nice guy, someone he could take into confidence. Nadeem got up as he could feel the mercury rise.

'I think I'd better take your leave now, I have some urgent matters to attend to . . .' Nadeem quaked.

'Sit your ass down, Nadeem. You aren't going anywhere!' Inspector Gaekwad pushed him back into the chair.

'What does he have to do with this?' Irshaad protested. 'All these minutes and seconds are costing him hundreds and thousands of rupees. Let him go home and sleep. The poor man has to go to work tomorrow morning. He has to earn a living.'

'You're not going anywhere, Chipkali,' grinned Inspector Gaekwad. 'Even if you have some business lined up, it can wait. Sit down! Relax! Make yourself at home! Would you like anything to drink? Tea, coffee, Coke, Pepsi, Mirinda, Mangola?'

Nadeem's face grew pale, slowly recuperating from the blows he had received. The blood trickling down his nostrils had by now dried up, turning maroon. He scratched his scar, picking at it with the habitual absent-mindedness of a woodpecker sabotaging a spot on the bark. It was broadening, creeping over to the lines that creased his forehead and folding up as it made its ascent. He smelt the blood on his fingernails; it smelt rotten. He was beginning to sweat as he settled, shifting about in the chair that was more comfortable than what he needed at this point. Irshaad turned to Nadeem who looked more shameful that he had reason to be. Irshaad winked at him, as if to tell him to think nothing of it, and that he had everything under control.

'So you plan to put a murder charge on me, is it?' he asked.

Inspector Gaekwad's stolid eyes grew suddenly thoughtful. The corners of his lips quivered, as he tried to put together an adequate reply, 'That's the idea.'

Irshaad glared at Nadeem, his bulging eyes softening into a kindly stare masked with apprehension.

'Rohini will be called in to testify,' continued Inspector Gaekwad. 'She'll be asked to supply the jury with all the sordid details of your brief yet tempestuous affair. That, added with the fact that her late husband owed you money, and that you owed money elsewhere, should provide enough of a motive. Also, your psychiatrist would be called in to testify about your character, and judging by his impression of you, I do not think his testimony would be favourable in your defence. I can only sincerely hope that you acquire the finest lawyer that money can buy, if you manage to settle your loans in time.'

'You'll be hearing from my lawyer in the morning.'

'I already heard from him,' Inspector Gaekwad smirked.

'You did?'

'Yesterday morning. He called on account of your pending trial for the half-murder case. Said he'd like to meet me to discuss the case. I told him to go take a hike.'

'That's funny,' Irshaad smiled. 'I didn't ask him to.'

'Perhaps he did it of his own accord.'

'Strange. I'll have a word with him tomorrow.'

Irshaad got up from the stool and looked out of the window, lost in thought. He then nodded with a customary shrug of the shoulders and signalled to Dilip and Srikant to tell his men that he was on his way out.

'Don't have to spend the night in judicial custody?' he asked.

'I'll give you that much leeway,' Inspector Gaekwad smirked with satisfaction. 'Twenty-four hours to say goodbye to your friends and family. I just hope to God you don't flee the country like your old man before I can get my hands on you!'

'Careful. Don't go on my family. You wouldn't like it if I went on yours.'

'You wouldn't be standing on your own two feet if you did.'

'I guess I'll see you in court,' Irshaad laughed.

'I guess you will,' said Inspector Gaekwad.

Irshaad looked towards Nadeem and then at Warren.

'Can I take these two with me?' he asked. 'I don't think you have any use for them since you seem to have made up your mind.'

'Sure,' said Inspector Gaekwad. 'Feel free to take them, provided you don't knock them off.'

'Rest assured,' laughed Irshaad. 'You have my word. I wouldn't want a double homicide.'

The Kiss-off

As Irshaad left the interrogation room, followed by Nadeem and Warren, Inspector Gaekwad asked Inspector Nagpal if it was possible to get a cup of tea for Dr Vengsarkar and himself. Inspector Nagpal called out for one of the junior constables, as Dilip and Srikant escorted the three men out.

Irshaad was silent all the way through the long walk past the corridors and out of Malad (West) police station. When they got to his car, the maroon Honda Civic that stood outside the main entrance, Irshaad put his arm around Nadeem.

'Why don't you get back to work for me, Chipkali?' he groaned. 'I'll pay you twice as much as what this son of a bitch Gaekwad is paying you.'

'Look, Irshaad,' mumbled Nadeem, 'I didn't tell him a goddamned thing about you!'

'I know you didn't,' Irshaad blinked, 'and he didn't tell you a goddamned thing about me. Not a word, you understand?'

'Not a word!'

'I didn't kill Makhija.'

'I know you didn't!'

Irshaad's tense face unfolded into a jovial smile. 'How do you know that?'

'Well . . . I don't know, I just know. You don't kill people without good reason.'

'Amen to that.'

'But we've got to find out who the hell did. Otherwise it's your ass on the line and the actual culprit will walk off scot-free.'

'I can do without the publicity. By the way, I hope you know what he said about me owing money all over town is all a load of horseshit.'

'I know that, Irshaad. Of course.'

'If my dad asks you anything . . .'

'I haven't heard a word of this conversation.'

'Take it easy, Chipkali,' said Irshaad, as he got into his car. 'Keep out of trouble. That goes for you too, Paolie. Call me if you need anything.'

'I don't know how I'm going to be able to do that,' said Nadeem.

'Oh,' smiled Irshaad, 'I'll have a brand new Samsung S6 sent to you in the morning.'

'New car?' asked Nadeem.

'Yeah. I got this baby souped-up. K&N air filter, rims, halogen, spoiler, 1.8-turbo charge, the works. The modifications set me back by half a peti. Forty-five G's to be precise.'

'Well, I hope it was money well spent.'

'I'll let my dad be the judge of that.'

'Goodnight, Batla!'

Irshaad got into the front seat and one of his guys closed the door for him and got into the back. Kaashif Bhai pressed his foot down on the accelerator sending the car growling off into the night.

Visitors

On their way home, Nadeem and Warren stopped at a 24x7 to get a packet of chips, but all they found there was moong daal, aloo bhujia and chana jor garam. They stocked up with namkeen and a bottle of Sprite, and headed home in the autorickshaw they had caught outside Malad police station. The autowaala was unduly inquisitive and asked what they were doing there so late at night, but they weren't in the mood to entertain his queries.

As soon as they had paid off the fare and entered the gate of Little Heights, Warren's phone started ringing.

'Who is it?' asked Nadeem.

Warren looked down at his phone and noticed it was Rohini's number. They had exchanged numbers in the waiting room at the hospital. She had asked Warren to call her if he needed some help later with Nadeem, as she had anticipated his condition to be far more serious than it actually was. Warren showed Nadeem the screen of his phone and put it on silent as they walked up the stairs past the lobby. Nadeem asked Warren to hand him the phone. Kishorie Lal was fast asleep. Once they reached their door, Nadeem called back on the number while Warren fished out the house keys.

'Hello,' said Nadeem into the phone, as he entered the flat. He closed the door shut and latched it from the inside.

'Hello,' he spoke again, louder and clearer as he could perceive a faint voice coming in from the other end of the line.

'Hello,' replied Rohini. 'Nadeem?'

'Yes?'

'Rohini here,' she spoke in a soft voice.

'I know.'

'I just got a call from your number.'

Nadeem raised his eyebrow higher than the crease of his forehead. He wondered how that could be possible as his phone had been smashed into bits in front of his own eyes. Just then, he remembered that Irshaad had stashed away his SIM card before doing so. Perhaps he had inserted it into his phone and called Rohini.

'Are you with Irshaad?' she asked timidly.

'I was,' he said. 'My SIM card is with him. Did he prank call you?'

'He told me to come over to his house. He said you were there with him and that it was an emergency.'

'What else did he say?'

'That they had found your body and that I was the last person seen with you.'

'Well, I'm alive and talking to you, aren't I?'

'Can I come over to your place right now?'

'I don't think that's such a good idea, Rohini.'

'I think he might have sent some people after me. He knows my address.'

'Listen, take it easy, Rohini.'

'Are you at home?'

Nadeem thought twice before giving an answer.

'Yes,' he said, hesitantly.

'I'll be there in fifteen minutes.'

'Listen, where are you, Rohini?'

Before he could get an answer to his question, she had cut the call. He sighed and threw Warren's phone back to him. He was not in the mood to deal with her. He lay down on the couch in front of the television and switched it on, as Warren spread out a mattress on the living room floor.

'What does she want?' he asked Nadeem, wearily.

'Irshaad Batla called her from my number.'

'Has he got your SIM card?'

'I forgot to collect it from him,' said Nadeem. 'Do one thing. Try calling my number from your phone.'

Warren dialled Nadeem's number but was told by a mechanized voice that the Vodafone customer he was trying to reach had switched off his mobile phone.

'It's coming switched off,' said Warren, tossing his phone aside and stretching out on the mattress. His yawn had in it all the noise and dreariness of exhaustion, but was beginning to reflect the absence of constant arduous employment and honest toil.

As Nadeem kicked off his shoes to put his feet up on the couch, four loud knocks were heard on the door.

'That was quick,' thought Nadeem, as he got up to answer the door. 'She reached already.'

On opening the latch, he was greeted by two men who stood purposefully at the door in height order. One of them was a tall wiry gentleman of about forty and the other was small and stout, slightly balding with a receding hairline and a handlebar moustache. They certainly fit the description and exhibited all the characteristics he had heard about from Mr Machhiwaala, and much to his amusement, Kishorie Lal had not left out any details in his description of them. Nadeem gladly welcomed them in.

'Mr Ganpat Shukla, I presume,' joked Nadeem.

'The name's Jayant Naagre,' said the shorter one, as he flashed a badge.

'And I'm Mangesh Raut, Crime Branch.'

'Plainclothesmen,' said Nadeem. 'Why, it's a pleasure to have you two at my house. What can I do for you?' he asked, sarcastically.

Warren immediately sat up on noticing them enter the house. The two of them looked around with an air of warrantable contempt. The tall one, Mangesh, shut the door and turned to Nadeem.

'We've been keeping an eye on you, Khatib,' he said.

'You two work for Gaekwad?'

'That's beside the point,' said the shorter one, Jayant.

'The point is,' began Mangesh, 'you're meddling with and snooping around what is potentially police business.'

'Where are the files, Khatib?' barked Jayant.

'What files?'

'You know what files! Don't try and be funny!'

'I don't know what you're talking about! Call up Inspector Gaekwad and ask him. I was with him just half an hour ago.'

The two of them started to look around the living room. Jayant immediately went to the dustbin and checked some of the crumpled up papers that had been thrown into it. They went over all the drawers, through each cabinet, folder and cupboard in the house.

'This is highly irregular,' complained Nadeem. 'I'm going to have to report you to Inspector Gaekwad.'

They didn't care about his idle threats and went about their search with much ease and tidiness, quite unlike their predecessors—Nagpal and Srikant—who practically tore apart the entire flat.

'So, you had two of your tippers living in the same building,' Nadeem sneered in defiance, looking at them go about their duty with contempt. 'How convenient! I'm surprised you've only paid us a visit once. Just for the record, when you guys signed in and told the watchman you were coming to meet me, who were you actually here to meet? Me or Makhija?'

The two men paused their rummaging, stood absolutely still and remained silent. As they straightened up, they looked at one another and then spoke, interrupting each other's sentences.

'We had actually come down,' began Jayant, 'to have a word with him.'

'And to collect the files,' added Mangesh.

'But unfortunately, we had to give your name to the watchman as we did not want to draw attention to him.'

'Why, of course, he was one of your most treasured informers, your prized possession,' said Nadeem. 'Inspector Gaekwad's personal courier. I'll tell you what I think. I think you two have been visiting this building more often than you say. But not by the front door, by the windows. The mali saw a man hanging off the parapet of the fifth floor. He thought it was the plumber, but I have some second thoughts about that. The terrace of the adjoining building slants right into the edge of the fourth floor balconies. A small jump is all it would take to leap from terrace to balcony and, with the help of the pipes, you could have climbed up to the fifth floor, straight up to 502.'

'It wasn't the plumber,' said Mangesh.

'And it wasn't one of us either,' added Jayant.

'Then who was it?' asked Nadeem, confoundedly.

'It was him,' sighed Mangesh. 'Makhija! That's where he used to hide his stuff.'

'What stuff?'

'His main pipeline,' began Jayant, 'which descended from his tank on the terrace and was connected to his bathroom, had a valve on the portion that converged with the fourth-floor pipeline. By rotating the lever, the knob opened up into another more complex network of smaller pipes, which constituted the combined pipeline supply of the building.'

'What did he stash there?'

'If what he stored there burst into the main pipeline, then the whole building's water supply would contain something unthinkable.'

The two of them looked at each other, wondering whether or not they should let him in on some of the facts. They didn't want to defame the dead, but Mangesh proceeded anyway with the necessary reserve required to prevent it from sounding like an unfairly inaccurate description.

'The last time we showed up here to have a word with him, he was behaving like a baboon,' he began.

'He was out of his head,' added Jayant, 'saying that he was hooked on to anti-anxiety pills, sleeping tablets and some other medication . . . that he needed to replenish his stock immediately since his doctor had cancelled his prescription.'

'He was doing all kinds of things as a replacement. Powder, dope, smack, ketamine, Dexedrine, Mandrax. He claimed Irshaad Batla had put him in touch with some people who supplied them.'

'The ketamine horse tranquillizer he claimed to have picked up from the same pharmacy where he purchased his medication.'

'So, we got hold of one of his prescription slips and copied it out on to an empty sheet of paper.'

'It worked with the chemist.'

'After all, he isn't exactly what you could call straight.'

'But we didn't want to waste our time on him, that's for the narcotics' department.'

'We got him his medication and went back to his house to give it to him. That was the last we saw of him.'

'He promised us the files.'

'Needless to say, he failed to live up to his word,' Mangesh concluded.

Just then, a soft knocking was heard from the door, as if the person outside intended to be discreet.

'That's probably Rohini,' said Nadeem.

'What's she doing here?' asked Mangesh, panic-stricken, as Jayant went coolly to open the door. He tried looking through the view hole, but could not see anyone outside.

'There's no one out there,' he said.

'I thought I heard knocking,' said Nadeem.

'Shhh . . .' Jayant hushed him up.

He opened the door just wide enough for him to peer outside and get a glance at whoever it was. Mangesh immediately pulled out his regulation automatic from his pocket and quietly went over to the door to back him up. Jayant looked back towards Mangesh, who nodded in reply. Jayant took out his revolver from his pant pocket and opened the door completely, poking his head out cautiously in order to scan the third floor. There was no one in sight, not even on the staircases going up to the fourth floor and down to the second. Once he was certain that the coast was clear, he stepped out of the doorway to take a proper look while Mangesh took cover on the back end of the open door. The third floor corridor was empty.

Perhaps they had just imagined the knocking or it was the wind, he thought. An approaching wind suddenly closed the door shut with a slam and Jayant was briefly trapped outside the flat. He tried turning the door knob and knocked a couple of times, but before either Nadeem or Warren could get to the door in order to open it for Mangesh, who was having a hard time figuring out how to unlock the latch, the automated sound of the lift music was heard, followed by the mechanized voice. The lift door was not closed completely, hence, it continued playing. Jayant turned around from the closed door of the apartment and went over to the lift to shut it. He tried shutting the lift door completely, but for some reason the irritating music would not cease. He pressed hard against the door in order to stop the music, but it still did not cease. He thought, perhaps, the lift door was spoilt.

Inside, they were struggling to get the door open as Mangesh had entangled the locking device by turning the latch in the wrong direction. The lift music could be heard inside as well, and just as Nadeem successfully managed to unlock the door, three loud shots rang out from the lift. They were most definitely from a semi-automatic and went off in quick succession. Mangesh immediately sprang up, pushing the door open and leaping out of the doorway. The lift door was closed and the irritating music was still playing. Jayant was most definitely inside the lift, as he could not have possibly vanished into thin air.

'Please close the door,' the mechanized voice said. '*Kripaya darwaza band kijiye.*'

It was followed by a beeping tune. Before Mangesh could get to the lift and open the door, in order to be sure of his partner's safety, the music stopped and the lift shot up to the top floor with a rumbling sound. Mangesh tried yanking the door open, but it was tightly sealed and would open only when the lift was back on the third floor. Mangesh pressed the lift button, calling for it numerous times before the distant sound of the lift door opening was heard from the fifth floor. The lift music was heard faintly this time. When Mangesh was sure that the lift door had been closed properly, he pressed the lift button, ringing for it again. It slowly came back to the third floor making its rumbling noises. Once it reached, Mangesh pulled the door open impatiently to find out where his partner had vanished, only to be startled by what lay at his feet. The lift was carrying the corpse of his partner with two bullet holes in the abdomen and one in the neck. Mangesh let go of the door handle and staggered back, retreating in utter bewilderment. His automatic pistol fell from his trembling hands and he nearly collapsed face down into the tiles in shock and disgust. The lift door fell back into place smoothly, closing completely. The lift was called back up to the fifth floor.

All Hell Breaks Loose

Nadeem and Warren rushed out of the flat to see what the commotion was all about.

'Get out of here!' Mangesh yelled at them, holding up his automatic pistol in firing position. He was pointing it in the direction of the staircase going up to the fourth floor and called out to whoever was upstairs.

'This is the police!' he yelled. 'Slowly come down the stairs with your hands in the air!'

The lift came back and stopped at the third floor. Mangesh fired two shots in the air to let them know he, too, was armed. Two shots were fired back at him from a disembodied hand that popped out of the lift door. Mangesh fired two shots at the lift, crouching back into the flat and taking cover behind the door.

Warren rolled under the sofa and Nadeem hid behind the television as another round of shots was heard outside. The sound of the lift music was audible in the silent intervals between the crossfire.

'Please close the door,' the mechanized voice repeated as the familiar jingle played over it. 'Kripaya darwaza band kijiye.'

Mangesh fired again, this time poking his hand out from behind the door. He hit the nameplate of the adjoining flat and had, no doubt, succeeded in awakening their neighbours. He slammed the door shut and ordered Nadeem to rush to the intercom and instruct the neighbours to not step outside their flat under any circumstances. He then switched sides from the hinges to the handle of the door and opened it slightly ajar, just enough for him to peep outside. As it opened, another shot sent the door handle flying halfway across the room. Nadeem and Warren were taking cover in the kitchen and were out of range of the firing that erupted across their living room. The door was almost off its hinges and kept swinging back and forth, as Mangesh literally emptied his revolver, shooting indiscriminately out of the doorway. Realizing that his gun was empty, he fled into a corner of the room and took cover in the balcony to reload.

In the silence that ensued when the firing stopped, and when the party outside was certain that the coast was clear, the lift door was heard closing. As the irritating music emanating from the lift door came to a halt, Mangesh rushed back into the living room. He called out for Nadeem and Warren, telling them it was all right to come out. But it took more than just a little reassurance to get them to budge an inch from their spots.

'It's okay,' he yelled again. 'They've gone.'

On hearing that, the two of them felt sufficiently secure and sprung out of the kitchen back into the living room. Mangesh was panting heavily and was still trying to catch his breath.

'What the hell was that?' he gasped.

'Irshaad Batla's men,' said Nadeem.

Mangesh ran out to the balcony to try and get a glimpse of the shooter. A black Mahindra 4x4 was parked in the compound with the boot facing the lobby. Two figures armed with double eagles were struggling hard to lift Jayant Naagre's body. They dragged him all the way to the vehicle and popped open the trunk, dumping him inside. Mangesh could get a faint look at them from the balcony, but he didn't manage to spot either of their faces. He wondered whether to take aim and fire or call for backup. He tried getting a glance at the number plate but could barely read in the darkness.

'Notify all units in the area!' he barked into his mobile phone. 'Night patrol, vans and two wheelers. Black Mahindra 4 by 4. Armed and dangerous. Approach with caution.'

'I think that's one of his shooters, Ghazfakullah Khan, goes by the name Ghazfak,' said Nadeem. 'He usually handles jobs like this. I've seen him before. Only the last time I saw him at work, he carved up a door with a Sten gun. He's seen me, but obviously never taken notice.'

'Why did they take the body with them?'

'Because they thought it was me. They've taken it along to show Rohini. Batla's going to get quite a shock when he sees who they're carrying. A murder of a police officer. That makes two for him. He's definitely not getting off this time.'

Mangesh immediately dialled Inspector Gaekwad's number. For the next half an hour, he gave out his report to him over the phone in Marathi. Warren and Nadeem could barely understand a word he was saying. For all they knew, he could have been trying to frame them, but he was an honest cop who was only trying to do his duty. He didn't want to wind up like his partner, so he told Inspector Gaekwad everything that happened without sparing the minutest of details. Tailing a couple of tippers around was one thing, but he knew who they were dealing with here. He insisted that Inspector Gaekwad come right down to the scene of the crime at once, but Inspector Gaekwad was smarter than he thought. He, instead, suggested that they try and identify the vehicle the men arrived in.

'Somebody must have seen them,' he said over the phone. 'The watchman, neighbours; just try and track these men. In the meantime, I'll try and find out where Irshaad Batla is.'

It was hopeless. As soon as he cut the call, Mangesh threw his phone down on the floor in anger.

'Fifteen years in the force and you see the man's lights go out in front of you just like a candle,' he sighed. 'What was it all worth? A pension, free parking, a pat on the back, another star on the uniform, an under-the-table bonus from the inspector. He served him loyally and faithfully, but now, he's just another stiff in the morgue. A tick off the list. He'll be lucky if he gets the coroner's blessing.'

The lift door opened, letting the sound of the mechanized music creep quietly through the open door into the flat. The lift door was firmly shut with a bang, and that put an end to it. Rohini's face turned pale as she got a glimpse of the bullet-ridden front door of Nadeem's flat. The watchman, Kishorie Lal, stood beside her with a bruise under his left eye. His eyebrow was swelling visibly and turning purple. He was the only one that the gunfire had succeeded in awakening and, judging by his wound, he had probably attempted to stop the assailants or had come in their way. The next-door neighbours didn't even answer the intercom when Nadeem tried frantically to reach them. They were probably fast asleep.

In an instant, Kishorie Lal recognized Mangesh's face and he too stepped into the flat with Rohini to take a look around at the mayhem that had disrupted the living room.

Getting Even

'Did you get a look at their car number?' Mangesh asked Kishorie Lal.

'No,' he replied. 'I was asleep when they came in. They opened the gate themselves; I told them they couldn't park inside the building.'

Rohini looked at Nadeem.

'Are you all right?' she whispered.

'I'm alive,' he replied. 'That's what counts.'

'I just got a call from Irshaad.'

'What did he say?'

'He was asking me where I was, saying that he was under my building. He said he had come to pick me up and that pretty soon the whole place would be crawling with cops.'

'What did you say?' he whispered, taking her to the balcony, away from Mangesh and Kishorie Lal.

'I said I wasn't at home.'

'Is the money still in your possession or have you blown it up?'

'What money?'

'The loan that he gave your husband,' he spoke in the same sly tone that she had heard from Inspector Nagpal. 'The sum of Rs 1 lakh is no meagre amount. I expect that if you have spent it, then you would have done so wisely, and utilized it to provide for a secure future, since you do not have the luxury of support from your family as most people from your social strata do. By the way, what do you do to keep the home fire burning? Provided you have a home to call your own.'

'What makes you think that I'm any different from you? What makes you think I've had it any easier? We're both made of the same metal!'

'Not me! You don't get to see these kinds of goods in my line of work. Most of us, we're just scrap metal. But you? You're a silver-plated wristwatch. Or no . . . a gold Rolex.'

'I need your help, Nadeem.'

'It's only fair and square that you get it, after that we're even. And you're on your own.'

'I need to hole up at your place for a couple of days, until this thing cools off.'

'My landlord will throw a fit!'

'Please,' she cried. 'Irshaad's men will be looking for me.'

Nadeem breathed heavily and rolled his eyes, flickering them to let her know that he was doing her a favour by talking to her in the first place. He had stayed up way past his usual bedtime and his faculties of judgement were not in the best shape.

'What about 502?' he asked. 'I'm sure you still have the legal right to stay there?'

'Don't try and be smart with me, Nadeem,' she snapped. 'Are you going to help me or not?'

'What's in it for me? How about the one lakh that you skimmed off your husband? We can split it fifty–fifty right down the middle.'

She remained silent. Didn't say a word, barely breathed even. She had her lips sealed, but her eyes spoke more than she could afford to reveal.

'If you want Irshaad off your back, I can arrange that for you, but there's gotta be a price, lady. You can even pay me off in information, works like currency for me, but anyway, tell me . . .'

'I didn't take a rupee of that one lakh from him. It was spent on running our kitchen, and when it ran out, I walked. I didn't want any of Irshaad Batla's money.'

Nadeem glanced at her sideways to try and spot a chink in her armour.

'How did a nice girl like you from a good family come to know a guy like Irshaad Batla?'

'Through a friend of mine . . .' she blinked. 'He helped me out in a jam.'

'What jam?'

'Shoplifting. I spent the weekend in jail. Was caught in Oberoi mall with twenty-five grand worth of perfume, nail polish, lipsticks and other shopping accessories.'

'Sounds like quite a heist.'

'My friend happened to know him, so he helped me out.'

'It's useful having friends like that. I suppose Irshaad Batla came into the picture to help out with the police.'

'That's how I came to be acquainted with him.'

'And what about Chintan?'

She turned away to look outside the balcony, her gaze yearning for some reassurance in the bewildering darkness. 'You know,' she turned back to look at Nadeem, the corner of her mouth curving into a strange smirk. 'This isn't the first time he's died on me.'

'What do you mean?'

'He'd cook up all kinds of stories, anything to get my attention. Once, he sent out emails to all of his friends and relatives that he had had a severe accident and was in the ICU. Just to get attention and sympathy from someone. Once I got a call from K.L. Hospital in the middle of the night saying he'd had a heart attack. I rushed over to find him hiding in the emergency ward in a wheelchair. Once they even laid him flat on the slab, embalmed and everything. He pretended to be still, but one look at him and I could tell he was breathing. I guess you could laugh at that and say what a stupid thing to do, and it is downright silly, not to mention inconsiderate. I had no idea what I was in for when I got involved with him.'

'He was unstable?'

'Not when I was married to him, but as the hours at the office grew longer and his pocketbook began to shrink, something within him began to change. He became more irritable, ill-tempered and even dishonest. He began to lie to me about trivial everyday things like whether he had put out the dustbin at night or paid the milkman.'

'I guess cheapskates stick together,' Nadeem remarked, his voice devoid of any compassion whatsoever.

Rohini still had her back towards him. She felt no need to challenge his assessment of her character. Her peacock eyes dwelt broodingly on the balcony railings. She slowly leaned forward on them and craned her head up to get a look at Makhija's window.

Inside, in the living room, Warren had brought out the ice tray from the fridge for Kishorie Lal. Mangesh had one eye on his phone and the other on Kishorie Lal's bruise. After a thorough inspection, he concluded everything was all right and that it was nothing: just a little cut.

Nadeem spun Rohini's shoulders around and looked her right in the eyes. 'You didn't know that he was lying to you about his profession?' he squirmed, specks of saliva hitting her forehead.

'I had suspected it from the outset,' she admitted, her eyes still hoisted up. 'But as he began to grow more secretive and kept to himself, I knew for certain that something was wrong. He'd spend hours locked up in the bathroom. God knows what he'd do in there. He was constantly glued to his phone. 24x7. I knew he was up to some scam or the other. It began to show on his face, he began balding, growing fat, all kinds of strange growths started erupting on his neck and shoulders. I guess a lie can only get you so far, sooner or later it gets into your skin.'

Nadeem let go of her shoulders, slowly pulling back, his clasp still hovering over her. She stood face-to-face

with him, yet her eyes were on the fifth floor. He tilted
her head down. 'I've heard that you spend a fair bit of
time on the phone yourself,' he muttered, his peripheral
vision scanning the living room. Warren was wiping the
drops of water that had spilt on the floor from the ice tray.
Kishorie Lal was still fussing over his black eye, trying to
convince Mangesh that it was a serious injury.

'Well, that one lakh wasn't the only thing Irshaad gave
him,' she said.

'I know,' he said, pointing towards the living room.
'According to Mangesh out there, Irshaad had been
supplying him smack.'

'I don't know about that . . . when I was with him, he
was clean. He wasn't doing any narcotics, but what he was
hooked to was far worse, I can tell you that. I happen to
know . . .' she paused, exhaling heavily through her nose,
'. . . because soon enough I got hooked to it too.'

'What?'

Her eyeballs quaked hesitantly into a blink. She
looked over her shoulders and closed in towards him,
murmuring softly. 'Show me your phone,' she said,
glancing at his pockets.

'I don't have one . . .'

'Okay, show me any phone, any other. Does your
friend have a smartphone?'

'Warren!' Nadeem called out to the living room,
popping his head in from the balcony.

'Huh?' Warren responded. Mangesh and Kishorie Lal
immediately looked towards him as he asked, 'Anyone
got a smartphone?'

'Mine's a smartphone,' Warren mumbled.

Mangesh instantly fished out his Motorola G6 and began to examine it. 'Is this a smartphone?' he pondered, displaying it.

'Mine's a Nokia,' Kishorie Lal mentioned, producing an obsolete 3310 from his chest pocket.

'Na, thanks,' Nadeem shook his head. 'His'll do.'

Warren tossed him his Samsung, which he failed to catch, dropping it on the floor and nearly cracking the screen. 'Uh . . . thanks . . .' he nodded, picking it up and stepping back into the balcony.

Warren remained expressionless.

As he stepped out and tried to unlock the screen, an incoming call caught his attention. It was Inspector Gaekwad's number. Nadeem cut the call, pressed down firmly on the right button and handed it over to Rohini.

In a matter of a few seconds, a phone began to ring in the living room. Nadeem turned back to see whose it was. As he had anticipated, it was Mangesh's.

She unlocked the screen and went straight to the App store. She typed in Q . . . then U . . . A . . . all in uppercase letters. A couple of options showed up. 'It's this new app that Irshaad introduced him to.'

'You gotta be kidding me . . .' Nadeem laughed. 'What was he addicted to? Some kind of a video game?'

'It's not a video game. It's a programme, a software.'

'What is this?' Nadeem wondered, looking at the screen.

'It's a morality calculator.'

'A what?'

'An app. It's called QUANTRA. It hasn't been launched yet, this is just the beta version.'

'What's so special about it?'

'Well,' she breathed, 'I wouldn't know how to begin.' She crinkled her lips, looking on into the distance.

'Suppose you begin from the very beginning.'

'Well, according to Chintan it was a thing Irshaad had picked up from the officials at the institution where he had been admitted for a while.'

'The Nandlal Pramod Functionality Centre?'

'I don't know. But he said the authorities had given it to Irshaad to help him out. He claimed that if utilized correctly, it could revolutionize law enforcement, render lie detector tests obsolete and be a mathematical judge that can measure right and wrong up to an accuracy of 85 per cent.'

'How does it work?'

'It calculates your moral wavelength and gives an approximate estimate of your morality index in accordance to your income group, the amount you donate to charity and what service you provide to society through your occupation. Your count, statistics, points, whatever you want to call it. There are three separate versions as per religious denominations. There's QUANTRA 3.1 for Hindus, QUANTRA 7.86 for the Muslim community, and a deluxe edition for Sikhs and Christians. The one for the Parsi community has not been developed yet. Apparently, they're in the process of studying the Zoroastrian scriptures. The Buddhist edition has been outsourced to Hong Kong. It measures each and every action of yours and tallies it with not just standardized measures of right and wrong, but also in comparison to what others are doing, and then imparts penance.'

'If you're taking an interest in my moral welfare, it's a lost cause,' he snapped, snatching the phone from her over-demonstrative claws. 'It's for sale. I'd be willing to loan it out to you at compound interest. Not at the cost of my convenience.'

'Well,' she smiled reassuringly, 'we've all done some things we're not proud of, Nadeem. Things that stay on one's mind and merit their worth once the deed is done. After the dust of excitement and the passing moment has settled. Maybe an act or an oversight or a simple convenience, but committed for the sake of one's own interest, disregarding that of the other, well, I think that constitutes a crisis of conscience.'

'Is that what you're trying to do then? Clean your slate? Wash away your sins? Get brownie points with that metal detector of right and wrong? That digital dogma? Is that why you helped me out earlier? So you could increase your score?'

'I helped you out because you needed the help. Not because I wanted to.'

'Must be quite a change for someone who's used to helping themselves,' he muttered, chewing on his fingernails and gently letting out a thought. 'The word on the street is that you emptied the one lakh out of him and bounced.'

She coiled up like a spring wire, the nerves poking out of her forehead and beginning to writhe up and down in intolerance. 'Who said that?'

'Someone.'

'Tell me,' she insisted, her nostrils flaring.

'Irshaad. But don't tell him I told you.'

'I'm not ever going to be meeting him to tell him anything.'

'That's what your husband told him, possibly to use as an excuse. But then they would have been after you.'

Her eyebrows curved up, slithering through her forehead. 'Tell me something,' she chewed on her lip, 'you sound like you have experience with what it's like to be in debt with the man.'

'I have more than that. I have the scars to show for it too. And a deficit on my chest that weighs more than twelve lakhs in rupees and sixty-four in kilos. It makes the time pass much slower, all that weight. Knowing that any second someone could walk into the room and lighten the burden.'

'You owe him twelve lakhs?'

'That's what I said.'

'I could help you with that.'

'First, you help him out with the one-plus interest, otherwise he's not going to be off your back. Isn't there anything you could sell of Chintan's to raise some money?'

'His car?'

'It's stolen. Tell me something. What about the seven lakhs he embezzled? Where's that?'

'He had to return it.'

'Oh,' Nadeem sighed. 'What about you?' he winked. 'What about the proceeds from your various escapades? I bet you've sent many a man to the cleaners in your time, baby!'

One smack landed flat on his left cheek. Nadeem turned back, slightly less cocky and more polite. 'You've got the palm of a kleptomaniac,' he spat, touching his cheek.

'Takes one to know one,' she smiled, gesturing towards the couch in the living room.

'We could make a hell of a team.'

'No, thanks. I held a joint account with my husband, and the more there were of us, the less there was in it. On our own we happened to get by, but as a duo we were a disaster.'

'You got the account dissolved?'

'After he was notified by the bank that I withdrew my share, I got a call from K.L. Hospital saying that he had been admitted for throat cancer and needed one lakh for chemotherapy. I asked them to courier me the medical reports. I received an envelope with an MRI scan, ENT X-ray and blood tests. I had them examined by a specialist to determine their authenticity. They were fakes beyond a doubt, or quite possibly someone else's, an actual cancer patient. I went over to the hospital, where he was supposedly admitted, and found out that he had made a deal with the staff to prepare the phony medical reports in exchange for blood donations. As expected, he was nowhere to be seen in the hospital. They had couriered the original tests and actual results to his home address for the sake of his own health. Trying to fake everyone with fractures, concussions, heart attacks and throat cancer, he had failed to realize what had actually happened to him.'

'What was wrong with him?'

'I saw the tests, with my very own eyes. The doctor showed them to me. He said he had been trying to get in touch with him urgently. He still had an outstanding debt at the pharmacy for a bottle of Phensedyl, which I had to clear up for him. But according to his CT scan, biopsy and chest X-ray, an abnormal outgrowth had been detected around his neck.'

'What!' Nadeem scowled, cupping his palm over his mouth.

'It was in the shape of a tumour, which was neither malignant nor cancerous, but was instead eating away at his respiratory system like a parasitic organism, not of a traceable origin, possibly a mutation of some sort. The doctor's theory was that this had been occurring ever since he started taking Synahydraloxide, an experimental drug that he had prescribed to him. It was causing an acute inflammation of the sinuses and windpipe, which required him to spend a considerable amount of time in the loo for nasal and throat discharge.'

'Oh my God!' Nadeem muttered under his breath.

'I immediately called him up for the sake of his own safety, to tell him what the matter was. But he kept crying, howling like a wild animal. I tried to hush him up and calm him down. I tried to console him even and tell him that everything would be all right. He kept begging me into talking to Irshaad, suggested I go see him even, but I told him it was out of the question. I knew he was in deep trouble, so I offered to help. I called up Irshaad but he didn't listen to me. He got angry; he gets crazy sometimes. He started yelling on the phone, saying he had been looking for Chintan for days. Finally, I decided the only course of action left was to go to the police. It was my idea. And it was my mistake.'

'Does Irshaad know this?'

'He doesn't know that I told Chintan to go to the police.'

'What did he say when you spoke to him on the phone that day? Did he ask you to clear your husband's debts?'

'I didn't have the money to do it. I was flat broke. The next day, he called me up when he was calmer and back in his senses, and asked me to pass on a message to Chintan.'

'What was it?'

'It was a mobile number. He also sent me a message with someone's bank account details, which I forwarded to him. So, he simply asked Chintan to pay off one of his debts and Chintan gladly obliged, since he had enough money to do so at the time. That bought him some time until Irshaad started calling again and again and again. It reached a point where I started getting calls from random numbers asking for Chintan, saying that he owed them money.'

'Those were Irshaad's creditors,' said Nadeem. 'The son of a bitch owes money all over town. He transferred them to Chintan Makhija. That's the loan-sharking food chain. The circle of life. If he owes them and your husband owes him, technically your husband owes them too.'

'That's what I thought. The last time I spoke to him, he said he was feeling better since he had been able to procure his medication from the pharmacy, thanks to some friends.'

Nadeem looked back into the living room through the balcony, throwing a narrow glance at Mangesh.

'I told him not to take the medication,' she said, 'that the doctor had said it was causing harm, but he didn't listen. He said he was feeling fine after taking it and that he was in the pink of health. He claimed he had found the answer to all his troubles.'

'What?'

'He told me he had the goods on Irshaad, and that he had something that could be used to blackmail him and extort money. Some files. He said they could be used to make a deal with the people who had been calling him.'

'Where are those files? Did he sell them?'

'Well, he told me everything was going to be all right, that he had made arrangements to sell the files to one of Irshaad's creditors, and that the person was going to meet him that evening.'

Nadeem took out Warren's mobile phone and proceeded to dial the number he had jotted down from the dhobi in order to clarify his suspicions. Thankfully, he had remembered it by heart, since the contacts on his phone were no longer available.

'Hello!' a sleepy voice answered.

'Hello,' Nadeem whispered politely.

'Speaking?'

'I don't think you know me, but I know a friend of yours.'

'Listen, can you call back in the morning?'

'No, excuse me! I'm afraid it can't wait. It's rather urgent.'

'Who am I speaking to?'

'My name is Nadeem Sayed Khatib. I used to work for Irshaad Batla.'

'Irshaad who?'

'He's a friend of yours! Or if I'm not mistaken, the last time we spoke, you referred to him as a client.'

'I don't know any Irshaad.'

'He owed you some money, which he had asked Chintan Makhija to pay off for him.'

'I don't know what you're talking about!'

'Your name has come up in his murder investigation.'

Nadeem could hear a pin drop in the silence that ensued. The man breathed heavily on the other end, thinking hard about what to say next.

'Are you with the police?' he stammered.

'I'm afraid I am,' Nadeem looked at Mangesh.

'Did you call me up earlier today with regard to Chintan Makhija?'

'Yes.'

'Why did you cut the call? I was about to mention that Makhija had cleared his debt; he had wired the money to my account.'

'How much?'

The man seemed to think twice before answering. 'Twenty grand.'

'Would it be possible to meet?'

The man took a long tentative pause. 'Where?'

Nadeem thought a second. 'Goregaon telephone exchange.'

'Okay,' he breathed heavily.

'I'll see you there in around twenty minutes?'

'Gimme thirty.'

'See you in half an hour.' Nadeem cut the call.

'Who was it?' Rohini asked.

'The person your husband wired the money to. It's got to be one of the creditors.'

Nadeem felt no need to continue the conversation and so he brought her back into the living room. Warren sat sullenly in front of the television. Kishorie Lal and Mangesh were arguing about what course of action to take. Mangesh insisted that the third floor be sealed and made out of bounds, as the ballistics experts were on their way to collect samples. By now, even Machhiwaala had been disturbed from his slumber. He stood outside the broken door, grumpily listening to every word.

'What's all the commotion about,' he quibbled.

On noticing the late Mr Makhija's wife, he immediately snapped out of his casual posture, conducting himself with the decorum expected of the esteemed position of landlord.

'Inspector V.M. Gaekwad of the Crime Branch should be here any minute!' Mangesh informed him.

'Good evening, Mr Machhiwaala,' Nadeem greeted him sarcastically. 'You're going to have a fair bit of explaining to do. Not like yesterday. I suggest you stay awake till Inspector Gaekwad of the Crime Branch gets here. He's not going to let you off that easy.'

'Inspector who?' frowned Mr Machhiwaala. 'I don't know him. I only know Inspector Nagpal from Malwani police chowki.'

'Is he coming down here too?' asked Nadeem.

'Nope,' said Mangesh. 'He's officially transferred both the homicide cases over to Inspector Gaekwad. It's a Crime Branch matter now.'

'Tell him to ask Nagpal for Makhija's phone. He's sitting with him right now at the station.'

'Wait a minute,' Mangesh protested. 'I'm not taking any orders from you.'

'It's our only chance. We've got to get hold of Makhija's mobile phone. He had been receiving threatening calls from people Irshaad Batla owed money to. He tried cutting a deal with them for the files in order to save his own ass. Obviously, one of them turned on him. Narrow down on the numbers you can get off his phone. One of those numbers on that phone belongs to the killer. Check the messages and all calls made and received in the last week. Rohini, you check if you can recognize any of the numbers. Also, do you have any of those numbers on your phone? You said they called you as well, didn't they?'

'I'll have to check in my call log. It was a while ago. The numbers may have been automatically erased as I didn't save any of them.'

Nadeem tossed the phone back to Warren, leaning out of the doorway with his feet on the shoe rack.

'Where you off to?' Warren asked Nadeem as he put on his shoes.

'To the Goregaon telephone exchange.'

Rendezvous with the Voice of Reason

Nadeem scooted out of the building without much explanation, leaving everyone unreasonably baffled at his doorstep. Much to Mangesh's protest, he had left him there to settle the matter pretty much all by himself. He promised he'd be back in the building before dawn, but he had nothing more than his own word to go on.

There was no one down in the lobby. Droplets of blood had trickled all over the white tiled floor of the small entrance to the building. The sewage pipes that hung over the protruding balconies were leaking fiercely all over the compound. He ran out of the unlocked gate, caught the first autorickshaw in sight and ordered the driver to speed to the nearest bus stop, where he hopped on to the 223 bound for 4 Bungalows and got off at the Goregaon telephone exchange. He waited at the signal for over half an hour. There was still no sign of the man. It was now getting frightfully late. The bus depot across the road was closing for the day and the entrance gate was being locked as all the empty buses lined up in their sheds. The traffic roared past Nadeem who stood on the main road on the divider, keeping a look out for the approaching vehicles. He kept fidgeting with his watch to check the time, looking out on to the road, hoping the next vehicle that took a turn at the distant signal for the Goregaon telephone exchange would be the one he was waiting for. He sat down on the divider in despair, sighing despondently, twiddling his thumbs and looking down at the road, having abandoned all hope. As he turned, kicking a stone in agitation, he noticed a small gathering of people about a hundred metres behind where he was sitting. They had congregated around a fenced-off construction area in the middle of the road. A section had been dug up and amidst the drills and other excavation machinery stood several municipal workers staring into the ditch in perplexity and amazement. Nadeem rushed towards them to see what all the fuss was about.

A rectangular 8x10-foot chunk of the cement had been removed and, under the sedimentary layer of gravel and asphalt, lay the corpse of a full-grown adult male, placed between two converging underground pipelines that were connected to an adjacent manhole. The man was covered in soot and dust and was indistinguishably grey. His body was beginning to decompose, but three bullet holes scattered across the upper torso were clearly perceivable despite the apparent mess of his condition. There was one in the abdomen, one in the left shoulder blade and another in the ribcage. The blood around the craters had dried up, turning maroon, and clung ferociously to the vicinity of the wounds.

Two municipal workers volunteered to lift him out of the pit and did so with a cast iron resolve. They could not help looking the other way when grabbing hold of his limbs, which hesitated to stay in one place. On getting a clearer look at his face, Nadeem instantly recognized him as Jayant Naagre.

A police jeep pulled up near the site and a hawaldar got out, putting a handkerchief over his nose and casually walking up to the dug-up area to supervise what was going on.

The excavation site had been a night-time operation. It was supposed to be cordoned off for traffic during the day, and it was now time for the labourers to begin work on it. The workers had just checked in for duty on the night shift when the man who drove the cement roller noticed something protruding from beneath the ground. The cement slab that covered the spot had not been reinstated firmly as yet. The cement on the upper layer of the slab had not even dried completely. It carried handprints scattered indiscriminately about it. The workers decided to call off the night's work in view of the irregular occurrence. They would resume in the morning. The spot, however, was sealed by the police in case it needed to be checked later on.

By the time the man Nadeem was waiting for reached the Goregaon telephone exchange, the cops and municipal workers had vacated the spot where the body had been found. It was covered with a series of boulders and shut off with a ramshackle tin covering. There were multiple excavations all around that section of the road, some for installing underground cables and pipelines, some for laying tar and cement, and others connected to obsolete MTNL switchboards that stood purposelessly on the corner of the road. Nadeem spotted a subway, which doubled up as an underground walkway, outside the entrance to the bus depot. The walkway appeared to be crossing the excavated section of the road where the body had been found. He was trying to trace the path when he heard a car careening into sight. He noticed a figure on the other side of the road stepping out of a totalled second-hand dark green Ford Ikon. It had a Maharashtra number plate: MH02NA0425. The entire front section of the sedan was heavily damaged, the windscreen had a crack on the top left corner, which spread out like a spider's web, denying any visibility. The right mudguard was hanging off the side of the car like the flap of a puppy dog's ear. The bumper was mutilated. The bonnet was dented and had a crease running all the way across it. It looked like at least Rs 80,000–Rs 85,000 worth of damage. The man who drove it seemed far from pleased at having to meet Nadeem.

'You the guy I spoke to earlier?' he slurred.

'That'd be me!' Nadeem stated, looking him over as he walked towards him, measuring each step with the stinginess of a salesman. He didn't strike him as particularly distinctive in any way, shape or form. Just kind of regular, like the kind of faces one sees on the local train on the way to work. It did appear from his manner, however, that he was not entirely alien to being awake at so indecent an hour. Nadeem sized him up to be about five-foot eleven, noticed that he had on a crumpled, full-sleeved rayon shirt with the sleeves folded up to the elbows, and a pair of creased semi-formal trousers with the brown leather square toes to go with it. Nadeem studied the facial hair scattered about his face with bemused wonder, observing the wavy hair that stood still over his forehead, masking a receding hairline. He felt casually intrigued at the man's appearance, which was just as bewildering as it was amusing.

'So?' asked Nadeem. 'You do know Irshaad Ahmed Sheikh!'

'Well, uh . . .' he mumbled softly. 'As I said before, he's my client.'

'What is your line of business?'

'Criminal lawyer.'

'I thought Razzaq Bhai was the family lawyer?'

'Well, you see, Razzaq Bhai had a bit of an accident.'

'Is he all right?'

'Oh, he's fine! Just a torn ligament and slipped disc. He's currently admitted in Holy Family Hospital. You ought to go visit him.'

'So since when have you been handling their affairs?'

'Well, you see,' he sniffled, 'I'm not exactly handling the family affairs. Just the minor scars and scrapes of Irshaad's personal misconduct. We have a sort of understanding.'

'I see, what's your name?'

'Hoseipha Khatri. You might have heard of me as HK.'

'I haven't heard of you,' Nadeem smiled. 'But if you're Irshaad's lawyer, I'm pretty sure you must have heard of me.'

'You're Nadeem Chipkali, aren't you?'

Nadeem's smile retracted. 'Talking to me is as good as talking to the cops,' he snarled. 'So, I suggest you gimme your statement or whatever it is that you can make up on the spot.'

'I swear to tell the truth, the whole truth, and nothing but the truth, so help me God.' HK put his hands on his chest, giggling away like a delinquent child caught by a schoolteacher.

'So, HK? When was the last time you spoke to Makhija?'

'Well, he paid me off. I had no reason to be in touch with him.' He began to cough, 'Whatever . . . ugh . . . ugh . . . business I had with him . . . ugh . . . ugh . . . was over as far as I was concerned.' He swirled the mucus around in his throat, trying to get enough to spit, but nothing came together in one piece. It was all floating around in his windpipe like a virus. He kept trying to clear his throat, making awful sounds that were more alarming than they were distracting. 'So, as I said, I had nothing to do with him in an official capacity after my payment was cleared.' He coughed again, this time managing to hurl a great big splotch of slime on to the sidewalk. Its colour was beyond description. Neither green nor grey. Black like the night.

'But then,' he continued, 'a couple of days later he calls me up, out of the blue.'

'What did he want?'

'He said he had some dirt on my client, some files which he was willing to sell provided the price was right, and if I knew anyone who was interested. I told him not to do anything of the kind. I, of course, didn't notify my client that he was in imminent danger, as you know his reactions tend to be . . . uh . . . a bit drastic.'

He spat again, this time with less vigour than before. 'And I am known to quite frequently act upon my own discretion and, as legal counsel, I am entitled to do as I see fit, provided it is within the scope of the law. I figured that if I got hold of those files, I could quietly hand them back to Irshaad, without him having a heart attack. So I told Makhija to hold on to those files for me, and that I would outbid anyone who was willing to purchase them. I took Irshaad's chartered accountant, Cheeku, with me to keep track of the expenses so that I would be duly reimbursed. You know Cheeku?'

'Yeah. I know Cheeku. I used to work under him.'

'So Cheeku and me got into my Ford Ikon and went over to Malad to meet this Makhija guy. We stopped at every ATM we could find in the area, scrounging together whatever dough we could pull out of our personal accounts.'

'Cheeku must have kept track of every rupee.'

'We managed to pull out about 40,000 bucks, which is the maximum withdrawal limit, and headed straight to Makhija's with a briefcase full of notes.'

'When was all this?'

'Uh . . . I'm not too sure. A couple of days ago. I can't remember the date.'

'Did you two sign in the register?'

'We did, at least we pretended to. But we didn't want to give out our details, so, when the guard wasn't looking, we pretended to write down our details and shut the register. He was half-asleep anyway, he probably doesn't remember. He'd even forgotten to lock the gate. He just mumbled to us in his sleep to write down our names. Seemed like quite an irresponsible watchman, if you ask me. Cheeku gave me cover and I did the same for him. It isn't all that difficult, you know. I usually never sign when I go into a building. Especially considering some of the buildings I find myself in. It's a mere formality and can be easily avoided.'

'Did anybody see you enter or exit the building?'

'I don't think so. It was way past lights out when we reached. He opened the door in his underwear and vest. I told him to dress up decently as he had company and that if he'd like we could wait about five or ten minutes for him to get changed. But he said it was all okay and that he had nothing to be ashamed of.'

'What condition was he in when you met him?'

'He was heavily sedated. He could barely keep his eyes open. I remember he popped a couple of tablets and, sure enough, that straightened him out. But I couldn't really tell. I'd done some nitro earlier in the evening and, in that condition, I can't tell a horse from a donkey. But I know how to carry myself when I'm on a heavy dosage, unlike some people who just fall to pieces.'

A gentle nip in the breeze lingered on Nadeem who wondered what next to say or add, but all that ensued was an awkward silence. The man looked down at the ground as if in resignation to the solemnity of the moment.

'Well, sometimes, a person comes damn near to cracking even when he's got all his faculties in constant motion,' he reflected. 'I've seen it in some of my clients. Take a guy like Irshaad for instance. He's been seeing a shrink. I put him in touch with a guy by the name of G.D. Vengsarkar. A miracle worker. He can pull the sap right out of a withered banyan branch. He helped me through some sordid years. Turns out this Makhija character had been seeing him too. I told him he was doing the right thing, that good old Dr Vengsarkar would have him back in tip-top shape in no time. I put the briefcase containing the dough on a small side table and cracked it open for him to get a good look, hoping that it'd bring some happiness to his hapless stupor.'

'Did it?'

'At least temporarily. He went over to the kitchen and brought out the files from a cabinet. I saw the doctor's name on the cover with the insignia of Healthy Mind Clinic. I recognized it instantly. But what lay inside of it, well, that was a different story altogether.'

Uncertain Confession

'I'll admit from the start, I was wrong in what I did. And I guess Cheeku'll vouch for me on that, considering he comes pretty close to being an accomplice. When I saw the files, I knew we were sunk. As long as they existed and this man had read what was in them, there'd be no peace. In this life or any other. It would forever nag at the consciousness. It would cloud even the happiest of thoughts, knowing that somewhere out there was a man who was fully aware that my client had been clinically diagnosed as criminally insane, that he came pretty close to be shipped off to Yerwada. He said that he smashed the A7 on the Eastern freeway and beat up the man driving it because he enjoyed it, that he'd beat up the psychiatrist if he came close. But, over the course of multiple counselling sessions, he began to thaw. And the good old doctor got to work on him. He got everything out of him, his whole life history, like a past-life regression therapist or hypnotist.'

'How come?'

'I don't know how he got Irshaad to talk. I guess having someone who'll listen is the only balm the good lord provided to any kind of illness, psychological or otherwise. That's the only time I've seen him open up. But I wish I'd never opened those files. Inside the folder were transcriptions of some of Irshaad's counselling sessions. Verbatim recordings of everything that he had said in the clinic. One of the pages contained a confession to the crime of assault and battery, given by him under oath following his incarceration. Now, how many judges and officials can you pay off to save a man from that kind of sentence? I'm known to do anything I can within a reasonable limit to get my client in the clear, but this was a lost cause. I know a little bit about the law, at least enough to get by, more so than an average person might be aware of. So, I'll admit it to you: I killed him. I killed Chintan Makhija. Took his life out of my own volition. Exercising my own free will. I had the chance not to, but I did. I don't know why. But it gave me a cheap thrill, like a child playing a prank on a schoolteacher and closing his eyes to the consequences. I locked him up in the bathroom from the outside when he went in to take a leak. And I left him there, thumping and banging on the door like a madman. Screaming at the top of his voice till it went hoarse. I stood there and watched. Cheeku looked at me like I was crazy, but then even he began to wonder. To him, it meant saving 40,000 bucks. We both smiled at each other with the camaraderie that mischief breeds and casually went about our own business, with our mouths firmly shut.

We left him there to see if he would make it. Almost like a friendly challenge.'

Nadeem gazed at him, perplexed, his mouth hanging open and his forehead stretching up in awe of the audacity of his claim.

'Now I'm telling you all this,' he continued, 'but I challenge you to put me in jail for it. There's no known soul but yourself and Cheeku who are aware of what I have just told you. It's your word against mine. And you won't be able to, I know it.'

'How do you know that?'

'I know the law. I know you need witnesses. I'm not likely to say ever again what I said to you just now. And now that I've said it, I feel kind of cleansed. Kind of got it out of my system. As I said before, sometimes, all you need is someone to talk to.'

Nadeem studied HK's cavalier manner. He didn't know what to make of him, whether he was telling the truth or gassing. There was something about him which seemed off-kilter.

'I wish I could say "don't worry", "I'll never do it again", but I just can't. I can never be too sure of anything, let alone myself. Not after I read what Irshaad had said. It kind of changed things for me, made me see things a whole lot clearer.'

'What did he say?'

'I don't have all night. You really want to know?'

'I do.'

'Then get in the car, let's go for a little drive. I can't tell you about it standing here in the middle of the road.'

Nadeem thought twice about the proposition. Getting into the car with a man claiming to be a murderer was not the most sensible thing to do in normal circumstances.

'Can I give you a lift till anywhere?' he asked Nadeem.

'No, thanks. I'd like to make it home in one piece.'

'Suit yourself,' he exhaled, looking back at the car. 'Then you'll never know.'

Nadeem hesitated, standing motionless, surveying the damage on the car. HK coughed, drew out some phlegm and rolled it about in his mouth, like he was chewing paan. He spoke with his mouth full. 'I guess I'll be seeing you around,' he gurgled. 'If you ever need any legal advice, let me know. I could do a thing or two about your predicament.'

'I don't know about that.'

HK nodded, kicking a stone out of his path and pranced off towards his car, waving back.

'What happened to it?' Nadeem asked.

'I smashed it into a silver SLR on Palm Beach Road.'

'Deliberately?'

'You could say that.'

'Why?'

'Because it was an SLR and I was driving an Ikon. I don't like things I don't have. That doesn't mean I want to have them, but sometimes I feel like I've gotta destroy them to save someone else the misery of want. You could say that I did Makhija a favour by putting him out of his misery.'

'What about the SLR guy? You put him out of his happiness.'

HK leaned on the bonnet, his car keys rolling around in the palm of his hand. 'I tend to simplify things by blaming it on envy,' he turned slowly to face Nadeem. 'There was an ulterior motive at hand. My client was in debt with him, so I just thought I'd put him in debt with his mechanic. I meant no harm. My client owed him a lakh of rupees over a poker game. Can you believe that? If he had an ounce of decency in him, he'd let it slide, but no. He insisted Irshaad pay up in a sporting fashion. So, you see, I had no choice. Anyways, I hate gambling, it's for sissies.'

'But you like to gamble with other people's lives.'

'What is a life? It isn't a physical tangible thing. It can't be measured. It has no real value in any quantifiable sense. It's floating in thin air to an inevitable conclusion. The only thing that's certain in life is death. Now, death has a physical presence. It hits like a sledgehammer, pops up out of nowhere and lays you down flat. You can hold it in your hand. But not life, life is like the wind. You gotta catch it or else it slips by.'

Nadeem walked over to the spot that was covered and kicked aside the tin covering, showing him the excavated pit where the body had been found.

'Well, I've got news for you!' Nadeem stated. 'Speaking of death and your casual regard for it. A body was found right about here. A police officer's, to be precise. The work of your client, no doubt. I can see you're going to have your hands full for the next couple of days.'

'Hmm . . .' HK mumbled, walking slowly towards Nadeem to inspect the spot he had uncovered. 'Now you're opening up a whole new can of worms with this,' he drawled, gazing through the cracks in the cement into the subterranean abyss. 'Did you know him?'

'He was at my house an hour ago. That's where he got tagged. The work of Ghazfakullah, I suppose.'

'Oh no,' he corrected Nadeem. 'Nowadays it's strictly Yunus for these kinds of jobs. He's the new trigger man, quiet as a dove.'

'Who Yunus?'

'Yunus Patel.'

'Yeda Yunus?'

'That was his moniker for a brief period, but one that would suit me better, given the circumstances. After all, it isn't only Yeda who's been doing his dirty work, you know.'

'I can see that,' Nadeem's polite smile contorted in scorn.

'I too am quite adept at making manoeuvres that could possibly involve the loss of human life. I've done things for Irshaad I'm not too proud of.'

'What things?'

'Things. I've killed a man. This wasn't a first, and I don't suppose it's going to be the last. I suggest you take that into consideration if and when you do intend to . . . uh . . .report me to the authorities.'

'Is that a threat?'

'It's an assurance.'

'Are you gonna sneak into my building one dark rainy night and put me out of my misery?'

'I'd be inclined to, if the odds were right and it was worth it. But, as of now, let's just say I'll let you live.'

He began to laugh. A fake laugh at first, but then it began to grow more genuine and almost impolite, as if he was scoffing at his new-found company and berating the very absurdity of having this conversation, standing in the middle of the road in the first place. Like he had better things to do, the laugh let out by one miraculously in command of his own hubris, one who supposes himself to be a superior being, lost in the company of strangers. As it progressed, it began to grow somewhat deranged, and Nadeem stared on in awe, trying to decode whether this insanity was an act.

'What are you?' Nadeem asked. 'Some kind of legal serial killer?'

'Ha!' he cackled. 'Serial killer! That's a good one, I can almost smell the headlines. I do suppose the common dictionary would refer to me as that particular brand of social misfit, often to be found dwelling amongst the multitudes, in a cruel unforgiving metropolis. Lonely and miserable, preying on the weaknesses of other. A menace to society. Public enemy! I'm not one of those. I'm not out of a textbook. You'll find me in the back columns of the newspapers, disguised in the classifieds as a chamber or a law firm of some sort, a corporate entity of remarkable significance. There's no denying my bona fides, I am an honest man, as was Makhija, and he came to a dishonest end. That about sums it up. There's really not much else to think about, now that it's over.'

'Tell me something. You ever hear of this medication he was taking?'

'Synahydraloxide?' he smiled.

'Yeah . . .'

'It was nothing. It was fake; it was rubbish . . . something stupid.'

'As in?'

'As in it was one of the good doctor's guinea pig attempts. I wasn't in the market for them. He had tried them on me but I caught him at the onset.'

'What do you mean?'

'It was junk.'

'Junk?'

'God knows what it was! I know what it did to you. I tried it.'

'What was it?'

'Look, it's a long story and I don't really have the time to get into it.'

'You might be summoned by the police for a questioning!'

'I have nothing that I wish to hide from the authorities. In fact, I'd be glad to meet them. I even tried getting in touch with a big inspector who's been on our trail for quite a while. But he didn't want to have anything to do with me.'

'All your commitment to your client?'

'Just trying to make life easier for him.'

'Making life tougher for yourself in the process,' Nadeem blinked.

'There's nothing that can happen to me! Unless they find my prints in the house on the doorknobs. Which, going by the police's track record of finding anything, is highly unlikely.'

'You actually killed Chintan Makhija?'

'Yup!' He blew his nose, wiping his hands on the side of his pants.

'You realize what you're saying?'

'I think I do.'

'You've just confessed to me about the murder of Chintan Makhija. If I go straight to the cops right now, there isn't a thing in the world that prevents you from being locked up.'

'Except for the law. That's the only thing that prevents you from convincing anyone else about what you believe to be the truth. The law's a stonewall. It's there to protect the guilty as well as the innocent, in equal measure, and give them both a sporting chance. Suppose you tell them I did it. What'll you say was the motive?'

'Protecting your client!'

'No lawyer will stretch that far. They know lawyers better than we know ourselves. No, what'd be the real cause? Insanity's an easy solution. But I've exhibited no real outward signs, unlike my client. In fact, I'd go as far as to say that my behaviour has remained wholly logical. Wouldn't you agree?'

'Then why'd you do it?'

HK faked a crooked smile, breathing gently through it. He turned his upper torso back towards the vehicle. 'Get into the car,' he chirped. 'You'll know.'

Nadeem followed him step by step to the side of the road towards the parked vehicle. He watched every move like a hawk as HK pressed the top button on the autocop, popping open the door to the driver seat. He got in, slamming the door harder than was necessary. Nadeem got into the passenger seat slowly. The entire car was reeking of air freshener. It was smelling like a Listerine leak.

HK stepped on the accelerator, clicking open the dashboard with his left hand. A large folder fell on to Nadeem's lap as the car slowly swerved to a turn.

'You see that subway over there?' HK asked, pointing towards the underground walkway outside the bus depot.

'Yes.'

'Well, I used to go there to score smack back in the late 2000s when it had just been built. Don't blame me. The job gets tough. We need all the healthy recreation we can lay our hands on. Now, I'm off it. I get my kicks out of whatever modern pharmaceuticals have to offer. It sedates the shit out of you, but it's nothing like the real stuff we used to get down there. There was an old lady who used to live down there. I forget her name. She used to sell vegetables as a front for powder, but I suspect she was nothing more than a beggar, setting up shop wherever convenient. She was the most sinister-looking bhaajiwaali I ever came across. Had great big craters under her eyes that swelled out through her cheekbones. But she was all there, had her faculties in place. She got busted eventually, but she'd carved up a little spot for herself behind the tiles.'

'Behind the tiles?'

'Behind or perhaps even under. Who knows? All I know is that a sewer system runs practically all the way across it. Whoever has the misfortune of having to use that walkway on a daily basis is likely to complain about the smell. It's no bed of roses.'

'Apparently, Makhija was doing smack.'

'Possible,' he coughed. 'Irshaad had asked me for some numbers. I even supplied him with the old lady's number. You think he might have gone there? There's people down there, you know.'

'People?'

'Yeah, if you wanna dispose of a body out there, they're the ones that do it for you. It's like an unofficial cemetery. An underground union. That's where you wind up if you've done somebody wrong on this earth. In Hindu mythology it exists. The *paatal ghar* they call it. Ha ha! If they start digging up this city, God knows how many more corpses they'll end up uncovering.'

The car took a left after the signal, straightening out on to S.V. Road. He seemed to be headed towards Goregaon (East).

'That manhole where they dumped the cop?' he mused.

'What about it?'

'Wonder where it leads to and wonder what the hell he was doing where he was found under the asphalt?'

'He wasn't there of his own accord. He was put there.'

'By fate, I suppose. A respectable police officer like that, crawling through the sewers in search of salvation. Seems highly unlikely, doesn't it? But free will is a strange thing. You never know where it makes you wind up. Like you. I have enough reason to ensure you don't leave this car alive, but you exercised your own free will by getting in.'

Nadeem's face shrivelled up. His heart skipped a beat and his eyes leapt towards his new-found acquaintance, contemplating the indecision on his face. He kept all eyes on the road, squinting through the beam of the headlights trying to decipher the routes. 'Where are you taking me?'

'To Chembur. To a eunuch communion at their holy temple, where they're going to dip a sickle in hot, boiling oil and cut off your pecker. You're going to join the holy order.'

Nadeem wondered for a brief flicker of a moment if he was actually serious or not but noticed him trying to suppress a smile.

'You got jokes, ha!' Nadeem grunted.

'I got you for a moment there, didn't I?'

The lawyer switched on the radio with his left index finger, twirling the volume dial with his pinky till he was satisfied. It seemed that he was keen on hearing the weather report in Marathi on 101.9.

'Hmm,' he responded to it. He pressed down on the accelerator, speeding to an alarming degree. The road was bumpy but he didn't seem too perturbed. His suspension was taking a beating. The car jumped across potholes in the road, rocking Nadeem back and forth, silently prompting him to put on his seat belt. The man's driving abilities were undoubtedly questionable, his manoeuvring skills had more reckless daring than good sense. He overtook a car which was a good deal ahead of them, honking at it a dozen times before it moved aside for him to pass through. Nadeem held on to the hand rest, his eyeballs scanning the road. HK was headed towards the depths of Goregaon, perhaps towards the forest in Film City.

'You going to tell me?' Nadeem trembled.

'I wonder what it must have been like for him.'

'Whom?'

'Makhija. Entombed in that bathroom. Alive in an 8x10 coffin, fit for a king. Wonder how long he must have lasted till he perished. There was no water at his house that day, no electricity either. We conducted the remainder of the transaction by candlelight. It was pitch black in the bathroom. I'd used it myself before him and had to keep the door slightly ajar to keep track of my aim. I sprayed a little bit here and there, but couldn't even wash my hands. Perhaps they'll find droplets of my urine, perhaps they'll find my prints on my money on the floor.'

'Your money?'

'I'd dropped some on the floor from the table and forgot to collect it on the way out.'

'How much was it?'

'About ten grand, I think.'

'You left ten grand at the scene of the crime?'

'I'm only human. I make mistakes.'

'It wasn't there when I found him . . .'

'I snuck back into the building last night. Hid in the shrubbery all night long till the watchman fell asleep. Tried going back up to collect it but realized that a guard was sleeping inside. Maybe the Gypsy parked outside saw me sneak in. Perhaps they'll catch me and I'll spend the rest of my life behind bars. But one thing they'll never know is why. Why I did the most heinous thing an upright model citizen could do. Why a lawyer was pathologically incapable of abiding by the very law he professed to practise.'

Nadeem's gaze tightened on him. He was speeding at an alarming rate, looking only at the road as he spoke. He didn't even turn to address Nadeem, he pretended almost as if he wasn't there, that he was all alone and talking to himself in soliloquy.

'You see, when we were growing up, we had been told by all the maulanas and maulvis of a promised land, a land where you were rewarded by the virtues you possessed, not by the whims and fancies of circumstance. Those that were rewarded on this earth were to be consigned to eternal damnation. After all, it was merely, as they called it, a "kaafiron ki Jannat", a place of sin and treachery where evil prevails. "Let 'em enjoy this life" was always their peaceful surmise. This one isn't for us. Those that found no peace or joy in the material world would console themselves with the cheering illusion that life would be kinder to them after it was over. That there would be real joy and real peace, which wasn't to be found in chicks and cars and money. A hell on earth was what their existence was about. A biblical purgatory of the everyday, where every step you took out of your house was a drop further away from sanity. Where the very air you breathed sucked the very life out of you, where your eyes were graced with only the sight of hideousness, where the only sounds that crept into your ears screamed misery, and where the forces of fate conspired against you, to keep you one step short of fulfilment. I'd never thought of it until Irshaad put things into perspective for me. What he said was that the only sentence that counts is the one the Almighty gives out, not the one notarized by some judge in a black gown. He should know, his account with the Almighty has suffered considerable deficits in proportion of his vices to his virtues. But as far as I'm concerned, I find that kind of liberating. The thought that the law and rules which apply to normal citizens don't really make that much of a difference in the scheme of things. That the ones toeing the line are actually just suckers.'

'Pull over!' Nadeem ordered him.

The speedometer was closing in on a hundred and fifty. Oncoming vehicles flew across with the beam from the headlights. The car leapt off an upward sloping road, the angle of which propelled them like a ramp, making them airborne for a couple of seconds.

'Woooohoooo!' HK exclaimed in nervous exhilaration as the car fell back on to the road. The smell from an adjacent sewage dump slipped into the car, making Nadeem even more ill at ease than he had good reason to be. HK continued rejoicing in his adrenalized elation. The pitch of his voice escalated beyond the boundaries of mania.

'Pull over, Hoseipha!' Nadeem screamed, his voice drowned out in the roar of the road.

'You know I kind of like that name. No one calls me by it. I like the sound of it. You know, it means Joseph.'

Nadeem grabbed hold of the steering wheel and twisted it around clockwise, sending the car straight towards the divider. The car skidded, going momentarily out of control, before HK pushed him aside, clearing his grasp off the wheel. Nadeem's shoulder pushed him back against the window, grabbing the gear and pulling it down from fifth to neutral. The car swerved across the divider and spun on to the other side of the road, with its rear end facing the oncoming traffic. A grey Innova screeched to a halt two inches behind, another truck cut across just at the right moment, missing it narrowly.

Just as the car came as close to being stationary, as HK would possibly allow, Nadeem flung open the door of the passenger seat to haul his torso out of it. HK immediately caught hold of the seat belt Nadeem had made the mistake of putting on and pinned his neck back to the headrest with it. Nadeem flapped about violently, trying to wriggle his way out of the headlock. He began to choke. The bewildered driver from the Innova got off to see what the matter was. He tapped at HK's window as the two men clutched vigorously at the seat belt inside. Nadeem bit HK's arm, trying to cry out for help. HK stuck his fingers up Nadeem's nostrils, jabbing him in the ribs. Nadeem's door was still open and HK's elbow was pressed firmly to the horn, making it scream across the empty road. On registering the gravity of the scuffle, the man outside immediately deserted the car and made back for his Innova, getting into it with undue haste. Nadeem tried to scream out to him as he zipped off, but HK stuck his hands over his mouth. Nadeem bit his hand again, this time managing to dig deeper. Blood spurted out of the side of his palm, leaving a tear of flesh hanging loosely over it.

'Aaaaarggghhhh!' HK screamed, retreating his hands and holding them up against the light to examine the wound. Nadeem took the opportunity to make a dash for it. He quickly turned around and tried to jump out but was catapulted back into the car by the strapped on seat belt. Before he could even reach for the red button to open it, HK slammed his foot down on the accelerator, sending the car hurtling forward. Nadeem's door swung back and forth, his left hand getting jammed between it. The car swayed wildly across the long empty road. The pickup was tremendous. It could lift off from 10 to a 100 in a matter of seconds. The car sped in the opposite direction, heading back towards the Goregaon telephone exchange. The road sloped forward, crossing a dilapidated bridge, which hovered aimlessly over a nala. The two men inside the car were battling fiercely over the steering wheel, causing a strange succession of screeching sounds that sent the vehicle staggering left and right. As it ran down the slope, Nadeem lifted his feet off and kicked the steering wheel, pushing HK's clasp aside. The car careened out of control and smashed through the crumbling concrete railings of the bridge, taking a nosedive straight into the filth of the creek.

Black water spilled in through the edges of the windows and the cracked windscreen. Bubbles swelled up all around them, submerging the entire vehicle in slime. It sunk slowly into the creek, filling up rapidly, almost to the point where it began to balloon out of shape. Nadeem held his breath, pushed open the seat belt and swam out of the open passenger seat door. HK was stuck inside with his door jammed. He struggled to open it but was bombarded by the influx of mucky water that poured in all around him, drowning him in sewage waste. Nadeem surfaced from the sea of sickness, his head popping out of the grey oblivion, paddling deliriously to the dirt-ridden shore. He heaved himself out of the creek, covered in slime from his head down to his toes. There were plastic bags and excreta everywhere. Every step he took was a living reminder of purgatory, almost of biblical proportions. He screamed for help, beckoning to the heavens above, but there was no one in sight for miles but for a few nocturnal cats and the resting swine rolled up to sleep in the sludge. Even the mangroves immersed in uncertain slumber at the edge of the creek seemed disinterested in his plight. The car had sunk completely and was no longer visible, taking with it the strange man interred in his own automobile down to the bottomless pits of hell.

The Nether Regions

Nadeem staggered through the marsh, trying hard to retain his balance, stepping on rodents here and there, and keeping a jittery eye on whatever path revealed itself in the pitch-black night. There was a navigable walkway back up towards the main road somewhere, but his eyes took some time to get accustomed to the darkness. He held his arms out, hoping to get a feel of anything that seemed even remotely familiar, anything that would guide him through the infernal swamp. As the blind haze began to subside and some vision presented itself to him, he could faintly perceive the grey concrete legs of the crumbling bridge that stood stooped into the shallower regions of the creek. Thankfully, there were indentations on the broad pillar-like structures that could be used as footholds to climb up till its top. He crawled up the bridge with the slithery grasp of a reptile. Once he had made his way up and was within reach of the railings, he lifted himself back on to the main road. He didn't want to turn back to look at what he had abandoned. It was no place for any human being in his right mind to be. He ran across the empty road, towards the Goregaon telephone exchange, stopping to ask a parked autorickshaw driver who was sleeping on the side of the road for help. The driver resisted on account of the way Nadeem was smelling. He had to walk all the way back to the telephone exchange, appearing in the darkness almost like a creature from the black lagoon. What had slithered past him as he swam to the shore was a matter only for the most depraved speculation. Whatever it was, he might have resembled it in that state—a mutant that had spawned out of the indifference of the great corporate carcass of our metropolis.

Gathering whatever strength he had left, he sprinted across the main road, dodging the speeding cars and trucks that stormed past, waving his hands wildly at them, in the hope of getting them to stop. None of the vehicles acknowledged his presence; he was simply a mild inconvenience that could be easily ignored with the blink of a headlight. Somehow, through sheer grit and brute strength, he managed to make it back to the telephone exchange. Once he reached, he hit the pavement at the divider and stretched himself out on it, panting heavily as if he was about to have a heart attack. He had depleted every last bit of wherewithal and laboured to catch his breath. His lungs began to squeak, a bloodthirsty cough enveloping his entire being till he looked no different from the derelicts in debauched slumber beside him. As he regained his bearings and attempted to straighten up, he turned gradually to the shut-up subway. It lurked like a concrete spectator in the illuminating gloom of the street lamp. He hurled himself towards it in an instant but paused at the entrance, glaring down at it incredulously.

He thought twice before entering it, but his curiosity outweighed his anxiousness. He walked in slowly keeping an eye on the stained, yellow cube tiled walls and floor. It was dark, the overhead tube lights had been switched off, but the moonlight still managed to seep its way in as he manoeuvred down the flight of steps. The dreary corridor seemed to stretch on into infinity. He wished he had a torch on him, but parts of it were vaguely perceivable in the darkness. Bits and pieces of the tiling on the walls were broken, the floors were slippery with paan stains and the grime and commotion of the day. He knew not what he was doing down there, but he carried on into the void as if obeying some unseen command from beyond. He could hear droplets of water dripping as he walked further into the bowels of the subway, keeping a stiff eye on everything visible. Stray dogs littered the path, some awake, some growling with malice and discontent, and some merely there as keepers of a forbidden alleyway.

The subway wound on indefinitely, curving left. Somewhere in the distance, a lamp illuminated a corner of the wall, making it appear faintly like a cave painting. Nadeem slowly closed in towards it, his eyes glowing with dread as he tried to get a glimpse of what had caused the light. He felt he could distinctly hear the sound of children playing, the noisome banter of a gathering of some sort. As he neared the lamplight, he noticed a crack in the walls from where the light arose. It had been covered with a board of plywood. The faint sound was emanating from behind it. He pulled it out with much force—one of the sides had been nailed in—and it swung open, giving way to a dilapidated view that struck him as foreboding, yet strangely inviting. Behind the cracks of the cube tiled walls, a dim passageway seemed to lead on to what appeared to be an underground drainage system, a network of tunnels and trenches in a crater that lay beneath even the lowest depths of the subway. He entered it, against his better judgment.

The hideous odours of the catacombs plagued him with delirious associations. 'This is where the sewage waste from the entire city winds up,' he thought. Everything that is flushed down, washed away or runs through a pipe lands up in this forsaken pit. As he walked through the scum, marsh and waste towards the illuminating abyss, he came across what at first glance resembled a settlement, a kind of ramshackle *jhopad patti*, an underground dwelling place where a family had camped for the night to avoid the wrath of the municipality. A stove was parked on the floor next to a tattered cloth which encircled a sleeping area, serving as a makeshift tent. Two adults were asleep inside it, as their two ragged children, a boy and girl, threw stones into the unending distance of the sewers. A small man sat quietly on the ground next to them, his stony visage sullen yet perceivably alarmed at Nadeem's intrusion. The two kids scarcely bothered to take notice of Nadeem, but the little man's wandering gaze settled on him, appearing remotely threatening in the shadows. He was a dwarf and was clothed in rags he had probably borrowed from the children. His eyes were large and the contours on his face resolutely unfriendly. The playful shrieking of the children took on an air of uncanny inappropriateness. So engaged were they in their trivial pursuits that they failed to acknowledge Nadeem's presence. As they glanced backwards and noticed him, the boy immediately shouted, 'Ehh! Police! Police!' The two children ran for their lives into the depths of the gutters, as if playing a game of hide and seek, abandoning their parents and the other man who sat silently, still as a rock. His face tightened as Nadeem closed in towards him.

'I'm not the police!' Nadeem informed him. 'And I'm not with the municipality, either.'

The two haggard adults, passed out in the enclosure, had failed to be awakened by Nadeem's intrusion. The dwarf did not speak a word; he just silently took in whatever explanation Nadeem had to give for himself. Nadeem himself did not have much of an explanation, much less a reason for being there in the first place.

'I heard you get 'maal' here. Smack. There was an old lady. Do you know her?'

The little man studied Nadeem's every gesture. He didn't have him squared for a junkie. He seemed too composed and in command of himself to be one, even though he was covered in slime.

'They found a policeman's body in this place,' Nadeem informed him.

The little man stared back at him, his eyes enlarging with every word that was spoken.

'I take it,' Nadeem continued, 'that the police are not your friend.'

The little man did not reply.

'Did you see the body?' Nadeem asked, cautiously.

The little man got up from his stoop and went over to a trash can that lay near the stove. He scooped out all the waste and removed from it a disembodied forearm. It had been severed from the elbow and was covered in slime, practically decomposed. It looked like it had been lying in the sewer for quite a while. The little man presented it to Nadeem almost as if he wished him to shake the hand. Nadeem retreated in disgust and outright horror. He had never had the opportunity to see anything quite like it.

'What the hell is that?' he gasped.

The little man still did not reply. Nadeem covered his mouth with the palm of his left hand, the one that had not touched the walls in the darkness and was presumably clean, at least in comparison to the rest of his body. He ran out of there, climbing back into the subway with the awful knowledge he had mistakenly gained and with the fearful realization that there were some truths that were better unknown. It took some doing for him to find his way back to the subway entrance, and as he emerged out into the outside world, he thanked his stars for being in one piece.

He walked all the way from the Goregaon telephone exchange to the nearest autorickshaw stand, near the Fire Brigade station, and rode home frightfully bewildered, telling the auto driver to step on it. The auto driver asked what the matter was and if he was all right, but Nadeem told him to keep his eyes on the road. Thankfully, he did not take objection to the smell. He'd probably smelt and seen worse.

Back from the Dead

By the time he got back to Little Heights, Inspector Gaekwad's jeep was parked outside the lobby carelessly, in a most indecent fashion. One of the doors had been left open and there was no one behind the wheel.

Nadeem rushed up to the third floor where Inspector Gaekwad and a team of ballistics experts were surveying the staircases. He flinched for a moment on registering Nadeem's condition.

'What the hell happened to you, Chipkali?'

'I rose from the dead.'

Inspector Gaekwad looked around at the rest of the assembled personnel, his face suddenly stricken with confusion. Rohini, Mangesh, Kishorie Lal, Mr Machhiwaala and Warren were still in the flat and hadn't budged from there. Warren was doing a miserable job at playing host; he tried his level best to make them tea but pretty soon, Rohini had to intervene.

'I think you'd better go attend to your guests and leave me to my job,' suggested Inspector Gaekwad, leading Nadeem back into his flat. He dispatched Mangesh to go and get his spectacles and flashlight from the open police jeep downstairs.

'What's that smell?' Mangesh asked, as he headed down the stairs.

Inspector Gaekwad proceeded up to the fourth floor. Warren shot a discreet look at Nadeem once he was away from the wandering eye of Inspector Gaekwad. He twitched his eyebrows and nodded silently, calling him closer.

'When did he land up?' Nadeem whispered to Warren who appeared to have more on his mind than he could communicate just at that moment.

'About fifteen or twenty minutes ago,' he groaned, suppressing what he actually wanted to say.

'How many people did he bring with him?'

'Four ballistics men, plus another guy in the bathroom. The psychiatrist.'

'The one we saw at the station?'

'Yeah, that's him,' he twitched nervously.

Nadeem's attention spun towards the bathroom. It was occupied, as was apparent from the lights that were switched on. 'Who's in the bathroom?'

'Him! Gaekwad brought him along handcuffed.'

The gentle sound of the flush rumbling into motion was followed by the crickety clank of the bathroom door being unlatched. Dr Vengsarkar emerged from the toilet, wiping his wet hands on his shirt. His crooked eyes had grown somewhat colder and less kind. He looked up at Nadeem, not knowing what to do or say.

'I hope you don't mind me using your bathroom,' he said politely. 'I just couldn't help myself. By the way, I think your toilet seat's busted.'

Rohini came around from the kitchen, carrying a tray with four cups of tea neatly arranged on it.

'Let me get that for you,' Warren insisted, fumbling at the tray and relieving her of the painful duty. Both of them moved into the living room where Mangesh, Kishorie Lal and Mr Machhiwaala were, leaving the two of them alone to have a little man-to-man chat, outside the bathroom.

'What are you doing here?' Nadeem asked.

'I got a call from Inspector Gaekwad earlier this evening in connection with the Makhija killing.'

'Killing?'

'It's actually a poisoning according to them, one that I engineered.'

'I see!'

'He seems pretty sure about it. He said it was "beyond a reasonable doubt". You see, after you left Malwani police chowki, the three of us had a conference. Inspector Nagpal had managed to procure Chintan's medical reports from K.L. Hospital and he shared them with Inspector Gaekwad.'

'What were you doing at the K.L. pharmacy earlier with Dilip? I saw you there.'

'I see,' he smiled. 'You did? Ah, yes, come to think of it, I think I saw you too . . . but only for a brief flicker of a moment.'

'What, may I ask, was the purpose of your visit?'

'Oh, it was merely scientific. Just a casual experiment. There is a particular medication of mine that is currently in the experimental stages, but easily procurable from your friendly neighbourhood chemist. The K.L. pharmacy is stocked with it. I had gone there at Inspector Nagpal's behest in order to test it on a specimen of mine admitted in the special ward on the third floor of the hospital.'

'I'm sorry?' Nadeem asked, as he tried to comprehend the purport of his account.

'That's where one of my patients is currently admitted. He's from the St Aloysius reformation and recreation centre, a former inmate at the Nandlal Pramod Facility in Pune. You see, K.L. Hospital has been kind enough to start a rehabilitation programme in association with the Nandlal Pramod Functionality Centre, where we run a programme that helps recovering addicts reintegrate into society through pharmaceutical assistance. I regret to mention that some of the patients in the ward were beyond saving and are presently in quarantine. Some of them are quite seriously infected and have, no doubt, picked up one or the other kind of neurological, physiological, skin and venereal disease from the various substances they had invariably been accustomed to. You see, Nadeem, when a person's moral compass collapses, there is no turning back from the point of no return.'

Rohini came along to hand Dr Vengsarkar a cup of tea, which he refused on account of his acidity.

'Look at this lady,' he said. 'A perfectly honest, hard-working woman. Works part-time at a handicrafts store. Vasundhara, isn't it?'

'Yes,' she said.

'Trying to get a degree in market research, studying for her MBA side by side, got married before her time. There's hope for her yet. For the likes of you and Makhija, who already had their shot and fouled it up, there's just one place—the dustbin. And what use is trash if you can't recycle it? That's where we come in.'

On re-entering the flat, Inspector Gaekwad immediately noticed Nadeem and Dr Vengsarkar talking to each other near the bathroom.

'Eh!' he called out. 'You two! Come here.'

Mangesh had by now come up with his torch and specs.

'Raut, separate these two men,' he instructed Mangesh. 'Put Nadeem Chipkali in the bedroom and lock him up there.'

'Wait a minute,' Nadeem stopped him. 'What's all this about him poisoning Makhija?'

'They showed the reports to a specialist,' Inspector Gaekwad spoke blankly with the dreary monotony of a newsreader. 'He claims there's been some medical malpractice involved.'

'What the hell are you talking about?'

'Eh! Watch your tongue, Chipkali!'

'This man had nothing to do with it,' Nadeem insisted, putting his arms around the doctor. The doctor shrugged his shoulders away from his grasp, wary of getting any of the sludge on his shirt.

'That's right,' Dr Vengsarkar added. 'Look, officer, if you want to put me away for medical malpractice, that's perfectly fine by me. That's a minor offence in comparison.

If you want, I can even sign a written confession. But not for murder. For God's sake. That I'm not guilty of. I've never killed anyone in my life. I swear on my mother. I swear on God.'

Inspector Gaekwad looked at him.

'Okay, not on my mother, but on God. I swear on God, I never killed anybody in my life.'

'Perjury's a serious offence, Dr Vengsarkar. If you intend to tell the truth, I suggest you tell the whole truth, not half.'

'What's all this about?' Nadeem asked, still befuddled by the recent progress of the case.

'Synahydraloxide,' Dr Vengsarkar proclaimed, holding up a rectangular glass bottle of pills with a yellow sticker running all the way across it. 'A concoction synthesized at one of the laboratories of a privately owned pharma company in Badlapur. One of the shareholders of the company, an acquaintance of mine, had a stroke of genius. You see, it is a widely known fact that some of the drugs floating around in the black market have been known to cause a wide variety of genetic abnormalities, mutations, birth defects, and so on. Where else does one procure smack but from the junkyards, where else does ganja grow but in the most squalid areas, feeding off of sewage water, where else does one procure a pharmaceutical drug but from a low-hygiene potentially bacterially infected hospital like K.L.'

Inspector Gaekwad looked at him morosely, his eyebrows thickening over the precariously balanced spectacles dangling on his nose.

'All the industrial, radioactive, biohazard waste that collects in the city can be used to a profitable purpose,' continued Dr Vengsarkar. 'If utilized correctly, it can be employed with startling effects, especially on the terminally ill. You can see results that would baffle science, give an answer to modern medicine. If implemented on living patients, one can study the outcome, psychological and physiological, and prevent any further such cases from occurring. It's kind of like trying to find a vaccine. You see, there are certain microscopic germs and bacteria which exist in all this waste. When isolated and extracted into a concentrate, they can then be injected into any substance or compound without altering the chemical composition. By doing this you can actually locate the disease and study the effects.'

'What the hell are you talking about?' Nadeem squawked. Inspector Gaekwad's eyes sparkled.

'Listen to me,' Nadeem broke in, much to Inspector Gaekwad's dismay. So immersed was he in Dr Vengsarkar's statement that he scarcely paid any heed to what Nadeem had to say.

'I know who killed Makhija!' he informed Inspector Gaekwad, in all earnestness. 'Listen, there is an advocate. Name of Hoseipha Khatri. HK, they call him. He's been handling all legal matters for Irshaad Batla. The ones that he doesn't want his family to know about. Hoseipha,' Nadeem cringed. 'Joseph. He's the one,' he said turning towards Dr Vengsarkar.

'How do you know that?' Dr Vengsarkar squinted. 'I know who you are talking about and he is a decent man. Law-abiding and an upholder of the law himself.'

'I was just with him. He confessed to everything. Said he locked up Makhija in the bathroom with the lights out and no water. He buried him alive in an 8x12 coffin.'

'They're going to institutionalize you if you carry on with that story. You don't really expect me to believe all this. What was the motive?'

'Protecting his client.'

'Where is he?' asked Inspector Gaekwad.

'You don't want to know. He's not alive, I can assure you.'

'You mean you killed him?'

'He tried to kill me. Call Cheeku. He was with him when he killed Makhija. He'll testify.'

'Who's Cheeku?' Inspector Gaekwad frowned.

'Irshaad's CA,' Nadeem told him.

'Do you have Cheeku's number?'

'Not on Warren's phone. I had it on mine.'

'Who can you call to get Cheeku's number?'

'Rohini! Do you have Cheeku's number?'

'Whose?'

'Cheeku, Irshaad's CA.'

'No, I don't think so. But it'll be on Chintan's phone. He had been in touch with him.'

'Rohini!' Nadeem yelled. 'Call Irshaad from your phone. Tell him you need Cheeku's number urgently so you can wire the money to him tomorrow.'

'Nadeem . . .' she mumbled. 'I can't do that.'

'It's our only choice.'

She clenched her jaw firmly, tightening her upper lip in resolution. 'No.'

'Look, Rohini, if you don't help me out here, your life could be in danger, and so could mine. With Irshaad Batla free and roaming the streets, no one's safe.'

Her lips parted slowly, letting out a faint murmur. 'All right,' she said, barely loud enough for herself to hear. She glared at Nadeem, fidgeting with her phone and dodging a couple of notifications from QUANTRA before finally deciding to dial Irshaad's number. It rang.

'Hello,' she spoke softly.

The voice from the other end of the line was clearly audible, as her phone volume had been set to its maximum.

'Hello!' Irshaad beamed, in a hollow crackle of a voice.

'Irshaad.'

'Tell me.'

'I need an urgent favour from you, right now.'

'Say it. Anything for you.'

'I need Cheeku's number.'

'Cheeku's right here if you wanna talk to him. Here, let me give him the phone.'

Rohini looked up at them, bewildered.

'Cheeku!' Irshaad hollered over the phone. 'Here, talk to Rinki!' He pretended to hand over the phone to someone else, putting on a fake voice which was easily recognizable. He tried to speak in Cheeku's high-pitched nasal tone.

'Haalllooo!' he squeaked, pretending to be Cheeku. 'Haaai, Rinki! Haaaw aaar yooo?'

'Irshaad!' she trembled, clenching her teeth. 'Stop fooling around.'

'I laaaw yooo, Rinki! Will yooo merry me?'

'Irshaad,' she growled, her temperature rising steadily. 'I have your money. I'm going to wire it to your account tomorrow. Give me your CA's number.'

'Take it down. It's zero, zero, double zero, double one, double zero. Sorry, triple zero. That's 000011000. Did you get it? You want me to repeat it for you?'

Suddenly, the voice coming from the mobile phone began to encroach into the living room from the surrounding walls. It got louder and louder as he repeated the number for the second time, until the voice from the phone and the voice from the lift were inseparable.

Inspector Gaekwad immediately reached for his holster. 'Everybody get back!' he firmly commanded, silently scanning the area outside the doorway from a distance. He shoved everyone from the living room into the bedroom and cranked out a 9-mm revolver from his belt. Mangesh flashed out his automatic and took his sahib's back. Inspector Gaekwad began to slowly close in towards the door with his revolver raised in the air, pointed at the ceiling. The ballistics experts were still on the fourth floor and their distant voices were vaguely perceptible, as was the voice nearing in towards the front of the doorway. Irshaad Batla came trotting along, his phone glued to his right ear, not in the least bit interested in where he was and what he was doing there. He was followed by two of his boys, who stood silently outside, refraining from entering out of polite courtesy.

'That's 000011000. Can you hear me, Rinki?' he kept hollering into the phone, scarcely even registering the presence of the two cops lined up to face him. He walked into the living room as if it was his house and was about to slip off his chappals and take a seat. 'Anyway,' he carried on, 'I'll talk to you later. I've just come to one place for some business. I'll call you once I reach home. You had dinner? Take care, ha . . . muaahhh . . . talk to you later. Bye! Love you!'

He turned to face the television as he stuffed his phone into his pocket, trying to fish another large object out of it. He struggled hard; his hand was getting stuck inside. On noticing the remote control lying over the television, he swiped hold of it and turned it on. The TV was tuned to Star Movies and an old World War II picture was roaring away. Bombs exploding, tanks hovering through the landscape, machine guns firing, the gyrating sounds of combat providing ambience to the dimly lit living room. Only a single lamp that stood on the wooden side table, on the left side of the couch, was on. The tube lights were not working properly and would flicker like disco lights when switched on. Irshaad cherishingly admired the warfare blasting through the screen. His pocket finally managed to spit out whatever he had been struggling with.

First came the handle, then the cartridge and then the mouth. He laid them all out on top of the TV and began to assemble a .22 Magnum, first, by sliding in the cartridge and then, by slipping the bullets into the magazine. He clicked it shut, unlatched the safety, pumped the cartridge and adjusted a silencer on the mouth of the barrel. Once he held it firmly in his clutched palm, he raised it into the air, swinging it around on his index finger. He had his back turned towards Inspector Gaekwad and Mangesh, who had by now pointed their firearms straight in his direction. He had two guns on his back and another set of ballistics experts shortly descending the staircase. Their voices could be heard as they came down the stairs, pausing at the doorway to greet the two flunkies who stood there. They entered, bemused, lost in casual banter, oblivious to the weapons on display in the living room. Inspector Gaekwad silently twitched at them, flicking his head aside, telling them to push out. Just as they were about to approach him with their findings, Irshaad blew a hole right through the TV screen. It exploded, letting out a profusion of sparks and fireworks.

'Get down!' Inspector Gaekwad yelled at the assembled personnel. A succession of shrieks and screams rang out across the living room with everyone reaching for the floor and ducking for their lives as Irshaad fired a second time, this time putting out the lights.

'Put the gun down, Irshaad!' Inspector Gaekwad screamed.

The two men outside had by now exhausted their courtesy and gained entrance. They had their firearms ready to use in service of their boss. Over the three ballistics experts who were laying flat on the floor, two sets of guns were pointed firmly at each other, while the fifth gun still lingered on the exploded television set.

'It's two against two. There's no need for crossfire.'

'Where's Chipkali?' Irshaad spoke, his back turned to the policemen.

'He's inside the bedroom,' Inspector Gaekwad told him.

'Bring him out here,' he ordered. 'I'm taking him with me as hostage.'

'Look, Irshaad . . .'

'You don't want anyone getting hurt. I suggest you bring Chipkali out.'

'Irshaad, if you tell your men to stop pointing their guns, I'll let you walk. Please, Irshaad.'

'Nadeem!' Irshaad yelled.

The bedroom door slipped open just wide enough to let a single person out. Nadeem walked out with his hands above his head. The muck he was covered in had by now dried up and occupied his entire face, as if he'd had it painted for some tribal ritual. He was practically covered in black.

'What the hell happened to you?' Irshaad asked.

'I was with your lawyer.'

Irshaad's glowering eyes floundered like a deer caught in the headlights. 'Where is he?'

'Twenty feet under. In the Goregaon swamp. Scattered among the waste yard.'

'Is he dead?'

'Most likely! He claimed to have killed Makhija. He told me.'

'He tells people a lot of things, only half of which are true. He likes to talk big, ever since he's been off the stuff.'

'What stuff?' Inspector Gaekwad nosed in.

Irshaad laughed, putting his gun away as he gazed about the apartment, inspecting every article with the keenest precision. One of the ballistics experts slowly rose from the floor, the rest of them stayed put.

'I guess you could say,' he began, 'that it took me less than a year to reduce him from a rehabilitated, reformed citizen, who had all his problems pinstriped away, to a pill-popping junkie with tombstones in his eyes.'

'He'd been trying to make life easier for you,' said Nadeem. 'It was all about his commitment to his client.'

'I always felt the fellow used to go out of his way to help me,' Irshaad stumbled across the room to the kitchen where he could hear faint whispers pouring out from under the closed bedroom door. He planted both his palms on the kitchen platform, searching in vain for anything even remotely appetizing.

'Nadeem, you got any chocolate powder?'

'There's some Bournvita lying around somewhere, I'm not quite sure. I'll have to look for it.'

'You got a mixie?'

'Yeah, but I don't know if it works.'

Nadeem pulled open a drawer from under the stove. An old mechanical grinder came out of it with its cap off. It was brown around the edges and probably hadn't been washed or even used in a while. The bottom unit it had to be attached to was plugged in next to the toaster, just a little ahead of the stove.

'Why d'you think he did it?' Nadeem asked.

'I don't know. I could never figure him out.'

Irshaad attached the mixer to its base and plugged it in. He cranked open the cabinets above the platform, fishing out a packet of milk powder.

'You got any milk?'

'I'm out!'

'Give me a bottle of cold water.'

Nadeem leaned towards the fridge.

'I guess he felt the strain of being my lawyer,' Irshaad continued. 'He used to visit Dr Vengsarkar and had, at one point, even been a patient at Nandlal Pramod Functionality Centre, where I was admitted. But apparently he escaped, changed his name and studied for his LLB, starting afresh. Kind of like you, I guess,' he smirked, pointing at Nadeem like a complaining classmate.

Nadeem fished out a half-empty bottle of cold water, as well as a quarter slab of ice cream from the freezer.

'We all want another shot, don't we?' Irshaad went on. 'Some with the law, some with life, some even with themselves. There wasn't a thing in the world he wouldn't do for me, HK. But what he did for himself, I never knew. How he lived, where he lived, with whom, for what. No one even knows his real name, if he's actually Muslim or not, where he comes from. I never even bothered to ask him. You see, like good old Dr Vengsarkar, I too consider myself to be a student of human nature. I like to know what it is that makes a fellow tick. It's good for business.'

'Who is this guy?' asked Insepctor Gaekwad, slowly lowering his gun.

'That's a good question,' Irshaad replied. 'I met him through an online app I had been told about by the psychiatric authorities.'

'What app?'

Nadeem's eyes glistened, his mouth split open, but before the words could come pouring out, Irshaad beat him to the punch.

'I've got the trial edition,' said Irshaad. 'I can get it for you too. Show me your phone.'

Inspector Gaekwad hesitantly handed him his brand new iPhone, keeping an eye on the screen to make sure he wouldn't sabotage it. Irshaad went to his app store where an incomplete command, C . . . O . . . N, still lingered on the keypad. He had been trying to download a game, Contra. Irshaad cleared that and typed in Q . . . U . . . A . . . N . . . T . . . R . . . A, reconfirming what his religious disposition was. He assured him it was Hindu.

'What's your Apple ID and password?' he asked.

Inspector Gaekwad typed it out for him.

'Voila!' Irshaad proclaimed, handing the phone back to him.

After having cracked his phone, he had successfully managed to download the application, and it was now stored on his desktop, right next to all the familiar logos. Inspector Gaekwad gaped at his screen in wonder. He entered his name, weight, age, height, sex, ethnicity and all the other regulars. In five minutes, after it completed a safety scan, he had an entire rundown of all his stats and info.

'It's kind of like Truecaller,' Irshaad stated. 'Apparently everyone's info is stored on the database. You see, the software searches cyberspace for all information about you and tallies together an array compiling your Google searches, mobile number, home and work address, pin code, email address and bank account number. It knows if you've been paying your taxes, how much you've been spending, how you've been conducting your social life, how many calls you've been returning in proportion to the calls you've been ignoring, how much data you use, how much talk time is wasted. This includes separate priorities for family members, friends, colleagues, batchmates, in order of importance. It also monitors the nature and content of your conversations and correspondence.'

'How is that possible?' Inspector Gaekwad asked.

'Easy,' he said, pointing towards his phone. 'Here you go. You see, this baby right here can perform just about any miracle that man or beast has been dying to be capable of since the beginning of time. It can defeat death, conquer the weather and even make a blind man see the light. The mobile phone has become the source of all life, an oracle, the cradle of experience. And it is through your characteristics, as manifested on that particular instrument, that your personal calibre can be judged. That, and your financial characteristics.'

'You've got to be out of your bloody mind.'

'You wanna know about this guy?' Irshaad asked, taking the phone away from Inspector Gaekwad's hands. 'Simple,' he said, as Nadeem and Inspector Gaekwad huddled around in rapt attention. He ran a check on Hoseipha Khatri. A single option popped up, not too many people had that name.

'Here's his profile,' said Irshaad. It said in big bold letters, PROFESSION: LAWYER. There were a couple of photos of him with scenic backdrops, the odd group photograph from the workplace, a picture of him with dark glasses staring into the lens, the corny quotable quotes and religious platitudes like, 'Do unto others as you would want them to do unto you.' It was the profile of a modest-looking man, not too different from the harmless company seekers one would scroll through on most platforms. He had a 95 per cent clearance rating on the moral latitude scale. It concluded that he was an 'upright, honest, hard-working citizen and pillar of the community'.

'Pillar of the community, my ass!' Nadeem grunted. 'He tried to kill me. He was going to run us into an oncoming vehicle and total his car to file for insurance, I suppose. It was already heavily damaged. I had your files in my lap.'

'You did?' Irshaad's eyebrow rose involuntarily.

'Your files were with him.'

'He can keep them! It's his files I'd like to see. Wouldn't you, Inspector Gaekwad?'

Inspector Gaekwad stuffed his phone into his back pocket and glanced at Mangesh from the corner of his eye. He breathed deeply and spoke under his breath, 'Just move out of here and you'll never have to deal with me again.'

'Is that a deal?' Irshaad grinned.

'It's a deal,' Inspector Gaekwad groaned, shoving his revolver back into its holster.

'You'll be off our backs?'

'I said it's a deal. What do you want? A written guarantee? I'm letting you go. Now go on, get out of here.'

'I don't think I will, inspector!' he grinned, gesturing towards the door. 'Come to think of it, I don't feel much like leaving now. I think I'll just stay.'

He caught Nadeem's attention swishing over to the closed door and glared at him in anticipation.

'Who you got in there, Nadeem?'

Nadeem didn't answer. He looked down at the floor instead, taking a gulp. The ballistics expert who had risen came cautiously tiptoeing over to the kitchen, trying to catch the inspector's attention.

'Excuse me, sir!' he called out demurely. 'Can we leave?'

'There's no one in there, Irshaad.' Nadeem shook his head.

Irshaad flitted over to the door and put his ear against it. He smiled in realization and went back to the kitchen platform, resuming his preparations.

'Irshaad!' Inspector Gaekwad quaked. 'Get out before anyone else comes here.'

'Sir!' The ballistics expert called out again. 'Uh . . . excuse me . . . Gaekwad Sahib.'

'I'm gonna have a glass of chocolate milk and depart at my own leisure,' Irshaad proclaimed.

He began to empty a bottle of cold water into the mixer, along with a heap of milk powder. Nadeem searched all over the kitchen for the Bournvita, finally managing to locate it in a container that had been stashed away in one of the bottom drawers.

'Sugar?' Irshaad requested.

Nadeem handed him the sugar from a jar behind the stove, growing increasingly restless. 'There's some vanilla ice cream in case you want it.'

'Hand it over,' Irshaad ordered. 'One day, if you want to feel real good about things, put all your possessions and belongings into this and shred them to pieces. They aren't worth a damn, anyway. It'll do you a world of good. You'll feel sort of . . . how shall I put it . . . purged. I do it myself sometimes. Break something just for the heck of it, because I can and I like to. I'll look at a vase, a perfectly handcrafted ornamental porcelain vase, with all sorts of intricate designs on it, and the first thing that comes to my mind isn't how beautiful it is or how long it took to make, but instead, what it would be like if I smashed it.'

Inspector Gaekwad immediately lunged over, putting his hand over the rim of the mixer in order to stop Irshaad from using it. 'Get out of here, Irshaad!' he repeated, this time with more severity than before. 'Quick! Before anyone gets here!'

Irshaad promptly jammed the cap of the mixer over the inspector's hand, pushing it down towards the swirling blades, which leapt into motion as the button was pressed. White water sprayed out of the open ends in terrifying profusion. Inspector Gaekwad wrenched in agony as he tried to pull his hand out. The entire wall over the kitchen platform was splattered with chunks of Bournvita powder, ice cream and sugar. The mixer shrieked away, its blades spinning like a metallic tornado. Inspector Gaekwad managed to get his hand out just in time, knocking the entire contraption over, spilling its contents all over the kitchen platform. Had he not possessed the strength to overpower Irshaad, his hand would have been mutilated in the whirlwind of the mixer.

Irshaad pounced on him with unbridled fury, grabbing his neck. Nadeem leapt between them, trying to tear them apart as they went for each other. The ballistics expert simply stood motionless, observing the mayhem in bafflement. Irshaad pushed Nadeem away, holding Inspector Gaekwad in a headlock before Mangesh could leap to his rescue. Inspector Gaekwad snuck hold of a plate that was drying over the sink and smashed it on Irshaad's head. He nearly collapsed with the blow, wading through bits of broken glass, blood spurting from his forehead. Gaekwad grabbed Irshaad's neck, this time from the front, with both his hands clasping his throat. Irshaad picked up a frying pan as they fell to the floor, breaking more crockery. Mangesh and Nadeem tried with best intentions to get involved and appease the aggravation, but it was strictly a two-way conversation. Gaekwad pressed his leg down on Irshaad's fingers. With the other hand, Irshaad smacked the frying pan on Inspector Gaekwad's forehead, quickly making a reach for a knife that stood in a utensil holder next to the washbasin. Inspector Gaekwad snatched it out of his hands and they tumbled against the kitchen sink, smashing everything that came in their path. Inspector Gaekwad finally caught the knife and twisted Irshaad's arms behind his back to excruciating effect. He pulled out Irshaad's gun from his pocket, despite much resistance and difficulty, and threw it aside.

'Raut!' he called out for help, pale with desperation. Mangesh came rushing to provide backup to his sahib.

'Get the handcuffs,' Inspector Gaekwad ordered, struggling to keep Irshaad down.

Mangesh ran across to the living room where the handcuffs lay on the wooden side table and brought them to Inspector Gaekwad.

'Keep still, Irshaad,' Inspector Gaekwad stammered, trying to hold both his hands tight. He clipped them together in the handcuffs and dragged him up to his feet, plugging his Magnum straight into Irshaad's shoulder socket. 'You move and you get it!'

Irshaad was shaking vigorously. His eyes seemed to spring out of their sockets and ploughed through the apartment like a tractor as he was pulled out. Inspector Gaekwad told both his cronies to keep away from the doorway. They looked at their boss with remorse and lowered their guns. Mangesh began to push them and smack them on the head as Irshaad and Inspector Gaekwad exited the flat. He started strong-arming them into surrender. By now, everyone had emptied out of the bedroom. They silently glanced at the destruction in the kitchen and parked their inquiries at Nadeem who told them to go to the living room.

From the balcony, Inspector Gaekwad could be seen hauling Irshaad across the lobby to the jeep. He shoved him into the passenger seat and locked the car, standing outside. He whistled to Mangesh who was awaiting instructions in the balcony. He rolled out his semi-automatic and waved it at the two henchmen.

'Come on!' he barked. 'Let's go! Chal, chal, chal!'

The rest of the spectators at the crime scene were visibly shaken. They all stood silently, avoiding each other, as though in attendance at a funeral.

'Uh . . . would anybody like some more tea?' Warren asked. No one answered.

Downstairs, Inspector Gaekwad and Mangesh piled all of Irshaad's men, including his driver, Kaashif Bhai, into the back of the jeep. They had to be pretty rough with them considering they were capable of retaliating. They were all armed and had to be emptied before they were stuffed into the jeep. Once they were all in, Inspector Gaekwad slammed the door, locked it from the outside and took out his phone, calling for backup.

Upstairs, the ballistics experts had emerged from the tiles, trying to regain their bearings. They had had the rug pulled out from right under them. In all their years of dealing with bullets, they had never been within firing range and so close to death as some of the victims of their arduous work.

Nadeem unfolded a brand new towel from his cupboard, fetched a fresh bar of soap from a toilet kit and limped towards the bathroom for a shower. Once he was inside, he felt momentarily at ease, shut off from the outside world. A faint spasm of relief ran through him. It was quiet inside, but he could still observe the commotion downstairs through the narrow slits in the windows. He hung his towel on a peg behind the door and began to peel off his soiled clothes, one by one, in preparation for a true cleansing. He unravelled in the bathing area, standing underneath the warm sanctity of the shower nozzle. He turned it down towards him and slowly rotated the knob. It came on with a spurt, stalling a few times before the water started flowing in a long continuous stream whose complexion grew darker as it poured out. At first, Nadeem drenched his hands and face in it, wiping away the muck that had been plaguing him. But on gathering a closer look once the water had cleared out of his eyes it became apparent that what ran out of the shower was not water at all. It was a great deal thicker, more voluminous and a shade redder, like blood! He recoiled, switching off the shower in an instant, and wiped the collected blood from his hands and face with the towel. He tried the washbasin and the flush. They were clean, but somehow, the shower seemed to be spewing blood. He leapt out of the bathroom in fierce urgency, half-naked, and scrambled to the living room, wrapping his lower torso with the towel.

Inspector Gaekwad and Mangesh had come back up to the living room and were briefing everyone as to what their official statements ought to be. They were headed for the Goregaon creek in order to fish the vehicle out.

'Wait!' Nadeem yelled.

'Put on some clothes, goddamnit!' hollered Inspector Gaekwad, as he turned towards him.

'The shower's pouring blood!' Nadeem informed them. 'Get someone to check the tanks.'

'What nonsense!' cried Machhiwaala. 'Kishorie Lal, go up to the terrace.'

'Do you have the plumber's number?' asked Nadeem.

Machhiwaala checked his phone as Kishorie Lal ran out. Inspector Gaekwad swept straight to the bathroom and stuck his head in. The water that had gathered in the bathing area was encircling the drain. It looked like someone had bathed there after playing Holi. He turned on the shower and, much to his surprise, nothing came out.

'You sure?' he cross-checked with Nadeem.

'I'm telling you!' Nadeem ran over to the washbasin, making sure it was still clear.

'Here it is!' Machhiwaala exclaimed, as he caught hold of the plumber's telephone number in his contact list. 'It's 0983134750.'

Inspector Gaekwad stepped out of the bathroom, balancing on his toes and heels, preventing his shoes from getting wet.

'What was that?' he asked.

'0983134750,' Machhiwaala repeated.

Inspector Gaekwad noted it down on his phone.

'Call him here!' Nadeem insisted, bathing himself at the washbasin with whatever water he could accumulate in a broken old bucket.

'What the hell happened to you, Nadeem?' Machhiwaala asked, visibly alarmed at his state.

Nadeem didn't have the time to get into it. He dried himself and went back into the bedroom to put on a clean pair of shorts and a T-shirt. Machhiwaala woke up the plumber and told him to come over to the building immediately, saying it was an emergency. Outside, in the living room, Mangesh was still busy taking down everyone's phone numbers. He said he would be in touch with all of them in case they were needed.

'Do you think he knew I was here?' asked Dr Vengsarkar, timidly.

'I doubt it,' Inspector Gaekwad assured him, as he stepped into the living room, wiping his shoes on the rug. 'He can't see through walls.'

'The plumber should be here any minute,' Machhiwaala informed him.

'Where does he live?'

'In the waadi (slum) at the back!'

Warren stood solemnly in the balcony, watching the locked police jeep downstairs. Its inhabitants were banging away at the windows, trying to smash them open and brawling amongst themselves, showering profanities at each other, startling the ground floor residents who awoke on account of the ruckus they were creating.

Nadeem emerged from the bedroom, having considerably freshened up, with the towel hanging around his shoulders.

'You already have my number,' he told Inspector Gaekwad.

'Not any more. I've deleted you off my contacts list.'

Nadeem looked around at the gathered company, nodding gently in agreement, wondering whether or not he should let spill what was on his mind. But he let it pass.

Departure from Duty

It was exactly 5.45 a.m. as per Nadeem's alarm clock when the plumber arrived. Two police jeeps and a van had reached downstairs. Assisted by two burly hawaldars, Mangesh escorted the gentlemen out of Inspector Gaekwad's jeep and transferred them into the back of the van, which filled up sooner than was customary with the likes of them, owing to the absence of a scrap. The men were by now tired and ready to hit the sack. They didn't have the energy for a scuffle with the cops. Usually, they'd take from morning till midnight just to make it up the metallic step above the exhaust, arguing with the apprehending authorities or even amongst themselves. Going into the back of a police 'dabba' was as good as going to jail. Irshaad Batla still sat awake though, his eyes swallowed in thought. He didn't look at anyone or say a word, just silently lamented his predicament like a disgruntled child being denied a toy, his demeanour regressing to the infantile state and his stupor worsening in anticipation of the procedural horrors to come.

The van drove off, leaving Mangesh by his sahib's empty jeep. It was headed straight for Arthur Road and then to Yerwada Mental Hospital. Those were Gaekwad Sahib's strict instructions.

Kishorie Lal had conducted a check of all the tanks on the terrace. One of them had a dead pigeon that had probably stooped in for a drink and ended up getting trapped. Apart from that, the other tanks were reasonably clean.

The plumber entered the apartment after taking off his chappals and lining them neatly at the doorstep. His hair hadn't been combed as yet, his sunken eyes drooped to the corners of their lids and it was too early in the day for him to have shaved.

'What's the matter, sahib?' he inquired.

'This is Inspector Gaekwad of the Crime Branch,' Machhiwaala introduced him.

'What have I done to get into trouble with the law?' he smiled nervously.

'Nothing,' Inspector Gaekwad said. 'We just want to know a few things. According to Machhiwaala, you were seen hanging off the pipes on the fifth floor.'

'That is not true, sahib.'

Nadeem stood silently in the corner, with Rohini and Warren, watching the two men harass the plumber into explaining himself. They started politely, talking nicely, but then as he failed to comply, they lapsed into rudeness, threatening to give him a smack on the back of the head. Finally, Nadeem had to intervene to make the two men see some sense. They had stayed up way past their bedtime to be able to exercise reliable discretion.

'Is there anything you haven't told the authorities yet?' Nadeem asked him calmly. 'If you haven't, then do so now, otherwise you're going to have to find out where that blood came from. And who it belongs to.'

'Look,' he quivered, 'I didn't know how to say this earlier, but you know I thought it would get me into trouble.'

'What?'

'You know how it is for a man in my station. They hit first and listen afterwards. I figured I'd better keep my nose clean.'

'What are you talking about?' Machhiwaala butted in.

'Well, you see, sir,' he spoke, looking at Nadeem but addressing the landlord.

'When I came in to work on Mr Goyale's bathroom the other day, one of the kids locked me in and put out the lights, as a joke I suppose, but I was stuck there for fifteen to twenty minutes before anyone bothered to open it. While I was inside, I tried calling out for help to the watchman downstairs but couldn't reach him through the slits in the bathroom window. As I waited for someone to come to my rescue, at length I became aware of a thumping or banging sound from the ceiling. It came from the flat above, the one that Mr Makhija occupied. I could hear a muffled voice yelling gibberish, loudly and with a fierce temper. I thought I was eavesdropping on some kind of domestic squabble, but it soon became apparent that the voice belonged to a single individual who was obviously crying out for help.'

'I told you!' Nadeem exclaimed. 'He was locked inside.'

'Before I could get any further with my assumptions, the door was opened by Mrs Goyale, who chastised her kids for having locked me in. She let me out, apologizing profusely on their behalf. I went out to the balcony to glance at the fifth floor windows. The glass blinds on the bathroom window were cracked and a hand was sticking out through one of the slits, trying to claw its way out. I got on to the fourth floor parapet and climbed up the ascending pipeline to the fifth floor. As I held on to the valve, where the pipelines converge, and hauled myself up to the narrow parapet beneath the bathroom window, I tried to peep inside but couldn't see anything clearly. All I could hear was loud, indistinct sounds, like someone smacking the walls, hitting things, items being flung around. It was all rather unsettling, so I made my way back down, deciding to mind my own business. When Mrs Goyale asked me what I was doing up there, I said that I thought someone there needed help. She agreed that the person who lived on the fifth floor certainly did need some help.'

Rohini walked up to him from the corner of the living room, keeping an eye on Dr Vengsarkar who was submerged in the couch. He was the only one in the room who had taken the liberty to sit. The door had been left open and the watchman stood outside, keeping a watch out for any resident who might inquire into the night's proceedings.

'I was never called by him during his entire stint,' the plumber carried on. 'Funny, considering he had often complained to Mr Machhiwaala about the pressure from his shower not being sufficient for his needs.'

All of a sudden, Dr Vengsarkar got up and sashayed past everyone to the front door to close it. He latched it shut with his hands behind his back.

'Then what?' he asked, coming face-to-face with the plumber.

'I collected my payment and was on my way with my mouth shut tight,' he said.

Kishorie Lal sneaked in, listening to every word, tired but attentive. He stared at the plumber, mute with astonishment and disbelief, his gatekeeper's sidelong glance for the first time reflecting a soldier's sincerity. He too had stood around and watched for far longer than intended. The only thing that kept him awake all those nights was the prospect that his being around would make a difference, and that without him, the building would be no safe place for anyone to tread.

'Uh . . . excuse me,' he broke in. They all turned to him. 'I think we'd all better get some sleep. It's getting late.'

'You can go now, Kishorie,' Machhiwaala told him.

'No . . . uh . . . but I think . . .' he continued, undeterred.

'What do you think?' Inspector Gaekwad asked him, his forehead straightening up like an exclamation mark.

'Uh . . . nothing, sir . . .' he muttered under his breath.

'What's the matter, Kishorie?' Machhiwaala asked, looking at Inspector Gaekwad.

'Well . . . you see, sir,' the plumber said, 'I think I know what the matter is.' He looked at the watchman, reassuring him with a friendly nudge.

'Wait a minute . . .' Kishorie Lal broke in.

'Well, you see,' the plumber continued, 'before I left the building, I happened to inform Kishorie Lal that I thought there was someone stuck on the fifth floor. He, of course, paid no heed to it at the time, asking me not to worry about it.'

'That's not entirely true,' Kishorie Lal waved his hands. 'I did inform Mr Machhiwaala. We just didn't realize it would amount to this.'

Feroz Machhiwaala turned to Inspector Gaekwad thoughtfully. 'Look, inspector' he began, 'let me start out by saying that had I known what kind of person Makhija was, I would have never accepted him as a tenant in the first place.'

Inspector Gaekwad looked at Nadeem and Warren. 'You have pretty high standards,' he remarked.

'I confess that I didn't want to have to deal with him any more than I had to. Would you? Who wants to have to deal with an undesirable? None of us,' he exclaimed.

Then, gesturing at the watchman and the plumber, he said, 'All three of us are as guilty as the next person in what we did, or in this case, didn't do. It was our negligence that resulted in his death. But what caused it we cannot be held accountable for. That's why I sent up another undesirable to deal with him.' This time, he pointed at Nadeem. 'I sent him to find out just what the hell was going on in that house. I didn't want to go myself, but I did want to know. It is my duty as his landlord to . . .'

'Cut out the "it is my duty as his landlord" crap,' Inspector Gaekwad snapped. 'You did the right thing by doing nothing about it. One Makhija more or less in the world doesn't make any difference. No one's gonna lose any sleep over it.'

He walked over to the door, fidgeting with his mobile phone. He shook his head, blinking at Mangesh, who promptly strolled out of the doorway in response. 'You made me stay up till 5:45 in the morning for this?' he yawned at Machhiwaala. 'For a moment, I thought we actually had something.'

'I'm sorry, sir!' the plumber said.

'I guess we can all close the books and call it a night,' he stated. 'Whatever your personal misgivings are about this mess is none of my concern. Keep them to yourself. I suggest you all keep your mouths shut about this. Don't go around propagating folklore about that flat just because someone died in it. After all, you do want to give it out on rent, don't you, Mr Machhiwaala?'

'I most definitely do.'

'Then start getting it ready for the next tenant. You wouldn't want to discourage people from considering it. If I was you, I'd try and sell it.'

'Thank you, sir!'

'Who knows, someday a big, bright and happy family may occupy it, or perhaps an enchanted couple, or a hard-working person who wouldn't spend all his time at home. I'm sure they'd look after it better.'

Inspector Gaekwad shook hands with everyone individually before heading out. The ballistics experts followed him.

'Can I go home now?' asked Dr Vengsarkar, sheepishly.

'Where do you live?' Inspector Gaekwad asked. 'I'll drop you home.'

'No, thanks! I can easily make it back myself.'

'I insist. I've kept you up all night. I owe you that much at least. Come on, I'll buy you a cup of tea.'

'Look, inspector . . .'

'Come on! Let's go. Never refuse a kind offer, you may not be so lucky to receive one the next time.'

'I know that only too well,' Nadeem snickered.

As Inspector Gaekwad was about to make his exit, Nadeem stalled him at the door with a casual inquiry, one that was still unsolved.

'What about the money?' he asked.

'What money?' Inspector Gaekwad retorted.

'The man I met earlier claimed to have left behind a sum of 10,000 rupees.'

'Quite careless of him.'

'Nonetheless,' said Nadeem, looking at the plumber and the watchman. They looked at each other.

'We don't know anything about that, sahib,' the plumber responded.

'We?' Nadeem wondered.

'We . . . as in me . . .' he blurted out.

'Speak for yourself,' Kishorie Lal moaned.

'One of you stole that money. I know it,' Nadeem smirked.

The two of them turned towards Machhiwaala.

'Well . . . uh . . . you see . . .' he began an evasive cough, a clumsy attempt at deflection. But as the cough fizzled out, it was dreadfully apparent that Inspector Gaekwad's attention had been alerted, and that his antenna had come back up. He hung on to the landlord's uncharacteristic pause in anticipation of an explanation. He had been quite adept at explaining himself earlier, almost suspiciously so.

'I forgot to mention that I had been into the flat earlier.'

'I see,' clipped Inspector Gaekwad, tight-lipped to the point of insincerity. 'When would this be?'

'The night before he was found,' he shamefully admitted, not particularly proud of what he had to share.

'I didn't see him anywhere around, so I . . . uh . . . left. It was dark, pitch-black. I couldn't see a thing. I could see his phase had blown, so I went up to the switchboard, opened the panel and turned on the main switch to get some light.'

'That is right,' Inspector Gaekwad agreed. 'According to the report, the first place the fingerprints expert checked was the switchboard, since all the electricity had been turned on. And apparently your fingerprints might have shown up on it. They're still confirming.'

'Well, I just picked up the fallen bundle and kept it for him, for safety, so to speak.'

'10,000. That's too much safety to be safe.'

'Well, I intended to return it to him, of course. Obviously.'

'There's nothing obvious about it,' Nadeem butted in.

'Chi, chi!' Inspector Gaekwad whistled at Nadeem under his teeth, referring to him the way he would address a stray dog. 'You keep out of this.'

'I swear. I was going to return it,' Machhiwaala insisted, his plea gradually degenerating into a pitiful appeal.

'You have it with you?' Inspector Gaekwad asked him in a decidedly different tone.

'Yes,' he whispered, looking left and right.

'I'd like it, please,' he instructed, as he stretched out his palm before him.

'Sure,' Machhiwaala conceded, putting his hands into his pockets and producing a rather large and overstuffed wallet.

'This is an incidental murder,' Inspector Gaekwad concluded, counting the cash, 'where circumstances were manipulated to appropriate convenience. Not premeditated, but a murder nonetheless, one that doesn't qualify for reassessment and one that does not, by any measure, deserve to go into the books. Plenty of them happen every day in the city.' He delivered his summation to a somewhat bewildered audience who were spread out in different corners of the living room. No one spoke; no one had anything to add. It is possible that the night's events were enough to shut a person up for good.

'Hmm . . . simplifies things for you, doesn't it?' Nadeem reflected, the sole voice of dissent in a room full of obedient stragglers. 'If we can all close up the books and get a night's sleep, forgetting all about whatever happened. Makes it easier for you, but not necessarily for us. We still have to live here.'

'Someday, come around to the place where I live,' Inspector Gaekwad smiled. 'See if you can call it home.'

'I guess I'll be seeing you . . .' Nadeem waved at Inspector Gaekwad after seeing him out of the door.

'I don't know about that, Nadeem,' Inspector Gaekwad sighed, pulling the elevator door shut. The lift shot down, carrying all the people who were in the building in an official capacity. Only the residents were left behind, those who actually had to conduct the rest of the day there. With the exception of Rohini, who didn't live there and was just passing through.

'Do you have the keys to my husband's flat, Mr Machhiwaala?' she asked him.

'Well…uh,' he fumbled. 'As a matter of fact, I do.'

'I would appreciate it if it were possible for me to take one last look at the place?'

'Uhh . . .'

'Well,' said Nadeem, 'I suppose we can permit that, can't we, Mr Machhiwaala?'

'Uh . . . well, yes, I suppose we can.'

Living Hell

The sound of the lock clicking open echoed through the corners of the empty apartment. The flat was excessively stuffy as all the windows had been shut since the forensic lab inspection. It was a fully furnished flat complete with microwave, sofa, cushions, lamps and cupboards. It seemed weathered, stayed in and weighed upon. Like a tired traffic cop wiping the sweat off his brow in the scorching heat of day. As if it had borne the brunt of many a human misery.

Next to a bookshelf beside the television stood a pile of discarded envelopes and old newspapers. Nadeem went through it and fished out a wrapped parcel from the very bottom. It was a courier addressed to Chintan Makhija, 501, Little Heights, Jankalyan Nagar 2, Pin code: 400053. The sender's address was 234, Shakuntala Building, Block number 3, B-Wing, Juhu Tara Road.

Nadeem tore open the packaging. There was nothing inside. Below it in the pile was an envelope, unmistakably bearing the insignia of K.L. Hospital, which contained his medical reports. All his bodily characteristics were neatly assembled in an authoritative document that aimed to be the final word on his predicament—the medical manifestation of all his internal maladies. It had taken the shape of a mutation; an aberration from what is usually considered normal, straying from the path of the straight and narrow.

How feeble was he in comparison to all that had been done. For what? And by whom? A lawyer pathologically incapable of following the very law he sought to practise or those who sat in judgment of people who broke the law or those that doled out salvation in the form of a supposed science, namely, medicine for those who needed a cure.

Nadeem looked at Rohini as they examined the medical reports, his eyes filled with the most awful knowledge. There were certain truths even she didn't want to know, and she probably figured there was a lot that was better off unsaid. She slowly walked away from the living room towards the terrace balcony. She opened the sliding door to look at what kind of view her husband had enjoyed in his brief stay.

It was nothing to write home about—just a couple of neighbouring buildings, the odd bungalow here and there, and just about enough greenery to ease the eyes every once in a while. The house had nothing to do with her. It was a part of his life she had never known. He had put it together with his bare hands, every lamp on every table and each picture on each wall. It was the hand of a man significantly different and deformed from who she had known. He was once a good man, an honest man, a person with the potential for kindness, who did all the things a good human being ought to do, all until being a human wasn't enough and began to entail more than goodness and more than kindness, more than generosity and more than what money could buy. Peace of mind. Reduced to what he was by the vagaries of circumstance, with the world by the tail on a downhill slide.

When they were together, he always paid up on time. He wasn't a miser in his more benevolent days. She always liked to say, it's the love you give out that counts, not the money. After all, he wasn't doing all that bad, his reputation was at stake and that takes money. To buy a reputation you have to sell a lot of guts! Maybe, that was why he got an ulcer so soon in life. Because he hacked his intestines out. He had pretty much lived in an office all his life. He liked the sickness of it all. The buzzing sounds and beeping electronics. It was like the sound of those planes taking off over his head every time he lay down for a wink's rest, when he used to shack up in a one-BHK in the Reserve Bank Quarters in Santa Cruz. Background music to the main concert! But no one played any violins to his sadness. It was swept aside, brushed under the carpet by his reassuring smile and instinct for self-preservation. But it wasn't just himself he thought about. In fact, he had put himself last on the priority list. He had better things on his mind. A happy family, a dog, a house with more than one bedroom, the roof higher over his head, a trip to the Bahamas, Sundays in the park walking with a baby carriage. What he wanted was the five-star package all wrapped up with a fancy bow on it. And here he was, on a one-way trip to oblivion.

Of all the ones to whom life had dealt out a bum hand, his had been the simplest and the plainest. Nothing fancy, nothing big. Imprisoned by the mundane, only stripes and squares all the way through the day. Choking under a starched collar.

She thought it seemed like a nice, happy house. A place worthy of living in. One that ought to be appreciated. It had the right layout, the right nooks and corners, all the Vaastu sorted. It was a place she thought anyone ought to be glad to occupy and Machhiwaala agreed with her most vociferously.

But to the tenant who had occupied it, it was just four walls and a ceiling. A cage. An enclosure from all his worries, a place to measure his deeds and live in silent contemplation. A living hell.

Whoever had killed him had robbed him only of the sanctuary and subterfuge of the passing moment, as the wheels of fate turned and conspired to bring him a day closer to his own doom, and to drown his fatal assassin in a sea of anonymity. The answer to which lay in the hundreds of debts of a hundred accounts, and in all the hundreds and thousands of phone calls made to restore the balance. To even things out and keep the essential equilibrium.

Acknowledgements

At the risk of sounding sappy, I would like to thank my parents for introducing me to the classics, and for always encouraging and nourishing any kind of artistic pursuit whether it be drawing comic books or even trying to put up a play, and my brother and sister for putting up with me, reading my work and introducing me to all kinds of cool stuff.

I would really like to thank the editor of this book, Anushree Kaushal, for her constant encouragement, patience and insightful feedback, and also for being a fellow crime fiction buff and sending me many interesting books. I would also like to thank the copy editor, Aslesha Kadian, and Aditya and Vaishnavi for their guidance.